Places, Please!

Published by
Smith and Kraus, Inc.
177 Lyme Road, Hanover, New Hampshire 03755
www.SmithKraus.com

Cover and text design by Julia Hill Gignoux, Freedom Hill Design
Cover artwork by Joe BelBruno

First edition: December 2001
10 9 8 7 6 5 4 3 2 1

The Library of Congress Cataloging-In-Publication Data
Varley, Joy.
Places, please! : a manual for high-school theater directors / by Joy Varley. —1st ed.
p. cm. — (Young actors series)
ISBN 1-57525-282-1
1. College and school drama. 2. Amateur theater—Production and direction — Handbooks, manuals, etc.
I. Title. II. Young actors series.

PN3178.P7 V37 2001
792'.0222'0233—dc21
2001020316

Places, Please!

An Essential Manual for High-School Theater Directors

How to Structure and Organize Your Theater Program

By Joy Varley

Young Actors Series

A SMITH AND KRAUS BOOK

First, this book is dedicated to my husband, Greg, who has attended more high school theater productions over the past twenty-one years than he ever bargained for. His love of theater and his willingness to see *everything* at least once has provided me with encouragement and endless support for every project. This book is a tribute to his belief that I can do anything.

Second, this book is dedicated to the talented and wonderful permanent members of my production staff. Their artistry, dedication, and professionalism cannot be surpassed. Thank you Howard Kilik, Maggie Paschke, Larry Loffredo, and Paul Morini.

And finally, I dedicate this book to the theater students and parents of Tallmadge High School (1980–1983), Eastchester High School (1983–1988), and especially Byram Hills High School (1988–2000). Collectively, your dedication, passion, and love of theater were motivating and inspiring to this director. Individually, the memories I have of you are treasured. You are the stage managers, actors, crew members, and musicians who live on in the pages of this book. Writing this manuscript rekindled memories of our most difficult challenges and our greatest achievements. It was my privilege to work with each of you.

Contents

Foreword

I grew up acting professionally on the television series "The Andy Griffith Show" (playing the part of Andy's son, Opie) and also performing in other film and television productions, so when I attended public high school, I stayed well clear of the drama wing and, instead, spent my time in the journalism department and playing on the basketball team. As a result, some twenty-five years later when two of my four terrific kids chose to make the theater department their focus in high school, I was rather ironically a backstage neophyte. I was pleased that they were exhibiting genuine passion for an aspect of their academic lives, but I must say I had little idea just how rewarding and complete an educational experience a well-run high school theater production could be for a student.

Bryce, my oldest daughter, had the good fortune to find herself in Joy Varley's theater program at Byram Hills High School in Westchester County, New York, for three years. Joy proved to be a wonderful influence and a fine educator, using the demands of a high school theater production as the platform for many practical and philosophical lessons. Some, I could have anticipated, and others were a pleasant surprise to my wife and I as parents.

There is something about the intense preparation and sustained coordination required to present a production to an audience that provides remarkably useful training for all kinds of real world circumstances the students may face in their lives. Preparation, teamwork, and coordination *are* rewarded in very tangible ways in a high school theater production, whereas in athletic competition, for example, despite all the conditioning, teamwork, and sacrifice, the difference between success and failure often comes down to luck, poor officiating, or a sudden act of superior athleticism from a single player that affects the outcome.

With a school production, hard work *will* be rewarded, assuming the show goes on as scheduled and individuals have carried out their responsibilities. If the props are where they are supposed to be, if the sets are standing and secure, if the lights are positioned and the cues practiced and organized, if the actors' roles are rehearsed, and if the ushers open the doors, take the tickets, and seat the audience, then the high school production will most likely be a resounding success and a memorable life experience for those students who met their deadlines, executed their prepared tasks, and worked in service of the show and the audience. A most valuable lesson will be learned. Certainly, inspiration and genius are wonderful when they can be found, but they aren't required in life to succeed. The simple acts of careful and dedicated preparation and earnest commitment to and execution of the plan will be rewarded with the respect of those in the audience, who appreciate that the challenge to entertain them has been successfully met.

What more could anyone ask of an employee, co-worker, boss, parent, or spouse than a well-organized and thorough effort to meet a deadline and achieve an objective that has agreed-upon value and merit?

Joy Varley's student productions leave participants with a sense of satisfaction, mental toughness, appreciation for each other's roles in the process, and, most important of all, enhanced self-esteem. These ambitious, demanding projects turn out wonderfully well, but the terrific result is no accident. Ms. Varley has the undertaking down to a science. If the students show up and are prepared to work, then they will learn a tremendous amount about every facet of production, both backstage and before the footlights. A few will discover a career path they wish to follow and will, indeed, have a wonderful head start in the world of professional theater. But they will all have an outstanding learning experience, reinforced by a shared moment of success they can build on as individuals.

Places, Please! is a soup-to-nuts schematic that reflects Joy's considerable experience and expertise in her field. A valuable organizational tool, the book thoroughly outlines each step in the daunting task of planning and presenting a high school theatrical production. Hopefully, with the aid of this text, those assigned the responsibility of a school theatrical production can stay ahead of the one zillion challenges and thereby leave themselves enough time to do the really important stuff, like teach the students, help them achieve, and make a difference in their lives.

Break a leg.

—*Ron Howard*

Preface

My parents used to take my brother, my sister, and me to our local university, the University of Akron in Ohio, to see the children's theater productions in Knight Hall. Sitting in a dark theater, we watched our favorite stories and fairy tales come to life. It was a thrilling and sometimes frightening experience. My memory is filled with wonderful impressions of those magical shows. I still remember the pumpkin carriage, the elaborate princess gowns, Rapunzel's hair, the frightening witches and villains, and the overwhelming experience of walking onstage after the production to speak to the actors and actresses.

My next theatrical experience occurred in the eighth grade when our school's new music teacher decided that our class should have the opportunity to perform a musical: *HMS Pinafore*. My best talent was playing the piano, so that is how I joined the company—as the "orchestra." I had special piano lights, sat alone in front of the stage in an area we called the orchestra pit, and watched the show through every rehearsal and performance.

During high school, I experienced two shows that forever sealed my love of musical theater. The first happened when I was fifteen and a part-time rehearsal pianist for a summer theater production of *Camelot*. The entire company was old (to me!); most were in their early to late-twenties. They were remarkably talented, very patient and kind, and inspirational to this inexperienced teen. To this day, *Camelot* is my favorite musical, and that production remains the hallmark of perfection for that play. The second experience happened when I was seventeen and a senior in high school. I was given the opportunity to act as music director for *Fiddler on the Roof*, the only student member of an adult staff. Finally, I was in the position of creating an element of the show. It was wonderful. And I thought it was the end of my theatrical career. I was heading to college as a serious music major. Theater was fun—not serious—and certainly not something to study in college.

Fast forward four years to my first teaching position as a high school choir director where it was expected that I would be involved in the high school musical. Theater re-entered my life. Several jobs and many productions later, I found myself working in Armonk, New York, in a school district that valued and supported all the arts. There, in my position as theater director, I was able to build a theater program that produced three to five plays and musicals per school year. Many students (and their families) made a strong personal commitment to the theater program. For some, the program provided a wonderful sense of community and an enjoyable artistic experience. For others, however, the school productions served a higher purpose. These students were interested in theater as a career. I found myself unprepared to answer their questions about college, career opportunities, and life in the real world of professional theater. I quickly became a student myself, reading and studying about all elements of theater, from methods of acting to elements of production design, to audition techniques, to professional career options. Over a short time, I reorganized my high school theater program so that it would meet the needs of *all* students: those for whom theater served as an avocation and those for whom it served as a stepping stone to a greater arena. This book is a summary of my twenty years on the high school stage.

Places, Please! offers an in-depth discussion of all the people who might be involved in a high school theater program and details their personal responsibilities and production relationships with one another. This book defines the roles of the adult staff and parent volunteers, describes the production skills and educational outcomes for all student members of the cast and crew, and provides a structure for organizing a production timeline that ensures you will never run out of time again.

I remain in contact with many of my former students and am in awe at the number of them who work professionally in the entertainment industry. They continue to inspire me as lighting designers, casting directors, script supervisors, television producers, music directors, and actors in theater, television, and feature films. I am a devoted fan of their work and am blessed to hear about their accomplishments and projects. These working professionals are my proof that what we teach about the art of theater and how we teach it is important. The high school theater experience can shape lives, inspire careers, and, above all, provide a unique opportunity to discover and develop the artist in each of us.

CHAPTER 1

WHO ARE YOU?

The Role of the High School Theater Director

The high school theater director does so much more than direct a play. He serves as teacher, role model, nurse, friend, counselor, boss, disciplinarian, mentor, and, finally, director. His responsibilities often include serving as producer, business manager, receptionist, custodian, and secretary. The director hires and administers a staff, raises funds and oversees a budget, monitors the growth of individual students, charts the progress of a production, and—oh yes!—must find the time and inspiration to be a creative and visionary artist. In short, the director often finds himself in the position of being all things to all people.

The successful theater director is a supreme optimist. He believes that all things are possible, that no challenge is beyond reach, and that every person is an important contributor and necessary for reaching the goals of the production. The director is the head cheerleader for his team: the company of staff and students pursuing the noble art of theater.

The high school theater director should be well trained. His repertoire of plays and musicals should be extensive. He should possess a basic understanding of stagecraft, lighting and sound design, production techniques, music form and structure, and theatrical technology. Additionally, the director should be an expert in acting technique, methods of actor training, vocal care and development, and stage movement.

In the realm of educational theater, the high school program is often the first step in training an actor or technical student who aspires to a professional career. The director identifies students with special theatrical talent and ability and provides a good pedagogical foundation of terminology, technique, and experience that will allow each student to pursue higher education in the theater and a professional career. This chapter identifies and defines the various roles and responsibilities that fall within the domain of the director.

The Director as Leader, Teacher, and Mentor

Your role as director is an enormous responsibility. It requires a complete intellectual understanding of the play, artistic knowledge of the varied elements of theater, and a deep level of caring for the people who are the staff, cast, and crew.

The director should inspire, challenge, and instruct the creative staff and members of the cast and crew. You provide energy and focus to all members of the production team. As director, you set goals and evaluate the rate of progress in meeting those goals and shape each element of a production. You guide and influence each person with whom you work. As director, you are the leader, teacher, and mentor for all members of a production company.

THE DIRECTOR AS LEADER

Directing a theatrical production requires several different kinds of leadership skills. All these skills are present in the most successful directors.

Organizational Leadership

The director is responsible for organizing the structure of the cast and crew for any production. The director creates the staff positions necessary to meet the specific requirements of a play, hires the best staff available, and assists the staff in recruiting membership for their separate crews.

As director, you are responsible for establishing a hierarchy for members of the production staff. In a play with rigorous set or costume requirements, those designers may be given a greater voice in determining the physical shape or size of the production. You are responsible for organizing the time structure of a production. This means creating a complete schedule that includes the days of the week when cast or crews are scheduled to meet, length of work sessions or rehearsals, and all dress rehearsal and performance dates.

You are responsible for ensuring the safety of all members of the staff, cast, and crew. The work and rehearsals spaces should be adequate for the needs of each department with an appropriate amount of space, lighting, and equipment available. Every rehearsal or workspace should include fire extinguishers, a first-aid kit, basic office supplies, and easy access to restrooms and a telephone.

By effectively addressing the needs of each department through staffing, cast and crew recruitment, and time management and safety concerns, the director provides the structure and organizational leadership necessary for a successful production.

The following diagram illustrates the most common organizational structure for a high school musical production.

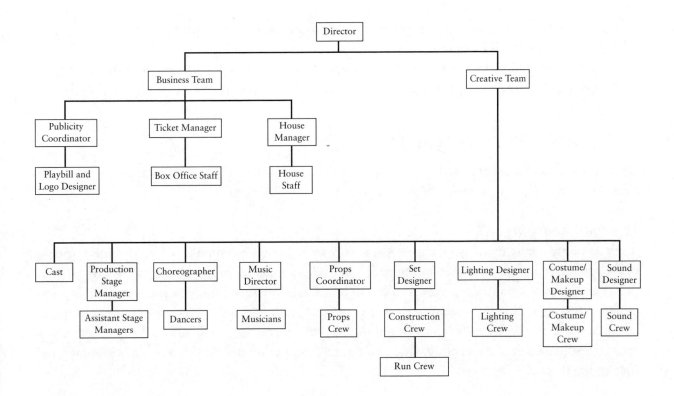

Creative Leadership

There are three general areas of creative leadership for which a director is responsible: creating a production concept, creating a rehearsal environment that fosters artistic growth, and creating standards for evaluating success.

As director, you are responsible for communicating your production concept to the members of the creative staff. The director's concept includes information about the period or location of the play, the number and style of sets required, the number and style of costumes required, any special color, look, or feeling that the production should reflect, and any special effects necessary for the production. You should also share your research about the play or past productions of the play with members of the creative staff.

The director is responsible for creating an environment that is disciplined yet nonthreatening. The rehearsal environment of the cast and work environment of the crew should foster opportunities for artistic experimentation and encourage creative growth and development for both the adult members of the staff and the student members of the cast and crew. The director should model the characteristics of a professional artist at work: one who is patient, calm, thoughtful, well prepared, respectful, courteous, and open to new ideas. When the adult and student members of a production follow this behavioral model, the resulting environment will be nurturing, thoughtful, and creative.

You are responsible for establishing standards—benchmarks or deadlines—by which all members of the production (staff, cast, and crew) are able to evaluate their progress and measure their success. Each member of the staff should assist the director by helping the student members of their crew to establish artistic goals and standards and participate in a process of artistic self-evaluation. If you teach all members of the production to define and evaluate artistic goals, the creative growth of each member of the staff, cast, and crew will significantly improve, and the artistic achievement of every production will be raised.

By effectively addressing the production concept, the rehearsal and work environments, and artistic standards, the director demonstrates leadership in the creative process of building a production.

THE DIRECTOR AS TEACHER

Using the play as your tool, as director you teach all members of your staff, cast, and crew about elements of theater and theatrical production.

Informal Teaching

You teach informally by daily example. Your words and actions communicate your understanding of the art and structure of a theatrical production to every member of the cast, crew, or staff in your presence. By being on time and prepared for all rehearsals and meetings, you teach punctuality and personal responsibility. By working together with members of the staff, crew chiefs, the stage managers, and the cast, you teach artistic collaboration. By treating all members of the staff, cast, and crew with equal courtesy and consideration, you teach respect. Your enthusiasm for your work teaches love of the theater.

Formal Teaching

As director you also give daily formal instruction to members of the cast, crew, and staff. When referring to parts of the stage, the theater, or equipment and supplies, you teach correct theatrical vocabulary. The director teaches technique in acting and vocal production when working in rehearsal with student actors. The director teaches methods of organization when instructing actors, stage managers, and crew chiefs in how to take notes and organize their rehearsal scripts and leadership skills when delegating responsibilities to student stage managers and crew chiefs.

THE DIRECTOR AS MENTOR

A high school theater program should be a place of opportunity for all members of your student population. New theater students and experienced thespians should be equally encouraged to take risks and explore new and different skills, gaining a wide variety of theatrical experiences. Students should be given multiple opportunities to develop skills in a particular area that interests them, or they should be able to move from crew to cast to crew in differing productions. By participating in the process of theater in a variety of roles, a student will begin to find a place where his talents and interests align.

While working on a production at the high school level, you are in a unique position to observe students learning new skills as they move from one crew position to another or participate in the cast at a variety of levels. You may discover a talent or special ability in a student that is new and unexpected. The talent may be in singing, acting, lighting, stage managing—anything! When you observe that a student has a particular strength or talent, assume the role of mentor and offer personal guidance and encouragement to that student.

The Director as Artistic Visionary

As director, you are responsible for the artistic integrity of a production. In this role, you balance the individual needs and goals of each department and ensure that all production elements are unified and are structured to meet the same goals. A director makes many artistic choices during the process of producing a play or musical. The most successful directors are able to verbalize their artistic choices.

CREATING AN ARTISTIC VISION

It is important for the director to develop a complete personal vision for every production. This vision, often called the director's concept, becomes the guiding force that shapes all production elements in each department.

When constructing an artistic concept of a play, it is important to begin with facts. You should research the play before making any important decisions about the production. When was the play written? Does the action take place in a specific historical time period? Does that historical period limit or expand choices of color, texture, movement, or action? Does the action take place in the past, present, or future? Are there performance traditions associated with this play? Why did the playwright create this play? When did the first production take place? Was it a critical success or failure? Was it a popular success or failure? Is this play relevant to the customs or traditions of your school or community? Are there issues or character types that are familiar?

Next, it is important to consider the property from several perspectives: the intention of the writer, the role of each actor, the experience of the audience, and the separate requirements of each production department.

Once you have completed your research and examined the play from each viewpoint, answer the following questions. The answers will provide necessary information for designers.

Mood
What is the overall impression or mood of the play or musical? Can that impression be interpreted through color? Through shades of light? Though shapes, form, or texture?

Characters
How many characters are needed for this play?
How does each character contrast with or complement the play's impression?
Do individual characters create a specific impression or function as part of a larger group?

Sets
How many sets are required for the play or musical?
Do those sets contrast with or complement the play's impression?
Are the sets of equal importance? Equal size?

Costumes

How many costumes are required for the play or musical?

Do the costumes contrast with or complement the play's impression?

Do the costumes distinguish the characters as separate individuals or as parts of a greater whole?

When the director is able to verbalize her thoughts about these conceptual interpretations of a play, she is ready to meet the designers and conduct the concept meeting.

THE CONCEPT MEETING

The concept meeting takes place very early in the production schedule, usually before the auditions occur. This the first planning meeting for the director and the design staff. When possible, all members of the design staff should be present: the set, lighting, costume, and sound designers. It is often wise to invite the properties coordinator, since props frequently overlap with the set and costume departments.

All members of the design staff should receive a complete script of the play at least two weeks before the concept meeting takes place. To ensure the productivity of this first meeting, each designer must have enough time to read the script several times and begin making notes about specific requirements relating to his department.

The concept meeting is your, the director's, meeting. During this meeting, you share your artistic vision with the designers. You should also share any general research you have done on the play, the playwright, former productions, the time period, architectural styles, or influences. Each designer should take notes while you are making your presentation. There should be some time reserved at the end of the meeting for the designers to ask questions or request clarification from the director.

THE DESIGN MEETING

The design meeting usually takes place approximately one week after the concept meeting and is the second planning meeting for the director and members of the design staff. When possible, all members of the design staff should be present. Again, it is wise to include the properties coordinator.

The design meeting should allow ample time for each designer to present her initial design concept of the production. The meeting should begin with the set designer presenting his sketches or drawings of the various sets. The costume designer is usually the second presenter, using sketches, photographs, and fabric swatches during her presentation. The lighting designer and props coordinator will make the final design presentations.

At the conclusion of the design meeting, the director and all designers should come to an agreement on the size of the performance space, number of sets, and the color palate and style for the production. Once these decisions are made, the designers can finalize their designs, submit their budgets, and begin organizing their work schedules.

The Director as Business Manager

In most high school theater productions, the director assumes the position of business manager. This usually happens by default, not by choice. The position of business manager, however, is critical to the financial success of a production and therefore to the long-term success of a program. A business manager has very specific responsibilities in a production company:

- Focusing everyone's efforts (staff and students) toward a specific goal
- Writing and signing contracts for hired staff
- Establishing budget priorities
- Creating a production budget; revising and updating as needed
- Organizing and overseeing technical elements of a production
- Scheduling staff budget meetings as needed
- Ordering and authorizing payment for purchased and rented materials
- Fundraising

MANAGERIAL SKILLS

Once the production goals are established through the concept and design meetings, it is the job of the business manager to keep everyone focused on meeting, not exceeding, those specific goals. During the process of building a production, members of the design staff, student members of the crew, or the director often propose creative additions to the original design concepts. Although these ideas may be wonderful and desirable, they can significantly impact the budget. The job of the business manager is to evaluate each suggestion as it is made, approve any idea that has little or no additional cost, and reject ideas that negatively impact the production budget.

CONTRACTS

All contracts for services or materials should be in writing. The contract may appear as a formal document or an informal agreement, but it should be written in a style that communicates needs, responsibilities, and any financial exchange.

Contracts for Hired Staff

Every paid member of your staff should receive a written contract to be signed by at least two parties: the business manager (or director) and the hired staff member. The contract should clearly state the following:

- The exact position and title
- A complete list of production responsibilities

- The times and dates of service expected
- Staff meeting schedule
- Rehearsal responsibilities (such as supervision of students)
- Performance responsibilities
- Strike responsibilities
- Any specific deadlines to meet
- The time and date of payment
- Penalties for failure to meet responsibilities

Contracts for Volunteer Staff

Volunteer members of the staff should also receive a written document clearly stating the responsibilities and expectations of their position. A written document validates the importance of their work in the production and helps to establish a good working relationship between you and your volunteer staff members. It is probably not necessary to sign and countersign the documents. Simply providing the information in writing allows each volunteer to organize his calendar, meet your deadlines, and complete his assigned responsibilities in a professional manner. Contracts should stipulate the same information as those for paid staff, lacking only payment schedule information and penalities for failure to meet responsibilities.

Contracts for Purchased or Rented Materials

When contacting a supplier to purchase materials or rent items for your production, be sure to have them send a written estimate or contract for the exact materials or supplies for which you expect to be billed. As your materials or supplies are delivered, check all estimates or contracts against the incoming inventory. If there is ever a discrepancy, call the vendor and resolve the matter as quickly as possible. Keep all receipts in your file.

CREATING A PRODUCTION BUDGET

The first step in creating a production budget is to calculate the total amount of money available to fund your production. Generally, this money comes from a variety of sources.

- The school budget
- Ticket sales
- The sale of ads or sponsor subscriptions
- Traditional fundraising activities

Once you finish calculating your total projected budget, subtract the following nonnegotiable expenses:

- Royalty and rental fees for all performances

- Fee to purchase scripts, and musical scores
- Salaries for hired staff members

The subtotal is the amount of money available for all the production expenses. You should create a budget sheet with a line for each department: set, lighting, costume/makeup, sound, props, musicians, office supplies, tickets, playbill, and advertising and publicity. Be certain to include a miscellaneous line item to cover such things as batteries for the microphones, posterboard and markers to create signs, masking tape to post signs and notices, paper towels, band-aids, and so on. If you overlook too many small items, they can quickly add up and greatly impact your budget.

Once you've created a master budget sheet, you are ready to review the budget requests submitted by the designers. It is important to establish priorities: Which items are essential to your production? Which items are desirable but not essential? Which items are completely unnecessary? Are items duplicated between departmental budgets? After each individual budget is carefully reviewed, make the necessary cuts and let each designer know her total final budget allowance.

If you find that your production requires additional financial resources, consider adding fundraising activities to your schedule. Some productions cost more than others by their nature and design. Over the course of a season, it is good to balance an expensive production with a budget-conscious show. The profits from one will offset the expenses of the other.

The Director as Communication Specialist

The director of a play must be a communication specialist if he is to be successful. You are the only member of the production team who must communicate with each separate constituency during the rehearsal and performance process. You need the skills and resources to communicate with large and small groups of people and individuals in a variety of forums. Your methods of communicating with members of the production team, the school, or community should include all of the following:

Informal Writing. Memos, announcements, reminders, e-mail, faxes, and schedules

Formal Writing. Business letters, personal letters, thank you notes, acknowledgments, calendars, and schedules

Public Speaking. In front of groups of students and adults

Telephoning Skills: With staff, parents, vendors, and students as needed

Responding to Daily Communications. Timely responses to voice mail, e-mail messages, and fax messages

Individual Conferencing. With students, parents, and staff members as needed

Meetings. Both formal and informal, business meetings, production meetings, informational meetings

As director, you must have a comprehensive vocabulary, possessing the ability to communicate equally with high school students, professional staff, and technical vendors. You must be able to exchange ideas and information at every ability level and with all members of the production team and community. Most important, you must be a good listener. If you are a patient, thoughtful, and considerate listener, students, parents, professional staff, school administrators, and community members will all feel at ease expressing their thoughts and ideas about the quality and growth of the theater program and its membership. When the director is a good listener, students feel valued and are committed to excellence in artistry, and staff members feel appreciated and will return for future shows when invited. Parents, community members, and school administrators feel included and will be supportive of the artistic goals and accomplishments of the theater students.

THE ART OF COMMUNICATION

There are a few general rules that will simplify all your communication woes.

1. Put everything that is important in writing. Be sure to date all important letters, notices, schedules, and memos.
2. Do not ever engage in idle gossip.
3. Keep private matters strictly confidential.
4. Treat all members of your staff equally. Give the same notice and professional consideration to paid and volunteer staff members.
5. Treat all student members of the company equally. Give the same notice and professional consideration to all students: leading player or chorus member, senior or freshman, cast or crew.
6. Be complimentary. In private, offer specific compliments to individual members of your staff, cast, and crew whenever possible. In public, compliment the achievement of groups: the cast, the costume crew, the orchestra members, and so on. Take every opportunity to recognize growth and improvement, however small, in each member of your program.
7. Say thank you whenever possible. It is a small but important courtesy to offer a word of thanks when anyone completes a task or performs an act of kindness. Thanks should be extended to staff members, students in the cast or crew, parent volunteers—everyone!

The general constituencies requiring regular communication with the director are:

Student Members of the Cast
The members of the cast have the greatest amount of contact with the director. They will work with you daily in rehearsal. Most members of a cast will develop a personal relationship with you and feel comfortable approaching you with questions or concerns.

Student Members of the Crew

The members of the crew do not have a lot of contact with the director, so it is very important for you to learn the names of all the student crew members and use their names whenever possible. Members of the crew should feel acknowledged by you and important to the success of the production.

All Members of the Production Staff

The members of the production staff will expect and require a high level of communication from you. If the members of the staff enjoy working with young people, have a professional attitude, and are committed to producing a great product, they will often seek your reaction to new ideas as they implement and tweak their design concepts.

Parent Volunteers

Parent volunteers, in general, come in two varieties: those who need to speak with you as often as possible and those who are afraid to bother you with their questions. It has been my experience that both varieties have equally good intentions, are volunteering to help the students reach greater success, and are deserving of the director's undivided attention. A high school play could not survive without parent support. All parents who volunteer want to make a significant contribution. It is critical to spend some time with each volunteer, to learn each person's name, to engage in personal conversation, and to say thank you whenever possible.

Vendors and Suppliers

Vendors and suppliers are both a necessary evil and a great resource. When you locate a friendly, reliable, professional vendor, develop a good relationship and keep it healthy. There is nothing more important than being able to ask a vendor for advice on a new product or service and know that you will receive honest information. Cultivating relationships with rental houses is also important. The pricing structure in much of the rental industry is flexible. One-time customers pay one price; loyal, repeat customers often receive a friendlier price. Long-term association with good vendors is a win-win situation. The vendor relies on loyal customers; the customer relies on the goods and services of a quality vendor.

School Administration

It is critical to keep the lines of communication open with the members of your school administration. Depending on the structure of your school, the administration might include the superintendent or head of the school, the assistant superintendent, personnel director, members of the board of education, the high school principal or headmaster, the assistant principal or dean, the director of guidance, the director of admissions, and any immediate departmental supervisor. Keep these administrators in the communication loop; be sure they know what play is in production. Extend a personal invitation to them to attend the performance of their choice.

School Staff

The school staff, faculty, support personnel, and clerical employees should receive notices and invitations regarding the current theatrical production. Little efforts can produce great results. Keeping in mind that the school staff members interact with the students daily, most of them have a genuine interest in the students. It is a good idea to give your school staff early notice of an upcoming production in the form of a memo, flyer, or cast and crew list. As the performance dates near, send an invitation to all staff members to attend the performance of their choice. If your budget allows, offer the staff complimentary seating. It is a nice perk and is usually well deserved.

Greater School Community (Elementary or Middle Schools)

If your production is appropriate for all ages, be sure to send a notice to all the schools in your district. Most schools have a weekly or biweekly newsletter and actively seek articles of interest. Have your publicity coordinator write a short blurb about your production, including the names of all the student leads and crew chiefs. Most families enjoy the opportunity to support school events. Communicating with all the families in your school district can greatly improve your ticket sales and expand your future audience base.

Local Community Members

It takes a great deal of effort to reach out to the members of your community not affiliated with the school. Many high school theater programs offer special performances for senior citizens, people with disabilities, or children. Posting flyers in local churches, synagogues, community centers, and shopping centers can attract new audience members to your theater.

Parents of the Cast and Crew

It is wise to invest a great deal of energy communicating with the parents of the cast and crew. Although you may be giving all students important paperwork and schedules, many teens are less than reliable about sharing these documents with their parents. It is a good rule to either require a parent signature on important documents or to mail each parent his or her own copy of critical production information. Remember, parents want to work with you to help their children succeed. Your written communication can make this possible.

The Audience

It is important to communicate with the audience. Following a performance, many audience members enjoy meeting the director and sharing their impressions of the production. Most of these conversations are sweet—very complimentary and short. When you make yourself available to audience members after a performance, you create a favorable impression. Audience members are more willing to become subscription members if the quality of each production is consistently good and you are a welcoming host.

Choosing a Property

Choosing a property, or play, is the most important decision a director makes in the preproduction process. If you choose a play or musical that is a good match for your talent pool, budget, facility, and community, you are on your way to a successful production. But if you choose a play or musical that is not a good match, every step of the journey to opening night will be fraught with difficulty.

THE FOUR-YEAR PLAN

The first step in choosing a property at the high school level is to review your past productions with the four-year plan in mind. In the four-year plan, a student who joins your theater program as a freshman and participates in your program for four years should experience four different types or styles of plays or musicals during his high school career. This should be true for all students in the cast and crews. Plays and musicals can differ in many ways. The following list offers examples of the most common differences between properties in content, style, structure, and physical or technical requirements.

Content. Is the play or musical comedic or dramatic?

Comedy Treatment. Is the show a comedy or a farce? Does the property require physical comedy? Is it overt or subtle? Silly or sophisticated?

Time Period. Does the show take place in a historical period or contemporary times?

Language. Is the use of language formal, idiomatic, or contemporary? Is an accent or dialect required? Does the script include prose? Does it include a foreign language?

Structure. Is the show an ensemble piece? Are there a few leading roles and many minor characters? Are all the principal roles equal? Do any actors play multiple roles? Is the property structured in one, two, or three acts?

Physical or Technical Requirements. Which is the primary physical or technical element of the play: the set, the lighting, the costumes, or the props? Any special effects?

Musical. Does the show require singing or belting? Does the show include dancing or musical staging?

SELECTION CRITERIA

When you begin the process of selecting a play or musical to produce, it is important to realistically assess the abilities of your students, the limitations of your facility, and the expectations of your community. There are many factors to consider when selecting a property. It is critical to prioritize your selection criteria.

Finding the Right Match

As director, you will want to choose a play that equally excites all members of your theatrical community—staff, cast, crews, parents, local audience, and school administration. To achieve this goal, each play or musical under consideration must be evaluated from several viewpoints.

- Will play and audience match? Does the community expect you to choose a family show? Is the show appropriate for young children? Does the subject matter of the play reflect the values and interests of community members?

- How does the play portray women, minorities, or ethnic groups? Does it re-enforce the values of the community? Is the subject matter appropriate for an educational environment?

- Does the property have an intrinsic educational value? What will the students learn about themselves and their world from working on this play? How will each student's knowledge of theater and stagecraft be advanced by participation in this play?

Availability

Once you've selected a property, contact the licensing agent to see if the play or musical is available for production. *Never perform a play or musical without a legal agreement from the licensing agent.* You should request permission to perform a property *before* you announce the play and hold auditions. If the play is unavailable, choose another property.

For a play, you should expect to purchase scripts for the members of your cast and crew and pay a royalty fee per performance . The fee is based on the number of performances, seating capacity of your theater, and ticket prices.

The licensing agreement and fee structure for a musical is more complicated. For a musical, you should expect to pay a royalty fee per performance *plus* a rental fee for scripts, vocal books, and orchestra parts *plus* a purchase fee for scores and miscellaneous materials that vary from show to show. Read all the fine print in your contract carefully.

Before you sign the licensing agreement for a property, be sure you address the remaining criteria. If at any point you decide the play under consideration is not a good match for your group, choose another property!

Physical and Technical Requirements

Once you've selected a property, you must determine the physical and technical requirements of the work. Does the play require one set or many? Are the sets complicated? Does each character require one costume or several? Are the costumes complicated? Does the lighting plot require more than basic illumination, such as storm effects, day or night, season of year? Does the production require special elements (fire, magic, running water)? Is the overall size of the production big or small? Do you have an adequate performance space? Do you have enough backstage or storage space?

Staffing

Once you've determined the physical and technical needs of your production, it is time to evaluate the abilities of your production staff. The goal of every director in assembling a production staff is to hire the best people possible. But, do you hire professional staff members or rely on volunteers?

Do you have a staff member to head each separate department or do you, the director, assume some of that responsibility? Is your staff (paid or volunteer) capable of meeting the demands of the production under consideration? Does each designer have the knowledge to create the necessary design elements in set, lighting, costume, and sound? Does each designer have the skill to implement the design and instruct student members of the crew? Are you able to meet your staffing needs for the production?

Student Enrollment

It is important for you to honestly evaluate the importance of the theater production in your school. Is the play important for a large population of the student body? Do 10 to 20 percent of your school's student body hope to be involved in the production in some way? Or do you service a smaller, more select group of students?

These are important questions. It is often impossible to provide a position for every student who might be interested in participating in a play. It is unfortunate, however, when a director chooses a property that doesn't match student interest or availability, thereby needing more students than are available or excluding interested students.

The factors to consider when evaluating student enrollment needs are:

• How many cast positions are needed? How many students do you anticipate auditioning? Will you have enough people to cast the show effectively? Enough men? Enough women? Enough singers and dancers? Do the students have the skills and experience required for the roles?

• How many crew positions are needed? How many students do you anticipate enrolling for those positions? Do the students have the skills and experience required? Can you fill all crew positions effectively? If your show requires a large crew for the construction period and a small crew for the performances, how do you address that problem?

• If your show requires a large cast and crew and you do not have enough student members for the crew, do you double the cast as crew? Or, if you have more members in the crew than the cast, do you double crew members in cameo acting roles? Is that an educationally or artistically sound choice for the property under consideration?

It is important to determine the needs of the theater students you service, and it is a challenge to meet those specific needs with any production. Every director needs creative strategies for including students in the educational theatrical process while maintaining an artistic overview of the production.

Time Management

Once you've addressed the requirements of your staff, cast, and crew, it is time to sit with a calendar and count your production days. A play usually requires six to eight weeks of rehearsal depending on the experience of the students involved and the complexity and technical elements of the production. A musical has greater production demands and requires more rehearsal time than a play, usually eight to twelve weeks. Even a small musical is more complex and demanding than a large play, because it combines acting, singing, and dancing and usually requires a large cast and an orchestra.

When counting the rehearsal weeks on a calendar, be sure you have at least the minimum number of weeks necessary to meet your production needs. Whenever possible, build an extra week or two into your schedule to allow for unanticipated interruptions due to illness, weather, or injury.

Budget

Finally, once you've met all the personnel and production needs for a property, it is time to address the budget requirements. At this point, you should total the fixed costs for the production, ask design staff members for a rough estimate of their projected budgets, and estimate the projected revenue from ticket sales and donations.

The fixed costs include all licensing fees and staff salaries. The designers should supply estimates in each major department: set, lighting, costume, and sound. If the combined totals of fixed and estimated costs equal (or near) the total projected revenue, you are ready to sign your licensing agreement and begin your production!

Preproduction Planning

Careful and insightful preproduction planning is critical for the success of every show. When a technical rehearsal runs smoothly, when a play looks easy, or when a director is complimented as gifted, it most often reflects the attention to detail in the planning process of a production. Careful, detailed planning is critical. This is the responsibility of the director.

During the process of preproduction planning, the director examines every aspect of a production from personnel to physical needs and limitations to calendar requirements. Preproduction planning requires documentation. The director will produce many lists, charts, and tables that itemize all elements of the play and all the players. These printed documents provide the information that unifies the production and keeps its progress on schedule.

The four major elements in the preproduction planning process are the production analysis, the scene breakdown, the contact sheet, and the production packet.

CREATING A PRODUCTION ANALYSIS

A production analysis is a written summary of the total requirements of a show. It usually appears in the form of a chart or table and details the needs of the production scene by scene as described in the script. The director creates the production analysis. The analysis helps the director gain a better understanding of the overall size and needs of a production and allows the design staff to clarify technical requirements and negotiate priorities and stage space during production meetings.

The first column of the production analysis designates the act, scene, and page where the action, set, technical requirement, special effects, or props take place. It is standard to use a Roman numeral for the act, an Arabic numeral for the scene, and *p.* for the exact script page. For example, act I, scene 3, page 12 would be written I/3/p.12.

The second column includes all information about cast members and their costumes. You will use this information later when creating the rehearsal scene breakdown. Some of the costume information included in the script may be very general (appears in elegant attire, in evening wear, dressed casually), but it should be included in this list. You should also look for costume clues that will assist the costume designer. If an actor is required to fight, or wear an ornate headpiece while dancing, or hide something in a jacket pocket, these functions must be considered during the design process.

The third column, which is used for musical productions, includes all the music that appears in the production: the overture and entr'acte, musical numbers, reprises, dance music, incidental music, scene change music, and bow-and-exit music. You should list both the music number (from the score) and the title of each selection in this column.

The fourth column includes notes on the set requirements. Descriptions of separate sets, necessary entrances or exits, staircases, moving walls or panels, space needed for furniture pieces or movement (a fight scene or chase scene) should all be included here.

The fifth column addresses lighting needs and should include time of day, season of year, and any practical lighting requirements (chandelier, bedside lamp, lanterns).

The sixth column details all props. Set furniture, critical set dressings, and personal props for actors should all appear here.

The seventh column describes the sound requirements for the production. In a play, this list might include recorded music, sound effects, and off-stage microphones. In a musical, the list includes all these elements *plus* specific microphone needs of individual singers and of ensemble singing.

The last column addresses special effects requirements. These can include real fire or the effects of fire, smoke, fog, explosions, rain or storm effects, gun shots, magic tricks, and any other novelty elements in your production.

PRODUCTION ANALYSIS

Act/Scene/Page	Cast/Costume	Musical Numbers	Set	Lighting	Props	Sound	Special Effects

The completed production analysis should be introduced first to the design staff at the concept meeting. This document provides a formal analysis of the needs of the show and complements the idealistic, wishful discussion that always occurs at the concept meeting. At the follow-up design meeting, the director should take careful notes of design proposals and decisions and update the production analysis as needed. The production analysis should be a living part of the production process. As philosophical or practical changes or choices are made during the rehearsal period, the production analysis should be updated and redistributed to the design staff. It should always reflect the most current decisions about the production elements of your show.

CREATING A SCENE BREAKDOWN

A scene breakdown is a detailed who's who of the cast. Two different types of scene breakdowns are commonly used. One features a full production overview, the other a full character overview.

One of these two types is usually better for the play or musical you are producing. Occasionally, for a very large-scale production, it is helpful to use both models. The scene breakdown is created by the director and is the first step in designing a rehearsal schedule for the cast of a show.

Scene Breakdown with Production Overview

The scene breakdown chart below details the cast requirements of each scene, including both actor and character names, reference to pages of the script, musical numbers, and set and costume requirements. The table design for this scene breakdown is similar to the production analysis, but it is limited to information needed by the cast for the rehearsal process. The scene breakdown will help cast members understand the overall structure of the show and specifically how their role fits into that structure.

As in the production analysis, the first column of the scene breakdown designates the act, scene, and page where the action, set, technical requirement, props, or special effects take place. The second column states the actor's name; the third column states the character name and costume for that scene. When the ensemble is needed for a scene or song, the second column should say full company and the third column should state their company roles (townspeople, soldiers, members of the court) and general costume descriptions. The fourth column includes all the music that appears in the production. The fifth and sixth columns list the location and props for each scene. The last column addresses special effects requirements.

SCENE BREAKDOWN WITH PRODUCTION OVERVIEW

Act/Scene/Page	Actor's Name	Character Name and Costume	Musical Numbers	Set Location	Props	Special Effects

The scene breakdown will be helpful to both the costume/makeup crew and the cast when they complete the wardrobe breakdown for each actor in the production. It will also be helpful to the stage managers when creating the large format running order of the show for dress rehearsals and performances.

Scene Breakdown with Character Overview

This scene breakdown chart details the appearance of every character in each scene of the play. If you are producing a play or musical with a large cast or where actors portray multiple roles within the cast, this model helps to organize your actors.

The first column of this scene breakdown designates the character by name. The remaining columns show each act and scene where the character appears.

SCENE BREAKDOWN WITH CHARACTER OVERVIEW

	Act I Scene:								Act II Scene:					
Character Names *In order of appearance*	1	2	3	4	5	6	7	8	1	2	3	4	5	6
Character 1	X	X		X		X		X	X			X	X	X
Character 2	X	X		X	X	X		X		X	X		X	X
Character 3		X	X				X	X	X			X	X	X
Character 4			X		X		X	X		X	X			X

CREATING A CONTACT SHEET

It is both courteous and professional to create a complete contact sheet including all student members of the cast and crew. The student contact sheet should be created on the computer and updated as changes are made.

The contact sheet should be organized by department, with all members of each department listed alphabetically. One method for organizing the information is to list the the stage management team first, then the cast, crews for props, set, lighting, and costume, and the house staff. Be sure all names are spelled correctly and all members of the cast and crew are identified properly by title or position. A typical student contact sheet could be organized with the following headings:

STUDENT CONTACT SHEET

Crew Title or Position	Name (last name first)	Grade	Phone Number	E-mail Address	Mailing Address	Parent Names and Phone Number	Parent E-mail Address

The contact sheet should be included in the production packet for distribution to all staff and student members of the cast and crew. Additionally, all parent volunteers will need a copy of the student contact list.

At the high school level, it is important to create a second contact sheet with information about all the adult members of the staff. This list should have limited distribution. It should be available to all members of the professional and volunteer staff, the stage managers, and school administration.

CREATING THE PRODUCTION PACKET

A production packet is a complete packet of information distributed to all members of the professional and volunteer staff and all student members of the cast and crew at the start of any production. The production packet gives every member of the company, adult and student alike, the same information, same set of expectations, and same schedule overview necessary for a successful production.

The director (and/or producer) is responsible for creating the materials in the production packet. Members of the creative staff may offer input during the process of creating the schedule and crew rules and expectations. The stage management team should assist with photocopying, assembling, and labeling the packets. Each production packet should include the following information:

A Complete Company List

The company list should include all members of the staff, cast, crew, and orchestra and should appear in a format similar to the listings in the playbill.

The staff list should include all adult staff, both professional and volunteer. The staff list should begin with the producer/director, then list the music director, choreographer, set designer, lighting designer, costume designer, sound designer, properties coordinator, publicity coordinator, ticket manager, and parent volunteer coordinator.

The cast should be listed in order of appearance. The character roles should be listed in the left column; the name of the actor portraying the role should appear in the right column. All minor roles should be credited to appropriate members of the company, followed by the chorus or ensemble members listed in alphabetical order. The orchestra list should include the student name and instrument assignment in the ensemble.

The crew list should begin with the production stage manager followed by the stage managers, and then student crew chiefs followed by the members of each crew. A complete crew list follows:

Production stage manager	Costume/makeup crew chiefs
Assistant stage managers	Costume/makeup crew
Properties crew chiefs	Sound crew chiefs
Properties crew	Sound crew
Set construction crew chiefs	House managers
Set construction crew	House staff
Run crew	Photographer
Lighting crew chief	Show logo designer
Lighting crew	

Contact Sheet

All student production packets should include a complete student contact sheet. All staff and stage manager packets should include both the student contact sheet and the staff contact sheet.

Master Production Schedule

This schedule should appear in calendar form. It includes a daily listing of cast rehearsal hours and crew work sessions, all run-through rehearsals, equipment load-in dates, the orchestra rehearsal, the costume parade, cue sessions and light walking, the tech rehearsal, dress rehearsals, performances, and the strike. The master production schedule should be included in the packets of all professional and volunteer staff, stage managers, and crew chiefs.

Complete Scene Breakdown

The scene breakdown should be included in the packets of the music director, the choreographer, the costume designer, the properties coordinator, and all members of the cast, stage management team, the props crew, and the costume crew.

Complete Rehearsal and Work Schedules

These schedules can be in a calendar format or appear as a weekly list, but the information should be as detailed and complete as possible. It is both courteous and professional to provide everyone with a daily rehearsal/work calendar at the start of the production.

For Cast. The cast rehearsal schedule should include all stage managers, members of the props crew, and members of the cast. It should include specific scenes and musical numbers or choreography scheduled for that day's rehearsal. It should also include deadlines for memorizing music, scenes, and choreography. Although your principal actors may be needed for almost every rehearsal, second leads, minor characters, and chorus members are rarely needed on a daily basis. The rehearsal schedule should detail which members of the cast are needed on each day, thus allowing parents to schedule necessary personal and medical appointments after school on days when their child is not needed in rehearsal.

For Crews. The crew work schedule should give the schedule of each crew: set, construction, run, properties, lighting, costume/makeup, and sound. Although each crew will have its own work schedule, the crew calendar should reflect the needs and requirements of *all* crews. The crew work schedule should include the name of the crew, days and hours of work, and the number of crew members required for each day. If you have twelve to eighteen students on the set construction crew, you will not need all of them on any one construction day. It is impossible to have enough project work or to supervise that many students at one time. Instead, your set, lighting, and sound designers should approximate the number of students they need on a daily basis. The crew chiefs should then assign students to staff the designers' personnel requests.

All Expectations, Rules, and Policies

Expectations. All students in the cast and all student members of each crew should receive a written, detailed job description in their production packets. The job description should include an overview of their position and a specific list of their production responsibilities. If each student (and her parents) understands what is expected and required of her, that student has a chance to be successful and meet the goals that you, the director, set before her. Clearly stating the responsibilities of each position also validates the role of each student in the production and allows him to see his specific contribution to the final product.

Rules and Policies. Every theater troupe has rules and policies that enable the group to operate, but few state these policies in writing. It is sound educational policy to state common rules of behavior and policy in writing so that all students and their parents have access to the same information. All rules about lateness or absence from cast rehearsals or crew work sessions should be stated in writing. Illness should be treated differently than "just forgetting" about a scheduled rehearsal or scheduling a dental appointment during that time. Policies on food, rehearsal breaks, open or closed rehearsals, open or closed backstage and dressing room areas should all appear *in writing* so that all members of the staff, cast, and crew have the same rules and abide by the same policies.

All Required Forms and Paperwork

These include a prior-conflict sheet, several ticket order forms, a T-shirt order form, a parent volunteer form, and any other general production paperwork necessary for your show.

A Complete Script of the Show

All members of the staff, cast, stage management team, properties crew, and all crew chiefs need a complete script. It is also possible for additional members of specific crews to want or need a script. If the script of your show is available for purchase, be sure to buy enough copies for every member of the company requiring the script.

Music

The vocal music for a show is published in one of two ways: in a vocal book showing only the vocal line with text (no accompaniment parts) or in a traditional piano/vocal arrangement. Each member of the cast and chorus needs copies of each song he sings in the show. Although the traditional piano/vocal arrangement is preferred, cast members can work from either version of published music. Each member of the stage management team, however, needs a copy of the piano/vocal arrangement of *all* the songs in the show.

Preparing the Script

It is the director's job to be sure that the script is complete and in good order before the production packets are made and the rehearsals begin. At first glance, this does not seem like a difficult job, but when there are discrepancies in the script, or when the text is illegible or incomplete, all members of the company are affected.

HONOR YOUR CONTRACT

The contract that you sign on behalf of your school to produce a play or musical usually stipulates that no changes can be made to the script or music without written consent of the author(s) or the licensing agent. Some directors choose to ignore this contract provision and change and cut the property. But once you make a commitment to a play or musical, you, as the director, are both legally and artistically responsible for maintaining the integrity of the show and of your production.If the play or musical is not well suited for your high school environment, if you feel a need to alter the language, remove a scene, or make any change that compromises the intent of the authors, *choose another play.*

PREPARING A PLAY

When producing a play, it is most important to be sure that everyone is working from the same edition of the printed script. Different editions have different page numbers, different notes and comments, and sometimes a different word here or there or different stage directions—enough changes to hamper the rehearsal process.

Scripts can be purchased from a bookstore, a theatrical store, or from the licensing agent for the property. Be sure to purchase enough copies for every member of the staff, all crew chiefs, and all members of the cast and the props and costume crews. Most plays are published in a small book form. This format is fine for reference and study, but impossible for rehearsals and recording cues for a production. You should create an enlarged master copy of the script on $8^1/_2$-by-11-inch paper. The master copy of the rehearsal script should be photocopied for selected members of the company who need to annotate their scripts with blocking notes or production cues. All rehearsal scripts should be *in addition to and not in place of* the purchased scripts. Each rehearsal script should be put in a three-ring binder.

PREPARING A MUSICAL

When producing a musical, your school will pay a rental fee for the use of the scripts, vocal books, and a conductor's score. These items are not available for purchase for most musical properties. It is important to place your order far enough in advance to secure the materials with enough pre-production time for the director.

It is difficult to prepare a musical script. There are often many discrepancies found in a musical script and all of them should be resolved before the production packets are assembled and the rehearsals begin. The director needs several sources of material before beginning the process of preparing the musical script: the musical score, the vocal book, an original cast recording, and the published script for the musical. Most of the errors in a musical will be in the printed lyrics.

First, carefully compare the original cast recording with the musical score. Are the lyrics sung on the recording the same as those appearing in the score? Are the verses in the same order? Are there more or fewer verses in the recording or in the score? Where there are differences, do you have a preference for one of the versions?

Once you have completed this exercise, then compare the lyrics printed in the score with those printed in the script. Ask yourself the same questions: Are the lyrics in the score the same as those appearing in the script? Are the verses in the same order? Are there more or fewer verses in the score or in the script? Where there are differences, do you have a preference for one of the versions?

It is wise to consult your music director when making some of these decisions. Once you arrive at a resolution for the conflicted lyrics, you must make corrections to the script. This means retyping some of the lyric pages. Be sure to carefully renumber the new pages.

Once you resolve all inconsistencies and finalize the complete script, create a master copy of the script on 8½-by-11-inch paper. Photocopy the master copy for selected members of the company who need to annotate their scripts with blocking and choreography notes or production cues. All rehearsal scripts are *in addition to and not in place of* the rented or purchased scripts. Put each rehearsal script in a three-ring binder.

THE DIRECTOR'S BOOK

The director's book is a complete record of the production. The book includes the script and all paperwork for the show organized in a three-ring binder. In the director's book are:

- Production analysis
- Scene breakdown
- Master production schedule
- Cast rehearsal schedule
- All crew schedules
- Staff/cast/crew lists
- Contact sheets
- Design notes

- Complete props list
- Complete production budget
- All staff contracts
- All contracts and rental agreements for materials and supplies
- All receipts for purchase of materials
- Musical score
- Script

Use tabs to divide the scenes in the script. All blocking, props, and costume notes should be clearly marked in the pages of the script. Fabric samples, costume photographs, and set design sketches relevant to each scene should also be included.

Creating Master Production and Rehearsal Schedules

Both the master production schedule and the master rehearsal schedule are master calendars. The production schedule includes all aspects of a production: all relevant meetings, rehearsals, and deadlines from preproduction planning through the strike. The rehearsal schedule has a detailed breakdown of each rehearsal—scene by scene, page by page.

Both schedules reflect the director's organizational overview for a production and help determine whether the play or musical can be produced within the time allotted. The director creates both the master production and rehearsal schedules. The production schedule should be in calendar form and is distributed to all professional and volunteer staff, the stage managers, and all crew chiefs. The rehearsal schedule can appear in calendar and/or linear form and is distributed to all staff members, the stage managers, the cast, and members of the props, sound, and costume crews. This schedule only records rehearsal and performance dates and is limited to information important to members of the cast during the rehearsal process.

CREATING THE SCHEDULES

To create a master production or rehearsal schedule, the director needs a copy of the script, the completed production analysis, the completed scene breakdown, and a blank calendar. Number the weeks of your calendar to indicate the number of weeks of rehearsal you have for the production. A play usually requires six to eight weeks of rehearsal, depending on the experience of the students involved and the complexity and technical elements of the production. A musical usually requires eight to twelve weeks of rehearsal time.

Begin both calendars by working backward.

1. Pencil in all performances and the strike.
2. Next add parent photo night (see chapter 7) and all dress rehearsals.

3. Schedule the technical rehearsal on the Saturday or Sunday prior to your performances.

4. Schedule the orchestra rehearsal and costume parade (see chapter 7) for the week preceding the technical rehearsal.

5. Schedule the lighting cue dates and light walking sessions (see chapter 7).

6. For the production schedule only: Schedule the load-ins for all rented lighting and sound equipment. Create a separate load-in date for each technical element of the production.

7. Schedule a pretech run-through for the week preceding the tech load-ins. All staff, crew chiefs and members of the props, sound, lighting, costume, and run crews should attend this run-through with their scripts, taking notes throughout.

8. Schedule a final run-through for the cast prior to the pretech run-through. Work carefully through this rehearsal, answering any final questions the cast may have about use of space, set, props, or costume changes. The cast should feel confident about all elements of the production at the conclusion of this last private rehearsal.

The Production Schedule

Once you have these dates logged on the calendar, continue working in this fashion until all rehearsals, meetings, and deadlines are scheduled. The master production schedule for a musical should include the following information:

- Ordering play or musical materials from the licensing agent
- Expected date to receive rented or purchased materials
- Audition announcement; crew sign-ups begin
- Concept and design meetings
- Dates for auditions and posting the cast
- Cast rehearsal information: date, time, and location of rehearsal
- Crew work session information: date, time, and location of session
- Orchestra rehearsals (without cast)
- Construction deadlines for set, props, and costumes; firm dates when parts of the set or the entire set is complete, when all final props are due for rehearsal, when costumes are complete and due for rehearsals and photographs
- Deadline for ordering additional rented materials: costumes, props, specialty set pieces, and lighting or sound equipment
- Date rented materials are expected to arrive: costumes, props, and set items
- Publicity and photo sessions and deadlines
- Company dinners and/or parties: tech rehearsal dinner, opening night dinner, cast party
- Final run-through (for cast) and pretech run-through (for staff, crew chiefs, and members of the lighting, costume, and run crews)
- Tech load-in dates: schedule separate deadlines for technical elements of the production

- Costume parade
- Orchestra rehearsal (with cast)
- Lighting cue sessions and light-walking sessions
- Tech rehearsal
- Dress rehearsals and parent photo night
- Performances
- Strike

Once the master production schedule is complete, each designer needs to create a schedule for her own crew, and the director creates the cast rehearsal schedule.

The Rehearsal Schedule

On the rehearsal calendar, log in all rehearsals and deadlines. The master rehearsal schedule for a musical should include the following information:

- Specific rehearsal information for each scheduled rehearsal. This includes:
  - The date, time, and location of rehearsal. If multiple rehearsals are scheduled simultaneously, list all information. When multiple rehearsals are scheduled, be sure to assign a stage manager to each location, for example music rehearsal in band room (list musical numbers), choreography rehearsal onstage (list musical numbers), blocking rehearsal in choir room (list script pages).
  - The exact act/scene/pages of the script scheduled for rehearsal.
  - The exact musical numbers scheduled for vocal rehearsals (identify by both title and number from the musical score or vocal book).
  - The exact musical numbers scheduled for choreography rehearsals (identify by both title and number from the musical score or vocal book).
  - When the rehearsal schedule is very complex, it is recommended that the character names and/or actor names be included with each scene/song listed.
- Deadlines for memorization of music
- Deadlines for memorization of script and blocking (called off-book)
- Deadlines for memorization of choreography
- Rehearsals requiring props
- Deadlines for final props
- Rehearsals requiring sound (music or special effects)
- Deadlines for final sound (music or special effects)
- Rehearsals scheduled on the set
- Publicity and photo sessions and deadlines
- Company dinners and/or parties: tech rehearsal dinner, opening night dinner, cast party

- Final run-through (for cast) and pretech run-through (for staff, crew chiefs, and members of the lighting, costume, and run crews)
- Costume parade
- Orchestra rehearsal
- Light-walking sessions
- Tech rehearsal
- Dress rehearsals and parent photo night
- Performances
- Strike

The scene breakdown and the master rehearsal should be posted in a prominent place on the theater announcement board. The rehearsal schedule should be amended and updated as needed.

SAMPLE MASTER CALENDARS

On pages 28 to 30 are models for the master production and rehearsal schedules. Both models will differ from your schedule in the following ways:

- The schedules should appear on actual calendar months: December, January, February, and so on.
- The schedules should include any school breaks or holidays: winter or spring break, President's Day, Martin Luther King, Jr. Day, special exam days when no classes meet, and so on.
- The schedules should include school events that present a conflict for your theater students or for the rehearsal spaces you need, such as concerts, sports events, or overnight school trips.
- The schedules should include the time and location for each rehearsal or crew work session that appears on the calendar.

Additional Production Schedule Information
- If your set designer only works on Monday, Wednesday, and Friday, only those days will say set design. That might open additional days for the cast to rehearse onstage.
- If you are able to target a midproduction deadline for Act I to be completed (props, dance costumes, set pieces, sound effects), add these deadlines to your master calendar.
- Include the orchestra rehearsals (without cast) on the master schedule.
- Include deadlines to place rental orders, complete playbill, order tickets, etc.

Additional Rehearsal Schedule Information
- Your schedule should include the exact material for each rehearsal (musical titles/numbers and script pages).
- On days when multiple rehearsals are schedules, it is recommended that the character names and/or actor names be included with each scene/song listed.

SAMPLE MASTER PRODUCTION SCHEDULE

	Sunday	Monday	Tuesday	Wednesday	Thursday	Friday	Saturday
WEEK 12		Announce Show and Performance Dates		Staff: Concept Meeting			
WEEK 11		Student Sign-ups for Cast Auditions and Crew Positions →	Staff: Design Meeting	Create Materials for Production Packets →			
WEEK 10		Auditions Crew Sign-Ups continue →	Auditions	Call-Back Auditions Assemble	Post Final Cast and Crew Lists Production Production Packets	Full-Company Meeting: Packets Distributed	
WEEK 9		Cast: Act I 3–6 P.M. in Choir Room	Cast: Act I 3–6 P.M. in Choir Room	Cast: Act I 3–6 P.M. in Choir Room Set Construction Begins	Cast: Act I 3–6 P.M. in Choir Room Tech Crews as Scheduled by Designers	Cast: Act I 3–6 P.M. in Choir Room Tech Crews as Scheduled by Designers	
WEEK 8		Cast: Act I 3–6 P.M. in Choir Room Tech Crews as Scheduled by Designers	Cast: Act I 3–6 P.M. in Choir Room Tech Crews as Scheduled by Designers	Cast: Act I 3–6 P.M. in Choir Room Tech Crews as Scheduled by Designers	Cast: Act I 3–6 P.M. in Choir Room Tech Crews as Scheduled by Designers	Cast: Act I 3–6 P.M. on Stage Tech Crews as Scheduled by Designers	
WEEK 7		Cast: Act I 3–6 P.M. in Choir Room Tech Crews as Scheduled by Designers	Cast: Act I 3–6 P.M. in Choir Room Tech Crews as Scheduled by Designers	Cast: Act I 3–6 P.M. in Choir Room Tech Crews as Scheduled by Designers	Cast: Act I 3–6 P.M. in Choir Room Tech Crews as Scheduled by Designers	Cast: Act I 3–6 P.M. on stage Tech Crews as Scheduled by Designers	
WEEK 6		Cast: Act I 3–6 P.M. in Choir Room Tech Crews as Scheduled by Designers	Cast: Act I 3–6 P.M. in Choir Room Tech Crews as Scheduled by Designers	Cast: Act I 3–6 P.M. on Stage Using any Completed Set with Run Crew	Cast: Act I 3–6 P.M. in Choir Room Tech Crews as Scheduled by Designers	Cast: Act I 3–6 P.M. on Stage Using any Completed Set with Run Crew	
WEEK 5		Cast: Act II 3–6 P.M. in Choir Room Tech Crews as Scheduled by Designers	Cast: Act II 3–6 P.M. in Choir Room Tech Crews as Scheduled by Designers	Cast: Act II 3–6 P.M. in Choir Room Tech Crews as Scheduled by Designers	Cast: Act II 3–6 P.M. in Choir Room Tech Crews as Scheduled by Designers	Cast: Act II 3–6 P.M. on Stage Tech Crews as Scheduled by Designers	
WEEK 4		Cast: Act II 3–6 P.M. in Choir Room Tech Crews as Scheduled by Designers	Cast: Act II 3–6 P.M. in Choir Room Tech Crews as Scheduled by Designers	Cast: Act II 3–6 P.M. in Choir Room Tech Crews as Scheduled by Designers	Cast: Act II 3–6 P.M. in Choir Room Tech Crews as Scheduled by Designers	Cast: Act II 3–6 P.M. on Stage Using any Completed Set with Run Crew	

	Sunday	Monday	Tuesday	Wednesday	Thursday	Friday	Saturday
WEEK 3		Cast Run-Through 3–6 P.M. on Stage Using any Completed Set with Run Crew	Cast: Run Act I 3–6 P.M. in Choir Room · · · Tech Crews as Scheduled by Designers	Cast: Run Act II 3–6 P.M. in Choir Room · · · Tech Crews as Scheduled by Designers	Final Cast Run-Through on Set with Run Crew	Pre-Tech Run-Through on Set with All Designers and All Crews	
WEEK 2		Cast: Run Act I in Choir Room · · · Lighting Load-In in Theater · · · Set: Final Painting in Theater →	Cast: Hair and Makeup Design Rehearsal in Dressing Room · · · Lighting Hang and Focus in Theater	Cast: Run Act II in Choir Room · · · Final Set Dressing in Theater →	Cast: Orchestra Rehearsal 7–10 P.M. in Band Room →	Costume Parade 3–6 P.M. on Stage Sound Load-In 3–6 P.M. in Theater Lighting Cue Session 6–11 P.M. in Theater	Final Dressing Room Set-up · · · Props Load-In Backstage · · · Lighting Cue Session and Light Walking in Theater
WEEK 1	Tech Rehearsal and Tech Dinner	Dress Rehearsal	Dress Rehearsal	Final Dress: Parent Photo Night	Performance and Opening Night Dinner	Performance	Performance, Partial Strike, and Cast Party
STRIKE	Complete Strike	All Rentals Returned Clean Theater					

SAMPLE MASTER REHEARSAL SCHEDULE*

This sample schedule assumes the following: The cast is scheduled for rehearsal every weekday; the music director is only available on Monday, Wednesday, and Friday; the choreographer is only available on Wednesday and Thursday; the set construction crew works Monday through Thursday; the props crew attends all blocking rehearsals.

	Sunday	Monday	Tuesday	Wednesday	Thursday	Friday	Saturday
WEEK 10		Auditions	Auditions	Callback Auditions	Final Cast List Posted	Full-Company Meeting: Production Packets Distributed	
WEEK 9		Cast: Act I 3–6 P.M. Music Rehearsal in Choir Room	Cast: Read-Through in choir room	Cast: Act I 3–6 P.M. Music Rehearsal in Choir Room	Cast: Act I 3–6 P.M. Blocking Rehearsal: in Choir Room	Cast: Act I 3–6 P.M. Music Rehearsal in Choir Room	
WEEK 8		Cast: Act I 3–6 P.M. Music Rehearsal in Choir Room	Cast: Act I 3–6 P.M. Blocking Rehearsal in Choir Room	Cast: Act I 3–6 P.M. Music Rehearsal in Band Room; Choreography Rehearsal in Choir Room	Cast: Act I 3–6 P.M. Blocking Rehearsal in Band Room; Choreography Rehearsal in Choir Room	Cast: Act I Blocking Rehearsal on Stage; Music Rehearsal in Choir Room	
WEEK 7		Cast: Act I 3–6 P.M. Music Rehearsal in Band Room; Blocking Rehearsal in Choir Room	Cast: Act I 3–6 P.M. Blocking Rehearsal in Choir Room	Cast: Act I 3–6 P.M. Music Rehearsal in Band Room; Choreography Rehearsal in Choir Room	Cast: Act I 3–6 P.M. Blocking Rehearsal in Band Room; Choreography Rehearsal in Choir Room	Cast: Act I 3–6 P.M. On Stage; Blocking Rehearsal on Stage; Music Rehearsal in Choir Room	

	Sunday	Monday	Tuesday	Wednesday	Thursday	Friday	Saturday
WEEK 6		Cast: Act I 3–6 P.M. Run Act I in choir room	Cast: Act I 3–6 P.M. Blocking Rehearsal in Choir Room	Cast: Act I 3–6 P.M. Run Act I on Stage, Using Any Completed Set with Run Crew	Cast: Act I 3–6 P.M. Blocking Rehearsal in Band Room; Choreography Rehearsal in Choir Room	Cast: Act I 3–6 P.M. Run Act I on Stage, Using Any Completed Set with Run Crew	
WEEK 5		Cast: Act II 3–6 P.M. Music Rehearsal in Band Room; Blocking Rehearsal in Choir Room	Cast: Act II 3–6 P.M. Blocking Rehearsal in Choir Room	Cast: Act II 3–6 P.M. Music Rehearsal in Band Room; Choreography Rehearsal in Choir Room	Cast: Act II 3–6 P.M. Blocking Rehearsal in Band Room; Choreography Rehearsal in Choir Room	Cast: Act II 3–6 P.M. Blocking Rehearsal on Stage; Music Rehearsal in Choir Room	
WEEK 4		Cast: Act II 3–6 P.M. Music Rehearsal in Band Room; Blocking Rehearsal in Choir Room	Cast: Act II 3–6 P.M Blocking Rehearsal in Choir Room	Cast: Act II 3–6 P.M. Run Act II in Choir Room	Cast: Act II 3–6 P.M. Blocking Rehearsal in Band Room; Choreography Rehearsal in Choir Room	Cast: Act II 3–6 P.M. Run Act II on Stage, Using Any Completed Set with Run Crew	
WEEK 3		Cast: Complete Run-Through 3–6 P.M. on Stage, Using Any Completed Set with Run Crew	Cast: Run Act I 3–6 P.M. in Choir Room	Cast: Run Act II 3–6 P.M. in Choir Room	Final Cast Run-Through on Set with Run Crew	Pretech Run-Through on Set with All Designers and All Crews	
WEEK 2		Cast: Run Act I	Cast: Hair and Makeup Design Rehearsal in Dressing Room	Cast: Run Act II	Cast: Orchestra Rehearsal 7-10 P.M. in Band Room	Costume Parade 3–6 P.M. on Stage	Final Dressing Room Set-up Props Load-In Backstage Lighting-Cue Session and Light Walking in Theater
WEEK 1	Tech Rehearsal and Tech Dinner	Dress Rehearsal	Dress Rehearsal	Final Dress: Parent Photo Night	Performance and Opening Night Dinner	Performance	Performance, Partial Strike, and Cast Party
STRIKE	Complete Strike	All Rentals Returned Clean Theater					

SAMPLE MASTER REHEARSAL SCHEDULE IN LINEAR FORM

This calendar includes the same information from the calendar model, but it is structured in linear form. This format allows more room for writing details in the master rehearsal schedule and is often a preferred option for a large-scale musical production. Again, your schedule will be different from this model in that it should reflect actual calendar dates (Monday, Jan. 5; Tuesday, Jan. 6; Wednesday, Jan. 7). And, as on the calendar schedule, it should should include any school breaks or holidays or any school events that might conflict with rehearsals.

WEEK 10	Monday:	Auditions
	Tuesday:	Auditions
	Wednesday:	Callback auditions
	Thursday:	Final cast list posted
	Friday:	Full-company meeting: Production packets distributed
WEEK 9	Monday:	3–6 P.M., Act I, Music rehearsal in choir room
	Tuesday:	3–6 P.M., Act I, Read-through in choir room
	Wednesday:	3–6 P.M., Act I, Music Rehearsal in choir room
	Thursday:	3–6 P.M., Act I, Blocking rehearsal in choir room
	Friday:	3–6 P.M., Act I, Music rehearsal in choir room
WEEK 8	Monday:	3–6 P.M., Act I, Music rehearsal in choir room
	Tuesday:	3–6 P.M., Act I, Blocking rehearsal in choir room
	Wednesday:	3–6 P.M., Act I, Music rehearsal in band room; Choreography rehearsal in choir room
	Thursday:	3–6 P.M., Act I, Blocking rehearsal in band room; Choreography rehearsal in choir room
	Friday:	3–6 P.M., Act I, Blocking rehearsal onstage; Music rehearsal in choir room
WEEK 7	Monday:	3–6 P.M., Act I, Music rehearsal in band room; Blocking rehearsal in choir room
	Tuesday:	3–6 P.M., Act I, Blocking rehearsal in choir room
	Wednesday:	3–6 P.M., Act I, Music rehearsal in band room; Choreography rehearsal in choir room
	Thursday:	3–6 P.M., Act I, Blocking rehearsal in band room; Choreography rehearsal in choir room
	Friday:	3–6 P.M., Act I, Blocking rehearsal onstage; Music rehearsal in choir room

The Director in Rehearsal

As director, you will spend more time with the members of the cast than with any other individual or group of people involved in a production. The relationship between you and the cast as an ensemble is unique. You must establish a relationship with the cast where each member feels equally valued and important, regardless of the size of his part. Establishing good relationships is a critical part of the your success as a director. A good director knows the strengths and weaknesses of each performer—what one is willing and able to do and what another shies away from. In building a personal relationship with each cast member, develop a bond of trust that allows you to challenge a performer to take risks, experiment with new ideas, and grow as an actor. It is through the rehearsal process that you, as director, teach, mentor, and lead the cast members toward their common performance goal.

WORKING WITH THE CAST

Every director has preferences for rehearsal policies and techniques. It is important to re-evaluate those preferences before each new production to be certain those policies and techniques are appropriate for the property at hand.

Rehearsal Policies

As director, you need to think of rehearsal policy as the rules and regulations that allow you to create the best rehearsal environment for yourself and for all members of the cast. Be sure the policies you desire are communicated clearly to your staff and the members of the cast. The most common rehearsal policies address these issues:

- Do you prefer open rehearsals (visitors are welcome) or closed rehearsals (open only to members of the company)? If you prefer closed rehearsals, how strictly will the policy be enforced? Does it include parents, family members, faculty members, or just friends of the actors? Do you have a pedagogical reason for the choice? Have you expressed your rationale to your staff and members of the cast? If you prefer open rehearsals, do you have a pedagogical reason for the choice and have you shared that with your staff and members of the cast?

- What is your policy on lateness? How do you define lateness? I have witnessed rehearsals where everyone arrives on time, but the rehearsal does not begin for twenty minutes while waiting for the director to complete discussions with individuals. Is late defined as arriving after the rehearsal begins or after the scheduled call hour? Is there a penalty for lateness?

- What is your policy for absences? If an actor is absent because she is sick, is that different than being absent because she forgot about the rehearsal? Or had an unresolvable conflict or a dentist appointment? Does your school have a policy regarding student absences from the school day and participation in after-school activities? Do you abide by the school policy? Is there a penalty for an unexcused absence?

- What is your policy on food in rehearsal? Do you mind if the actors, stage managers, or props crew snack throughout the rehearsal, or do you prefer a formal break for everyone at once? Do you eat during rehearsal?

- What is your policy on preparedness? If an actor forgets or loses his script, how will you handle the situation? If one or more actors misses a deadline to be off-book, how will you conduct the rehearsal? Is there a penalty for the student who does not meet your expectations? If not, what message does that send to other students who worked hard to be prepared and responsible?

It is critical for the director to think these kinds of policy situations through before they occur. Your reactions should be thoughtful and well considered. It is unwise to react severely to a difficult student and mildly to a leading player or favored individual. Enforce policies fairly and equally for all students.

As the director, you must be a good role model for the policies you endorse. If you expect your students to be prepared, you must always be prepared. If you expect your students to be punctual, you must be punctual and begin each rehearsal promptly as scheduled. It is also important to end a rehearsal punctually and not hold the cast for an extra five, ten, or fifteen minutes. Be a good time manager; be courteous and respectful of all the people with whom you work.

Rehearsal Styles

There are two common approaches to a script during the first rehearsals of a play. In the first approach, the director puts the play on its feet immediately. Stand up, get going, let's act! In the second approach, the director spends the first few rehearsals sitting and reading with the actors, working for character, interpretation, and objectives. Both these approaches have merit and should be considered by the director when planning the first rehearsals for a new play.

Once the rehearsal process is underway, you, as director, hope that each actor will grow in her understanding of her role and the play. To achieve this goal, you should ask questions that stimulate each actor to think about his character's motives and desires. Ask: Why do you think he is saying that? What is your character's goal in this scene? How does he conceal/reveal his motives through his actions? These types of questions promote thoughtful exploration of the script by each actor and produce results that students more easily internalize.

Some directors talk a lot in rehearsal. All directors should examine their methodology to discover what percentage of each rehearsal is filled with their words instead of the words of the playwright! Avoid explaining the play to the actors. It is best if the cast discovers the play together rather than learn all the answers about each character from you.

Some directors expect immediate results from the instructions they give during a rehearsal. They give the actors one chance to perform new blocking, then when it is not perfect, launch into additional explanation. Once you give blocking instructions, allow the actors several opportunities to rehearse the new blocking before offering additional instruction, adding more blocking, or changing the blocking that was just given. If the actors do not get it right the first time, ask if they need help or if they would just like to try it again. In most cases, the actors need the opportunity to redo (thus, rehearse) the new movement. For complicated blocking, work a few lines at a time. Once those lines feel comfortable, add a larger section, gradually building to a whole scene. Frequent interruptions during rehearsal slow the learning process and interrupt the continuity of a scene. In every rehearsal, be sure to spend most of the time allowing the actors to act!

Finally, stick to your rehearsal plan. Nothing is more frustrating to a performer than preparing for a rehearsal, then arriving to find out that the director has changed her mind and would rather rehearse a different part of the play. That is unprofessional and unfair to the actor who is now unprepared. Once you announce a master rehearsal plan, try to meet the goals of that plan whenever possible.

Rehearsal Notes

Take written notes during each rehearsal. The director's notes include personal reminders as well as comments on the current scene, suggestions for individual actors, and ideas for future consideration.

Begin the process of giving rehearsal notes from the very first time the cast meets. The process of giving rehearsal notes should be formal and should take place during the last five to ten minutes of the rehearsal, after the cast has assisted the stage managers with the rehearsal cleanup. To formalize the process, say, "Okay, everyone, it's time for notes."

For daily rehearsals, you could deliver your notes and comments in oral form. The director's notes should always include a general overview of the progress of the rehearsal and should state goals for the next rehearsal. Special recognition or thanks should be awarded any student who had an outstanding day. The notes should be positive and motivating, even if the rehearsal was slow and frustrating.

The cast should be given an opportunity to ask questions or state concerns. The stage managers should *always* be expected to make a comment during the daily rehearsal notes.

Rehearsal notes for the tech and dress rehearsals are a much more complicated event. First, you have notes for everyone: members of the staff, the production stage manager, members of each crew, and members of the cast. Delivering these notes orally would take forever—sometimes as long as the play itself takes to perform! Second, the tech and dress rehearsals will provide a different experience for many members of the company. The lighting crew may have had a great rehearsal and be energized; the run crew may have broken a chair and missed two important cues and be upset; the costume crew may have misplaced a hat and is worried about finding it; the chorus might have performed brilliantly, but your lead player may feel he let everyone down. It is hard to give specific notes to members of a group with such diverse reactions to the same experience. Instead, following tech and dress rehearsals, give notes in four ways:

- Oral comments for the entire company
- Written notes posted on the company bulletin board
- Written notes given to specific members of the staff, cast, or crew
- Private conferences with individual members of the company

Although it takes a lot of effort to organize your notes in this way, the results will be spectacular and will be evident by the progress shown at the next rehearsal.

Oral Comments for the Entire Company. Following a tech or dress rehearsal, after everyone has assisted with the daily cleanup, the entire company should sit together for the director's rehearsal notes. The director should begin with a general thought (great rehearsal, this was an interesting night, we're getting better), then immediately ask the members of the staff if they have general comments or reminders to offer the company. After the adult staff has a chance to speak, the production stage manager, stage managers, and crew chiefs should be given an opportunity to give brief comments or reminders to the group. Then the director should conclude with her own final thoughts and remind everyone to check the company bulletin board tomorrow for additional notes. A brief staff meeting often follows the tech or dress rehearsal.

Written Notes Posted on the Company Bulletin Board. Written notes to be posted should be directed to a crew or group of cast members. They should include general comments, simple reminders, or points of clarification. These notes should not be directed to individual problems or performances, which could embarrass a student. There are two effective ways to post written notes to the company: the first is by department; the second is by act and scene in show order. If you post by department, place a heading on the top of a sheet of paper with the name of the department. Then list the act/scene/page in question, and state the problem or concern in as few words as possible. It should be the responsibility of each department's crew chiefs to incorporate the changes and improvements in the next rehearsal. If you post by show order, use the act, scene, and page as a heading, then list the department, then state the problem or concern in as few words as possible.

BY DEPARTMENT:
Run Crew
    I/1/p. 8 (*problem or concern*)
    I/4/p. 19 (*problem or concern*)

BY SHOW ORDER:
I/1
    Sound: p. 2 (*problem or concern*)
    Chorus: p. 4 (*problem or concern*)

Written Notes Given to Specific Staff, Cast, or Crew Members. Following a tech or dress rehearsal, the director often has specific comments or reminders for individual members of the company. These often require no response from the individual; the notes are self-explanatory. Written notes should be identified by act/scene/page and stated in as few words as possible. They should be distributed to each individual well in advance of the next rehearsal.

Private Conferences with Individual Members of the Company. When the director has questions, concerns, or ideas for a specific individual, it is sometimes best to address those notes in a private conference. I post a "see me" list of names on the company bulletin board. If a student's name appears on the list, he sees me at his earliest convenience to get his private notes. Most private conferences are only five minutes long, but they provide the opportunity for the personal attention that some matters require.

Rehearsing with Technical Elements
When planning the master rehearsal calendar, the director should try to schedule the rehearsal agenda in such a way that the cast never faces more than one new production element at a time. Whenever possible, create a different completion deadline for each technical element of the production and integrate each element as soon as it is completed. Adding only one technical at a time allows the cast to focus on the new element and provides the opportunity to solve any problems created by adding that element without disrupting the entire rehearsal.

Differences Between Rehearsing a Play and a Musical
When planning a rehearsal, the director should have a good understanding of how students learn a play or musical. For a play, much of the student learning can take place at home by individuals. Students can rehearse and memorize lines on their own, and their progress is easily demonstrated during each rehearsal. In a play, the entire cast advances quickly because each student can progress individually. For a musical, however, most of the student learning takes place during the rehearsal process and not at home. Choreography is taught in rehearsal step by step, and most dance numbers require the other members of the company to rehearse. Music is taught in rehearsal by the music director. Many students do not have the ability to learn their music on their own, especially ensemble numbers where the chorus sings in harmony. Combining the music and choreography can only happen in rehearsal. The lines and blocking are the easiest elements of a musical and are often the only parts of the show that members of the cast are able to rehearse individually at home.

The Rehearsal Process for Learning a Musical

It is best to learn the music, blocking, and choreography separately. As each element is mastered, it should be combined with other elements into scenes. Scenes are often learned out of order. Finally, completed scenes are put into sequence to complete each act. This process allows the students to rehearse each element of a musical separately, then gradually put the different elements together.

1. Begin with the music. The music is what makes the property special and unique. It makes it live at a larger dimension than a play. It is also impossible to make much progress until the music is mastered. Begin with the company numbers. They are often the longest and most complex. Devote a lot of time during the early rehearsals to the company production numbers, then ensembles and duets, and finish with the solos. When setting music memorization deadlines, set the earliest deadlines for the company numbers so the choreographer can begin working with the cast.

2. While the cast is in the process of learning the music, begin blocking the scenes, and adding props, costume pieces, and set pieces as soon as possible.

3. As each musical number is memorized, begin the choreography.

4. As the choreography is learned, integrate the musical numbers into each scene as soon as possible.

5. Finally, rehearse the completed scenes in order.

TYPES OF REHEARSALS

Every play or musical requires many specific types of rehearsals during the process of learning the show. It is important to recognize the goal of each specialty rehearsal when planning a master rehearsal schedule.

The Read-Through

Most productions begin with a read-through of the script. At the read-through, the cast should start at the beginning of the script and read through to the end, taking an intermission break. The director should avoid making corrections or comments during the read-through. This rehearsal provides the actors an opportunity to experience the play for the first time. A stage manager should read all staging notes that appear in the script.

The Blocking Rehearsal

During the blocking rehearsal, the director gives instruction for the actors' movement on the stage. This movement (or blocking) is timed with lines in the script. Blocking instructions often include many elements of the actor's surroundings: the use of the set, props, and sometimes costumes. During a blocking rehearsal, each actor should record his own blocking notes in his script. The director should take the time to teach correct blocking notation to all members of the cast. All blocking notes should be made in pencil to allow for changes or modifications in future rehearsals.

The Vocal Rehearsal

During the vocal rehearsal, the music director teaches the music for a show to the entire cast, small ensembles, and soloists. The director and music director should establish a standard of behavior and responsible work ethic from the first rehearsal. During the music rehearsals, the cast begins to develop a personality as an ensemble. Structure the music rehearsals in a way that promotes the behavior you desire from your young actors.

The Choreography Rehearsal

During the choreography rehearsal, dance numbers and musical staging are taught to the entire cast, small ensembles, and soloists. The choreographer should team with the director and music director and require the same work ethic, standard of behavior, and rehearsal etiquette established in the ensemble music rehearsals.

The Orchestra Rehearsal

The orchestra rehearsal takes place near the end of the rehearsal process. During this rehearsal, the cast and the orchestra are combined for the first time. There is no blocking or choreography during this rehearsal. The exclusive goal is mastering the music. The music director is in charge of this rehearsal.

The Tech Rehearsal

The goal of the tech rehearsal is to integrate the technical elements of the production into the structure and flow of the show, making sure that everyone present understands how the separate elements fit together (set changes, props, lighting and sound cues, costume changes, and special effects). The focus of this rehearsal should *not* be on cast members or their performances. After spending many weeks of working exclusively with the cast, this is a difficult habit for many directors to break. The most important person monitoring the tech rehearsal is the production stage manager. Above all, she must understand how the production elements combine in order to call the show correctly.

The Dry Tech or Cue-to-Cue Rehearsal

The dry tech or cue-to-cue rehearsal is a tech-only rehearsal. No actors are present. The production stage manager calls each cue, and the crews (lighting, props, and run) rehearse their part and solve any problems that arise. The director attends this rehearsal and offers comment and instruction when needed. Again, the most important person monitoring this rehearsal is the production stage manager who must understand how the production elements combine in order to call the show correctly.

The Dress Rehearsal

The dress rehearsal provides the opportunity to see a show under performance conditions but without an audience. There is usually a moment during the first dress rehearsal when each student recognizes the importance of his individual effort in the total production. This generally provides an increased level of energy for the rehearsal.

During a dress rehearsal, the company should try to establish a flow and tempo for the production. The director should not interrupt a dress rehearsal unless there is a problem that prevents the rehearsal from moving forward. All noncritical errors should be addressed in the director's postrehearsal notes.

It should be agreed upon in advance by members of the creative and design staff who has the authority to determine what qualifies as an event serious enough to stop the rehearsal.

Your priority, as director, during dress rehearsals is to focus the energy and concentration of all members of the staff, cast, and crew toward a common goal. Before any changes should be introduced in a dress rehearsal, be sure all the rehearsed blocking, set changes, and lighting cues are coordinated and executed as planned. If the plan is faulty, then the director should feel free to make minor adjustments to achieve a specific goal.

WORKING WITH STAGE MANAGERS

The director should treat all stage managers with the same respect as other members of the adult staff. Since the stage managers control the show during dress rehearsals and performances by calling cues and managing the cast backstage, it is your job, as director, to teach leadership skills to the stage managers during the rehearsal process and provide them with opportunities to practice those skills.

There are many ways you can empower stage managers and help them achieve successful peer leadership. The first is to *always* include them in the rehearsal note process, beginning with the first rehearsal. Allowing the stage managers to offer comments and observations about the progress of the show on a daily basis separates them from the cast and elevates them to a staff position. Allow them some opportunity to run mini-rehearsals with the cast or parts of the cast. If there is a particular scene with difficult blocking, and if the director has rehearsed and re-rehearsed the scene with cast members and they still seem unsure of themselves, and if the stage managers feel confident about the scene, then the director can include a stage manager's brush-up rehearsal as part of a normal daily rehearsal. To frame the stage manager's rehearsal, the director should clearly state specific goals to all members of the cast: accent the movement, pick up the pace, fewer stops and starts within the scene, and so on. Then, give the stage managers a specific amount of time to rehearse the actors. The director can then turn his attention to other work—paperwork, assisting the props crew—during this period. At the appropriate time, the director should have the cast, directed by the stage managers, perform for his critique. Using this rehearsal technique provides multiple benefits. The stage managers practice and improve their leadership skills, the members of the production learn to work together, and the students begin to examine and evaluate their own progress and improvement.

WORKING WITH THE CREATIVE STAFF

During the early rehearsals, each member of the staff meets with the director, then works independently with the members of her crew, creating the part of the production for which she is responsible. When the tech and dress rehearsals arrive, however, it is time to combine all the separate efforts into one cohesive whole. Although all members of the creative staff are present and are interacting with the students during the tech and dress rehearsals, all members of the staff should defer to the director when a conflict arises. The director may consult with his staff during a conflict or problem, but the final decision on all matters lies with the director. It is his show, his vision, his concept, his problem, and his responsibility. The director always has the final word.

CHAPTER 2

ADULT STAFF MEMBERS

A Who's Who of
Production Options

Theater is a collaborative art form with each department making a unique contribution to the whole. Each department has a set of parameters that are constantly challenged and requires leadership that is creative, well trained, experienced, and highly motivated. The adult staff members—the directors, designers, and coordinators—guide students through a rehearsal process that culminates in a show, teaching artistic discipline, creative thought, and the art of collaboration.

Every high school theater staff is comprised of three types of adult staff members: professional members who are paid, professional members who are not paid, and volunteers who are not paid. Most high schools do not have the resources to hire professionally trained personnel in all leadership positions. Fortunately, many schools are blessed with an abundance of volunteerism from parents and other adults in their community.

The most important qualities to seek in any staff member are the desire to work with students, to create in a collaborative forum, and to put on a show. Adult staff members should have experience organizing and running groups, creating a work schedule, meeting deadlines, and staying within budget. They must enjoy working with young people; be articulate, patient, and kind; and possess a good sense of humor. It is their responsibility to instill professional work habits in the students.

This chapter defines the roles and responsibilities of the adult staff members: music director, choreographer, set designer, lighting designer, sound designer, properties coordinator, costume designer, ticket manager, parent volunteer coordinator, and publicity coordinator.

The Music Director

The music director is responsible for all elements of music in a musical theater production. In some schools, the responsibilities of the music director's position are divided among several members of the high school music staff. But though several members of your school music staff may participate, it is still best to have one individual act as the music director, to whom the other members of the music staff report.

QUALIFICATIONS OF THE MUSIC DIRECTOR

The music director should be a professional musician with an understanding of the styles and traditions of musical theater, and dance, and knowledge of the human voice. It is helpful if the music director is also a strong keyboard player. He should be a highly skilled conductor and a strong and willing collaborator.

RESPONSIBILITIES OF THE MUSIC DIRECTOR

Preproduction
- Consult with director/producer during selection of show
- Participate in the audition and casting process
- Coordinate responsibilities of the music staff
- Create budget request for all music needs

During Production
- Consult with director to create weekly rehearsal schedule of musical numbers
- Consult with director and choreographer to edit dance music and incidental music
- Recruit student musicians for the orchestra
- Recruit and hire professional musicians for the orchestra
- Implement rules of conduct for student orchestra members
- Supervise and instruct principal cast members during vocal rehearsals
- Supervise and instruct chorus members during vocal rehearsals
- Teach correct vocabulary to student actors and musicians
- Make rehearsal recordings of the cast singing musical numbers and of dance/incidental music to be used in staging and choreography rehearsals
- Conduct all instrumental rehearsals
- Conduct the orchestra rehearsal
- Conduct the tech rehearsal and all dress rehearsals
- Conduct all performances
- Supervise the set-up of the orchestra pit
- Keep orchestra pit clean and orderly during dress rehearsals and performances

Postproduction

- Collect and erase marks from all orchestra books
- Package orchestra books for return shipping
- Plan and supervise strike of the orchestra pit

WORKING WITH OTHER STAFF MEMBERS

- Attend scheduled meetings of full creative staff
- Consult with lighting designer to discuss installation of orchestra lights in the orchestra pit
- Consult with sound designer to discuss sound needs of the orchestra
- Work with director and choreographer editing dance music and incidental music

DIVIDING THE MUSIC DIRECTOR'S RESPONSIBILITIES

If you, or your school, opt to assign the music director's responsibilities to several members of the music staff, it is common to divide them among the vocal coach, rehearsal pianist, and conductor.

Vocal Coach

This position is usually awarded to the high school choir director. The responsibilities of the vocal coach include assisting the director during the audition and casting process and teaching the vocal music to the cast during the rehearsal process.

Rehearsal Pianist

This position can be occupied by the vocal coach if she possesses strong keyboard skills, but it is frequently awarded to a talented student (or two), another member of the school music staff, or to a talented parent. The responsibilities of the rehearsal pianist include attending all vocal music rehearsals with the vocal coach, attending staging rehearsals with the director, and attending dance rehearsals with the choreographer. The rehearsal pianist usually plays one of the keyboard parts in the orchestra during the performances.

Conductor

This position is usually awarded to the high school band director. The responsibilities of the conductor include recruiting student members for the orchestra, hiring additional orchestra members as afforded by the budget, and conducting the orchestra during the orchestra rehearsal, all dress rehearsals, and all performances.

When the position of music director is divided between several people, problems can occur because some parts of the musical score, such as dance and incidental music and the overture and entr'acte, do not fall neatly under the auspices of either the vocal coach, rehearsal pianist, or conductor. Be sure that these musical responsibilities are assigned to one of those individuals.

Dance Music

The score of a Broadway musical that includes a significant amount of dance is a challenge to navigate. The piano reduction of the dance music is usually very intricate and difficult to play. Sometimes, the dance music that is printed in the score is different from the music on the original cast recording. And very frequently, the length of the dance music (written for professional Broadway dancers) exceeds the talent and endurance abilities of the high school performer. Although the choreographer makes the final decisions when altering or cutting dance music, a member of the music staff must work with the choreographer playing the score, notating any cuts and communicating this information to the conductor, and making a rehearsal recording of the new version of the dance music.

Incidental Music Requiring Staging

This is another gray area in the musical score. Incidental music is instrumental, and therefore assumed to fall in the domain of the conductor. If that incidental music requires staging by the director, however, it reflects all the same rehearsal problems that affect the choreographer. A member of the music staff must work with the director playing the score, notating any cuts and communicating this information to the conductor, and making a rehearsal recording of the incidental music.

The Overture and Entr'acte

The overture and entr'acte are traditionally instrumental pieces and fall in the domain of the conductor. In some shows, however, these pieces include vocal elements (*City of Angels*) or require staging (*Guys and Dolls*). Again, a member of the music staff must work with the director playing the score, notating any cuts and communicating this information to the conductor, and making a rehearsal recording of the overture or entr'acte.

The Choreographer

The role of the choreographer varies from show to show. A musical requires an extensive amount of movement, either in the form of dance or musical staging. This work is usually divided between the director and the choreographer. Traditionally, the choreographer is responsible for major production numbers, small ensemble dancing, and featured dance solos. The stage director often covers the numbers requiring musical staging.

QUALIFICATIONS OF THE CHOREOGRAPHER

The choreographer should be a professionally trained dancer with an understanding of the styles and traditions of musical theater. She should be highly skilled in a wide variety of styles of dance and movement. It is helpful if the choreographer is also knowledgeable about the human voice.

OVERVIEW OF THE CHOREOGRAPHER'S RESPONSIBILITIES

Preproduction
- Meet with director to discuss script and create initial movement concept
- Participate in the audition and casting process

During Production
- Consult with director to create a rehearsal schedule for dance numbers
- Consult with director and music director to edit dance music
- Consult with music director to discuss making rehearsal recordings of the cast singing musical numbers and of dance music to be used in choreography rehearsals
- Supervise and instruct cast members during dance rehearsals
- Attend the tech rehearsal and all dress rehearsals

WORKING WITH OTHER STAFF MEMBERS

- Attend scheduled meetings of full creative staff
- Consult with set designer to discuss the amount of stage space available for dance movement in each separate set
- Consult with costume designer to discuss issues related to movement and costume design, such as footwear, clothing style, hairstyle, and the use of hats or other headwear.

The Set Designer

The set designer is responsible for the physical definition of stage space in any production. A set can include walls, doors, windows, partitions, platforms, stairs, and any type of furniture and can be rendered in any style—realistic, minimalistic, fanciful, or historic.

QUALIFICATIONS OF THE SET DESIGNER

The set designer should be a skilled builder with a strong sense of form, structure, and dimension. He should be able to draft building plans to scale and create a model of a proposed project. In many high schools, the set designer does not have a college degree in theatrical design, yet brings a wide variety of life experience to his stage work.

OVERVIEW OF THE SET DESIGNER'S RESPONSIBILITIES

Preproduction

- Meet with director to discuss script and create initial set concept
- Draft blueprints and create model of the set
- Create budget request for all set needs
- Create shopping list of items required to build and complete set
- Shop for construction supplies
- Finalize set design

During Production

- Create weekly work schedule
- Supervise and instruct student crew during construction process
- Implement backstage rules of conduct for the run crew
- Teach correct construction vocabulary
- Assist run crew chiefs in assigning run crew positions and specific set/strike jobs
- Keep supply inventory
- Locate required furniture, specialty items
- Dress the set
- Hang painted drops, cyc, or scrim as required by the production
- Install hard and soft masking as needed
- Supervise spiking of set
- Supervise painting of set
- Complete set by agreed date
- Rehearse set changes
- Attend all light cue sessions
- Attend full runs of acts, coordinate crew to move sets as completed
- Attend tech rehearsal and all dress rehearsals
- Attend all performances
- Clean stage before tech rehearsal, store unused set items
- Keep backstage in good safe condition

Postproduction

- Plan and supervise complete set strike
- Clean stage following show
- Update inventory list

WORKING WITH OTHER STAFF MEMBERS

- Attend scheduled meetings of full creative design staff
- Consult with costume designer to discuss common set/costume concerns (for example, period costumes require extra room for hoop skirts)
- Consult with properties coordinator to discuss common set/props items
- Coordinate rehearsal space and work schedule with lighting designer
- Coordinate rehearsal space and work schedule with sound designer
- Assist lighting designer with lighting hang by moving the set as needed
- Work with lighting designer to install running lights backstage
- Work with lighting and sound designers to secure all cables and equipment that are backstage to create a safe environment for all cast and crew

The Lighting Designer

The lighting designer is responsible for illuminating all parts of the theater space in any production. The lighting includes the audience seating areas, the backstage work areas, onstage performance areas, onstage transition scenes, practical lights on the set, and all special effects.

The lighting crew is exposed to the most danger. Members work with large quantities of electricity, manipulate stage pipes heavily weighted with lighting cable and equipment, and are often required to climb ladders, scaffolding, or hydraulic devices to work at great heights. Because of the risks assumed by the members of this crew, it is imperative to hire a qualified, well-trained lighting designer.

QUALIFICATIONS OF THE LIGHTING DESIGNER

The lighting designer should be professionally trained in the rudiments of lighting and principles of design. He should be a skilled and experienced electrician and should be able to draft a lighting plot to scale.

OVERVIEW OF THE LIGHTING DESIGNER'S RESPONSIBILITIES

Preproduction

- Meet with director and set designer to discuss script and create initial lighting concept
- Draft lighting plot
- Create budget request for all lighting needs
- Creating complete shop order for rented items
- Create list and shop for lighting supplies to be purchased
- Finalize lighting design

During Production

- Create work schedule for hang and focus
- Assign lighting crew positions for the show
- Supervise and instruct student crew during lighting process
- Implement rules of conduct for the lighting crew
- Teach correct lighting vocabulary
- Keep supply inventory
- Assist set designer with hanging painted drops, cyc, scrim
- Assist set designer with installation of hard and soft masking as needed
- Complete lighting hang by agreed date
- Rehearse lighting cues
- Attend all light cue sessions
- Attend tech rehearsal and all dress rehearsals
- Attend all performances
- Clean stage of unused lighting equipment and supplies before tech rehearsal
- Keep all lighting equipment that is backstage in good condition

Postproduction

- Plan and supervise complete lighting strike
- Supervise the restore of repertoire plot
- Update inventory list

WORKING WITH OTHER STAFF MEMBERS

- Attend meetings of full creative design staff
- Consult with set designer to discuss common design concerns
- Coordinate rehearsal space and work schedule with set designer
- Coordinate rehearsal space and work schedule with sound designer
- Work with set designer to install running lights backstage
- Work with conductor to install orchestra lights in pit

The Sound Designer

The sound designer is responsible for all the sound requirements of a production. These can include an internal communication system using headsets, creating and playing back sound effects, sound amplification using microphones, and music playback through computer, CD, or cassette recording.

QUALIFICATIONS OF THE SOUND DESIGNER

The sound designer should be trained in the principles of sound design. He should be familiar with all types of sound equipment (microphones, speakers, playback devices, amplifiers, sound effects machines) and should be able to make minor repairs to that equipment.

OVERVIEW OF THE SOUND DESIGNER'S RESPONSIBILITIES

Preproduction

- Meet with director to discuss script and create initial sound concept
- Create budget request for all sound needs
- Create complete shop order for rented items
- Create list and shop for sound supplies to be purchased
- Finalize sound design

During Production

- Create work schedule for load-in of house communications system
- Create work schedule for load-in of all other sound equipment
- Assign sound crew positions for the show
- Supervise and instruct student crew
- Implement rules of conduct for the sound crew
- Teach correct sound vocabulary
- Keep supply inventory
- Complete sound load-in by agreed date
- Attend tech rehearsal and all dress rehearsals
- Attend all performances
- Keep all sound equipment that is backstage or onstage in good condition

Postproduction

- Plan and supervise complete sound strike
- Update inventory list

WORKING WITH OTHER STAFF MEMBERS

- Attend meetings of full creative design staff
- Consult with lighting and set designers for placement of onstage or backstage microphones
- Consult with costume designer to discuss body mike placement
- Consult with music director to discuss sound needs of the orchestra

The Properties Coordinator

The properties coordinator is responsible for all the props used or consumed during a production. She is also responsible for props that are not used but function as set dressing, such as artwork hanging on a wall, desk accessories, or magazines on a coffee table. In general, all the small stuff that makes its way onstage falls under the domain of the properties coordinator.

QUALIFICATIONS OF THE PROPERTIES COORDINATOR

The properties coordinator should have an eye for detail and be well organized. She must be able to teach basic life skills (table settings, proper food storage), basic organizational skills, and be familiar with elements of set dressing and decorating.

OVERVIEW OF THE PROPERTIES COORDINATOR'S RESPONSIBILITIES

Preproduction
- Meet with director to discuss script and create initial properties concept
- Create budget request for all prop needs: perishable items, rental items

During Production
- Attend cast rehearsals as scheduled
- Supervise and instruct student crew during rehearsal process
- Implement rules of conduct for the props crew
- Teach correct props vocabulary
- Create complete props list for each act
- Keep an accurate inventory list
- Locate required specialty items
- Make props as needed
- Dress the set
- Complete prop acquisition by agreed date
- Attend full runs of acts; coordinate crew to set and move props as needed
- Keep all props clean and in good condition
- Create safe storage for props during all rehearsals and performances
- Assign props crew positions for the show
- Attend tech rehearsal and all dress rehearsals
- Attend all performances

Postproduction
- Plan and supervise a complete props strike
- Coordinate the return of rented or borrowed props

WORKING WITH OTHER STAFF MEMBERS

- Attend scheduled meetings of full creative design staff
- Consult with set designer to discuss common set/prop items
- Consult with costume designer to discuss common costume/prop items

The Costume Designer

The costume designer is responsible for all articles of clothing worn by every actor on the stage from footwear to headgear, often including undergarments. In productions where the run crew appears onstage with the cast, the costume designer also dresses those crew members. She has a wide variety of responsibilities that vary from show to show, depending on the specific needs of a production. These responsibilities can include:

- Designing original costumes for a production
- Shopping for fabrics and building original costumes
- Coordinating all rented costumes
- Shopping for costume accessories: gloves, hats, spats, parasols, and so on
- Providing actors with a list of required personal costume items; these can include footwear, tights, socks, undergarments, and basic black pants
- Providing actors with list of local shops to purchase required items, often coordinating a bulk purchase of those items for all members of the cast
- Making personal props to coordinate with costumes
- Making set dressings to compliment color palate of show (making tablecloths, curtains, or drapes; reupholstering chairs or other furniture pieces)
- Coordinating the purchase of all hair and makeup supplies
- Keeping all costumes clean, pressed, and in good repair

The costume designer rarely works alone; coordinating all the wardrobe needs for an entire production is not a one-person job. The two most common assistants are the head seamstress and the milliner. The head seamstress works most closely with the costume designer. She is a highly skilled dressmaker possessing a thorough knowledge of fabric, color, and design. Her principal job is sewing. She is the designer's primary partner during the process of building original costumes and fitting each actor. The milliner specializes in headwear, specifically women's fancy or exotic hats. He is an invaluable member of the costume design team in a big musical or period show. The milliner possesses a thorough knowledge of fabric, color, and design and is a highly skilled seamster.

QUALIFICATIONS OF THE COSTUME DESIGNER

The costume designer should be trained in the principles of wardrobe design, hair styling, and makeup styling. She should have a keen eye for color and balance and be familiar with all styles and periods of dress.

OVERVIEW OF THE COSTUME DESIGNER'S RESPONSIBILITIES

Preproduction
- Meet with director to discuss script and create initial color palate and costume concept
- Create budget request for all costume needs
- Finalize costume design

During Production
- Create work schedule for the student members of the costume crew
- Create dresser assignments for the show
- Implement rules of conduct for the costume/makeup crew
- Supervise and instruct student crew during design sessions or rehearsals
- Teach correct vocabulary for wardrobe, hair and makeup
- Complete measurements for each actor and crew member requiring a costume
- Design and build original costumes
- Create a complete order for all rented costumes
- Provide actors with list of required personal costume items
- Keep an accurate supply inventory for costumes and makeup
- Complete the production wardrobe by agreed date
- Rehearse costume changes
- Attend costume parade
- Attend tech rehearsal and all dress rehearsals
- Attend all performances
- Keep all wardrobe items in good repair

Postproduction
- Plan and supervise complete costume strike
- Return rented costumes
- Clean and store all school costumes
- Update inventory list

WORKING WITH OTHER STAFF MEMBERS

- Attend scheduled meetings of full creative design staff
- Consult with set designer to discuss common set/costume concerns (period costumes require extra room for hoop skirts)
- Consult with sound designer to discuss body mike placement
- Consult with choreographer to discuss issues related to movement and costume design
- Consult with properties coordinator to discuss common costume/prop items

Ticket Manager

The individual responsible for tickets and seating is a very important member of your staff. The ticket manager processes all the advance ticket orders, gives regular sales updates to the director/producer, and runs the box office for all the performances. If you use a reserved seating plan, the ticket manager is responsible for creating a master seating plan, assigning patrons to seats, and issuing the correct ticket to each patron. Additionally, she collects and records payment for all ticket sales and manages the parent volunteers who assist at the box office.

The position of ticket manager is a big job. There is usually a rush of advance ticket sales during the first weeks of rehearsal for a show, followed by a lull in sales, followed by a frenzy of sales during the final two weeks before the performances.

QUALIFICATIONS OF THE TICKET MANAGER

The position of ticket manager requires a high level of computer skills, organizational strategies, and management skills. She must record all advance ticket sales information in a spreadsheet format. This information includes keeping an accurate record of all sponsor subscriptions for the playbill listing. The ticket manager will use this information to provide the director/producer with regular updates on ticket sales and show revenue. This information will also be used during the week of dress rehearsals and performances to create a master seating plan and assign seats to all advance-sale patrons. Using a mail-merge program, this same spreadsheet information will produce labels for the ticket envelopes (if you use a reserved seating plan in your theater). The producer should provide the ticket manager with printed tickets and blank ticket envelopes in a timely manner. The ticket manager must create an organized system of filing all ticket paperwork for a show. The ticket orders must be accessible through the final performance of the show.

The ticket manager should be a skilled coordinator. She will need the help of parent volunteers during the final weeks to create reserved seating assignments, stuff ticket envelopes, and staff the box office during all performances. She will assign positions to the parent volunteers and assist them in performing their jobs. If the show sells out, the ticket manager (with the producer's knowledge) is responsible for creating and selling standing room tickets. At the conclusion of each performance, she counts the box office receipts and gives that money to the producer for deposit.

OVERVIEW OF THE TICKET MANAGER'S RESPONSIBILITIES

Preproduction

- Consult with the director/producer to discuss any specific ticket requests or concerns about the upcoming production
- Proofread the advance sales ticket order form for the new show
- Create blank spreadsheet documents

During Production

- Process advance sale orders weekly during the early weeks of rehearsal updating the spreadsheets often
- Process advance sale orders as often as necessary as the show approaches
- Consult with the producer as often as possible, providing updates on advance ticket sales and total revenue
- Provide a complete list of sponsor subscriptions (in alphabetical order) to the producer for inclusion in the playbill
- Coordinate parent volunteers for box office staff
- Create reserved seating assignments
- Stuff ticket envelopes
- Manage box office during all performances

WORKING WITH OTHER STAFF MEMBERS

- Consult with producer/director regularly
- Consult with parent volunteer coordinator to discuss the number of volunteers needed to assist with ticket and seating

SPECIAL RECOMMENDATIONS

Reserved Seating

If you do not currently use a system of reserved seating for your advance ticket sales, it is a subject worth reconsidering. When a patron knows that purchasing an advanced sale ticket guarantees him a reserved (better) seat, that patron is more likely to buy in advance. If many patrons purchase their tickets in advance, your show will have greater revenue up front and the producer will have a more accurate financial picture of the production. Since ticket sales are the major source of revenue for most high school theater productions, obtaining that capital up front is enormously helpful in meeting your show expenses.

Sponsor Subscriptions

Many high schools have some form of special sponsorship that increases their ticket revenue. A sponsor is a patron who is paying a specific amount of money with the understanding that part of that sum gives him a pair of tickets for one performance and the remaining amount is a donation to the production. For this donation, the sponsor receives recognition in the playbill.

The easiest formula to use in determining the price of a sponsor subscription is this:

Normal ticket price:	$5.00	$8.00	$10.00
Multiply by 2; the sponsor subscription includes two adult tickets	X 2	X 2	X 2
Subtotal:	$10.00	$16.00	$20.00
Now multiply by 2.50 for the Sponsor donation	X 2.50	X 2.50	X 2.50
Total cost of sponsor subscription	$25.00	$40.00	$50.00

Sponsor subscriptions provide a wonderful way for community members to support your theater program and increase your revenues at the same time.

The Parent Volunteer Coordinator

The parent volunteer coordinator acts as a liaison between staff members who need assistance and the parents who want to offer that assistance.

QUALIFICATIONS OF THE PARENT VOLUNTEER COORDINATOR

The position of parent volunteer coordinator requires good organizational skills. The producer sends a parent volunteer form home with every student member of the cast and crew. When the forms are completed and returned, the coordinator sorts through the forms and places the volunteers in appropriate job assignments. Once that task is completed, the coordinator remains in contact with the producer. If the staff needs additional parent help, the coordinator continues to act as a liaison between the staff and the parent volunteers.

PARENT VOLUNTEER OPPORTUNITIES

Parent Chaperones

Parent chaperones are invaluable to the director and the entire company during tech and dress rehearsals, the performance, and the strike. If an emergency arises with a student, it is wonderful to have a parent available to assist. For example, if a student feels sick or is injured during a rehearsal, the parent chaperone can attend to the needs of that student and the rehearsal continues uninterrupted. Otherwise, the director would care for the student and the rehearsal would stop until the director returns. Chaperones can be assigned to work in four-hour shifts.

Chairperson and Volunteers for Company Dinners

Two chairpersons, assisted by additional parent volunteers, will be needed for the two company dinners that occur during the final weeks of the show: the tech rehearsal dinner and the opening night dinner. Both dinners serve several purposes: They ensure that all students have an opportunity to eat at that time; they keep all the students on campus, which makes the dinner break shorter and puts students at less risk of injury when rushing out for fast-food in their cars; and the company dinners provide an opportunity for camaraderie between cast, crew, staff, and parents.

The tech rehearsal dinner occurs in the middle of the tech rehearsal between Acts I and II. The opening night dinner occurs after the opening night performance of the show. Because many students will likely be too nervous to eat much before the show, everyone will be famished when the show finishes. This dinner is a wonderful way to celebrate the show and provides another opportunity for camaraderie and community building.

Additional Volunteer Opportunities

Providing and Selling Refreshments. Refreshments sold during intermission generally raise a lot of additional revenue for the production. Volunteers must like working with people, or must be willing to bake for the refreshment table.

Assisting Box Office. Assisting with advanced sale tickets and seating, and selling tickets before each performance.

Running Errands. Picking up items during the school day when the director is normally unavailable.

Assisting Costume Designer: Sewing, ironing, shopping for costume pieces or supplies.

Assisting Set Designer. Assisting with building or painting the set, or dressing it.

Assisting the Properties Coordinator. Assisting in procuring, organizing, and arranging the props.

Assisting the Publicity Coordinator. Writing press releases or distributing and posting flyers and posters in the community.

OVERVIEW OF THE PARENT VOLUNTEER COORDINATOR'S RESPONSIBILITIES

Preproduction

- Meet with director/producer to assess volunteer needs for the production

During Production

- Collect parent volunteer forms from all members of the cast and crew
- Organize the volunteers into appropriate job assignments

- Recruit additional volunteers as needed to fill spots
- Create a master list of all volunteer positions and photocopy; send to all parents and post a copy in the rehearsal area of the theater
- Make reminder calls to parent volunteers as needed
- Consult with each committee chair and offer assistance as needed
- Consult with the director/producer frequently; when they request assistance, act as a liaison between the director/producer and the parent volunteers
- Consult with the designers requiring volunteer assistance; act as liaison between the designers and the parent volunteers

SAMPLE PARENT VOLUNTEER FORM

Parent Volunteer Form

Name of Show: _____

Name(s):_____

Home Phone Number: _____

E-mail Address: _____

Please check all areas possible for you to volunteer. The volunteer coordinators will distribute the jobs equitably between all parent volunteers. Thank you for your support of the production. We look forward to working with you.

_____ Coordinate the refreshment sales

_____ Assist with the refreshment sales

_____ Coordinate the tech dinner

_____ Assist with the tech dinner

_____ Coordinate the opening night dinner

_____ Assist with the opening night dinner

_____ Coordinate the box office:

   All ticket sales and seating

_____ Assist with the box office

_____ Chaperone tech rehearsal (a 4-hour commitment)

_____ Chaperone a dress rehearsal (a 4-hour commitment)

_____ Chaperone a performance (a 4-hour commitment)

_____ Chaperone the strike (a 4-hour commitment)

_____ I am available to run errands during the day

_____ Assist with costumes

_____ Assist with the set

_____ Assist with props

_____ Assist with publicity

Publicity Coordinator

The publicity coordinator works with a student crew to create a comprehensive publicity plan for a production. He oversees the implementation of the publicity plan, which should include:

- Designing a show logo
- Designing publicity posters and flyers
- Writing a press release about the show for the school and community papers
- Taking publicity photos to include with the press release
- Coordinating the call-board headshots
- Creating attractive call-boards
- Creating and sending invitations to neighboring school districts

QUALIFICATIONS OF THE PUBLICITY COORDINATOR

The position of publicity coordinator requires organizational skills and writing and graphic design skills. To be successful, it is critical to establish firm deadlines for each separate publicity project and to meet those deadlines. The coordinator must research and meet deadlines imposed by outside sources: newspapers, printers, and photo labs.

OVERVIEW OF THE PUBLICITY COORDINATOR'S RESPONSIBILITIES

Preproduction
- Meet with director/producer to assess special or unique aspects of the show and begin to develop logo concept
- Create budget request for all publicity needs

During Production
- Complete logo design; submit to producer for approval
- Complete design of publicity poster and flyer; take to printer
- Oversee the writing of a press release
- Oversee the taking of publicity photos to accompany the press release; develop film immediately
- Submit press release and photos to school paper; mail same to community papers
- Coordinate the call-board headshots
- Write captions for all headshots
- Create attractive call-boards
- Create special invitation for neighboring school districts; mail them in a timely fashion

- Create a unique publicity campaign within the school to raise the level of excitement about the production

Postproduction
- Strike all signs and posters from the school and the community

Working with Other Staff Members
- Attend scheduled meetings of full creative staff
- Consult regularly with producer offering updates on the progress of the publicity campaign

CHAPTER 3

STAGE MANAGING

The Student
Stage Management Team

S tage managing is people managing. The stage manager interacts with every element of a production and with every person in each department. He works most closely with and receives instruction from the director, but he also works with all members of the cast, crew, and house staff. Stage managing requires a variety of skills. The stage manager must be able to think rationally under the most trying circumstances. He is the calm in the middle of a storm. A successful stage manager is energetic, organized, patient, and kind.

The Stage Management Team

In professional theater, usually one person fills the position of stage manager. But for high school productions, it is best to have a team of students. For a play, two students are recommended; a musical usually needs three or four. The head of the team is the production stage manager; the other members are the assistant stage managers.

All should have had successful experiences in the cast or on a variety of crews—props, set construction, run, sound, lighting, costume/makeup, and house staff—and should be familiar with the protocol and priorities required by each department. These experiences will enable each stage manager to do her job more completely and effectively.

Stage managers should be respectful of the theater, of all the equipment and supplies, and of all the people with whom they work. If the members of the stage management team are disciplined and focused, the entire production will run more smoothly.

SKILLS OF THE STAGE MANAGEMENT TEAM

Stage managers occupy the highest positions of student leadership. The stage managers should be experienced members of your program and should be given substantial responsibilities throughout the entire rehearsal and performance process. The production stage manager should be the most experienced member of your theater program; when possible, a senior should occupy this position.

To meet the responsibilities of his position, each student stage manager needs to possess or develop and perfect the following skills:

Leadership Skills

The stage manager accepts and meets responsibilities. She is punctual, responsible, reliable, and trustworthy. She is knowledgeable about all production departments. She is able to work comfortably with both students and adults. She should model a good work ethic for the other members of the cast and crew: how to carefully listen to and follow directions, how to complete every task that is begun, how to ask for assistance when needed, and how to assist others when asked.

Communication Skills

The stage manager should possess both oral and written communication skills. He should be able to speak before the cast and/or crew with confidence. He should communicate effectively with the members of each crew using appropriate vocabulary and technical terminology.

Organizational Skills

The stage manager must be an organized person and possess good time management skills. It is the job of the stage manager to keep the whole production organized and on schedule.

Interpersonal Skills

The stage manager is a collaborative worker. She is energetic, optimistic, and outgoing. Being a stage manager requires patience. An effective stage manager is able to stay calm, cool and collected when chaos looms. She never loses perspective that the individuals in the cast and crew are more important than the production. She should make each member of the company feel valued and important. The stage manager is sometimes the parent, sometimes the friend or counselor, sometimes the boss. She needs a quick mind and a big heart.

RESPONSIBILITIES OF THE STAGE MANAGEMENT TEAM

The stage managers are the first students to join the production team and have the most influence on its success. Their job begins the week before auditions are held and ends at the conclusion of the strike. They are involved in preproduction work, every blocking rehearsal, every music rehearsal, every choreography rehearsal, every student leadership meeting, the orchestra rehearsal, the tech rehearsal, all dress rehearsals and performances, and the strike. They should know the structure and details of the show as well as the director does.

In general, the stage managers have the following responsibilities:

- Are role models to the members of the cast and crew in meeting behavior expectations and production responsibilities (see side bar on page 62).
- Act as a liaison between the director/producer and other crew chiefs
- Work with director and music director to create the weekly rehearsal schedule
- Work closely with the director on all elements of the production
- Work with the director, set designer, lighting designer, sound designer, and all crew chiefs during the tech rehearsal and all dress rehearsals to create the cues for the show
- Call cues for all dress rehearsals and performances
- Collect and process all paperwork; keep production and rehearsal records; photocopy and file paperwork as needed; create checklists for cast and crew on the computer; post schedules, announcements, reminders, and deadlines on the production board

The stage managers' job responsibilities can be broken down into three categories: preproduction, during production, and postproduction.

Preproduction
- Assist the director with preparing student audition packets
- Encourage students to add their names to the posted sign-up lists
- Attend the preaudition meeting; assist the director in distributing audition materials and scheduling actors for their first auditions
- Neatly type and post the final audition schedule
- Attend all auditions and call backs; check in the actors as they arrive
- Collect student contact information forms from each cast and crew member
- Assist the producer and director assembling a production packet for each member of the staff, cast and crew

During Production
- Collect and organize all student paperwork: T-shirt order forms, parent volunteer forms, student bio forms
- Collect advance ticket order forms as they are submitted; forward them to the producer or ticket manager
- Collect playbill advertisements as they are submitted; forward them to the producer
- Assist the production stage manager recording daily cast attendance at all rehearsals
- Attend daily rehearsals of blocking, music, and choreography, taking notes as required
- Attend the orchestra rehearsal
- Attend the costume parade
- Organize a rotating schedule of chorus members for light walking; principals attend the entire light-walking session

- Attend all cue sessions; work with the director and lighting/set/sound designers
- Work with all crew chiefs to record and synchronize cues between departments
- Attend tech rehearsal; call cues
- Record final cues in cue script
- Call cues for all dress rehearsals
- Call cues for all performances

Postproduction
- Assist the director during strike
- Clean out stage manager files from current show

SUPPLIES AND WORKSPACE FOR STAGE MANAGERS

To do their jobs correctly, stage managers need the following supplies:

Two complete copies of the script. The production stage manager should read the script several times before the rehearsal process begins. He should have a clear understanding of the plot of the show and what is required of the actors. He should also have a clear understanding of the physical needs of the show: the set, props, and costumes. The production stage manager's rehearsal script should be in large print in a three-ring binder. Dividers should separate each scene.

The second script will be the production stage manager's final cue script. It will not be needed until the dress rehearsals begin. This script should be in large print and in a separate three-ring binder with dividers separating each scene.

Notepads, pencils, pens (black or blue and red), highlighters, ruler. The production stage manager needs these supplies to accurately mark her final cue script. All rehearsal blocking should be recorded in pencil. The completed script should be as professional and organized as possible. When completed, each marked script reflects all requirements for calling the lighting cues, set changes, and sound cues.

Work space. The production stage manager works with the assistant stage managers collecting and processing all student paperwork. To do this effectively, the stage management team needs access to a work space. They need a large table or several desks to check, sort, and file paperwork daily and a place to store their completed files. One drawer in a file cabinet or one shelf of a bookcase should be enough space. The stage management team also needs basic office supplies: file folders, envelopes, pens, tape, stapler, etc. It is best if the stage managers have their own supplies and are responsible for them.

Multiple copies of all paperwork. The production stage manager and assistant stage managers should keep a master file of extra copies of all required student paperwork. This file should include the audition form, audition packets, student contact information form, T-shirt order form, ticket order form, student bio form, parent volunteer forms, the complete cast rehearsal schedule, and a complete crew work schedule. The stage management team needs several copies of a complete cast/crew checklist to record which students have or have not turned in required paperwork.

BEHAVIOR EXPECTATIONS AND PRODUCTION RESPONSIBILITIES FOR ALL STAGE MANAGERS AND MEMBERS OF THE TECHNICAL CREWS, HOUSE STAFF, AND ORCHESTRA

Behavior Expectations

- Be on time for all calls.

- Wear appropriate clothing to all work sessions. The dress code for all dress rehearsals and performances is black shirt, pants, shoes, and socks. All clothing and footwear should fit well and be comfortable and safe. Loose clothing might catch on set pieces and tear; tight clothing might restrict movement. Clothing should not make noise. Shoes should be flexible and have soft rubber soles. Some work boots are a good option; black sneakers are the best choice for comfort, safety, and silence of movement.

- Never leave your job to talk with friends. Friends are not permitted to visit during rehearsals.

- No eating or drinking backstage or in the control booth during dress rehearsals or performances.

- No talking, whispering, singing, pantomiming, or dancing backstage or in the control booth during any part of the dress rehearsal or performances.

- Be courteous, polite, helpful, respectful, and outgoing.

- Be willing to assist the director, any member of the adult design staff, any parent volunteer, or any other student member whenever needed.

Production Responsibilities

- Selling tickets for the production

- Selling sponsor subscriptions or advertisements for the production

- Report for a call-board photo on the assigned day and time

The Role of the Stage Managers During Auditions

The stage managers play an important role during the audition process. They assist the director by organizing the audition materials, recruiting actors for the production, assisting in all preaudition meetings for actors, creating and managing the audition schedule, and assisting with callbacks.

PREAUDITION

During the week of cast sign-ups, the stage managers should offer assistance to the director in two ways:

- Recruit and encourage a wide range of students for the cast and crew of the show
- Assist the director in creating, photocopying, and assembling the audition information into audition packets

Once the director and music director select the audition materials for a production, the stage managers should join the team to assist in creating each actor's audition packet. Each audition packet should include:

- Dates of performances
- Dates and approximate times of rehearsals
- Dates and times of auditions and callbacks
- Required monologues or scenes to prepare
- Required songs to prepare
- Clearly stated minimum performance standards
- Any dress requirement

Once the materials for the packet are created and put in order, the stage managers should make photocopies for each actor and all members of the creative staff. A master copy should be placed in a file.

On the day of the director's preaudition meeting with the cast, the stage managers should arrive at least fifteen minutes early to assist the director with preparing the meeting space, setting up appropriate check-in areas for the actors, and organizing audition materials and required paperwork.

As the actors arrive for the meeting, they should sign-in with the stage managers and receive an audition packet. The director will conduct this meeting, introducing the show, explaining the audition requirements, and answering questions from the actors.

As the student actors leave the preaudition meeting, they should stop by the stage managers' table to schedule an audition appointment. There are many ways to schedule audition appointments: by age (all seniors, all juniors), by ability (actor/singer, singer/dancer), by gender, by character type, or by voice type. Appointments should be scheduled according to the preference of the director.

When the meeting ends and all actors have been scheduled for audition appointments, the production stage manager should neatly type and post the final audition schedule. He should make copies of the final schedule for the director, members of the creative staff, and members of the stage management team.

THE AUDITION

It is the job of the stage managers to keep the auditions organized and running on schedule. The stage managers should arrive at least fifteen minutes before the auditions are scheduled to begin. They should assist the director with preparing the audition space, setting up the lobby area with appropriate check-in areas for the actors, and organizing audition materials and required paperwork.

Preparing the Audition Space

The stage managers should assist the director in setting up a table and chairs for the artistic staff. The table should be large enough to provide each staff member with enough room for her script, audition materials, and private writing space. The table should have adequate lighting and all members of the staff should have an unobstructed view of the performance area. The staff table should be set with water, pens and pencils, and tissues. The stage managers should also assist the director in preparing the performance area for the actors. It might be necessary to spike mark the best performance spot (for lighting or sound). Be prepared with tape and markers.

Greeting the Actors

The stage managers should prepare an area where the actors sign-in and wait for their audition appointments. This should include a large table and enough chairs for the stage management team. The stage managers table should be set with extra pens and pencils, copies of the rehearsal and performance dates, extra copies of the audition materials, character descriptions, and tissues.

As the actors arrive for their scheduled audition appointments, the stage managers should greet them and have them sign-in. Each actor should be given an audition profile and student contact information form to complete and return to the stage managers before his audition begins. The stage managers should collect and alphabetically file each actor's contact information form. The production stage manager should escort each actor (or group of actors) into the audition space at the appropriate time and hand all audition profiles for that group to the director.

It is important to remember that no two auditions are alike. The role of the stage managers might be redefined from show to show to include tasks specific to a particular audition. During a music audition, one of the stage managers might be needed to assist the pianist as a page-turner while she plays for each singer. During a dance audition, one of the stage managers might be needed to assist the choreographer by operating the cassette or CD during the session.

During the scheduled hours of first auditions, all students who signed up for membership in a crew should stop by the stage managers' table and complete a student contact information form. The stage managers should have a master checklist of all members of the student crew and should file their contact forms alphabetically by crew as they are completed. The stage managers should keep the lobby area quiet and neat while the auditions are in progress.

The Callback

Once the first round of auditions are over, the director, music director, and choreographer may wish to see specific actors for a second audition, or callback. The director should give the list of students to be called back and any important instructions to the production stage manager. It is the job of the production stage manager to personally call each actor on the list and give the same instructions to each person. These instructions usually include the time and place of the callback, the role(s) for which the actor is being considered, any dress requirements, and any special songs or skills the director would like to see performed at the audition. If the list of actors needed for callbacks is long, the production stage manager should divide the calls between the members of the stage management team.

On the day of callbacks, the stage managers should arrive at least fifteen minutes before the auditions are scheduled to assist the director with preparing the audition space, setting up the lobby area with appropriate check-in areas for the actors, and organizing audition materials and required paperwork. As the actors arrive for the callback audition, the stage managers should greet them, have them sign-in, distribute the callback materials to each actor for review before his scheduled audition time, and escort each actor (or group of actors) into the audition space at the appropriate time.

The Production Book and Cue Script

It is the responsibility of the production stage manager to maintain a complete written record of all elements of a production. The production stage manager accomplishes this task by creating a production book. She should begin assembling the production book as soon as she begins working on a show. Traditionally, audition materials are not included in the production book; they should be filed separately.

THE PRODUCTION BOOK

The production book should be a large three-ring binder. The production stage manager will need dividers and page protectors to effectively organize the information included in this book. Every production book should include:

1. All preliminary show information, including research on previous productions, period, style, writer/composer/librettist, elements of design, and so on.
2. Contact sheets for all cast, crew, creative staff, and business staff
3. Checklists for cast and each separate crew
4. Master production schedule
5. Publicity information and schedule
6. Parent volunteer information and schedule of volunteer personnel
7. Cast list
8. Complete scene breakdown
9. Cast rehearsal schedule

10. Actor's conflict calendar
11. Attendance sheets for cast, props crew, and stage management team
12. Script: Act I and Act II(in a musical, have tabs for each scene, sometimes with retyped pages for corrected lyrics, sometimes with pages from the musical score)
13. Lighting notes
14. Props notes
15. Complete props list
16. Costume, makeup, and hair notes
17. Sound notes

Items 1 through 11 on this list are important organizational items for every production. In most cases, the production stage manager will be asked to assist in creating these schedules, checklists, contact sheets, and calendars. The production stage manager should make each document he creates look as professional as possible. These materials will be distributed to most members of the professional staff and student members of the cast and crew. The documents should be proofread, spell-checked, and proofread again. All documents created on the computer should be saved and a back-up copy created. As personnel or calendar information changes, updated copies of each list, schedule, or calendar should be created and distributed to appropriate staff, cast, or crew. When creating updated documents, try to make the new document easy to identify by photocopying on a new color of paper or placing a new date (such as "Updated on March 12") in the heading

Items 12 and 13 on the production book list are the actual script pages of the play. It is crucial that the production stage manager's script be complete, accurate, and well organized. When working on a musical, it is smart to use dividers to separate each scene. This helps to organize the needs, requirements, and responsibilities of each department as rehearsals develop. This method of organization also supports the structure of the show as it is outlined in the scene breakdown.

It is also a good idea to insert selected pages of the printed music (from the score) in the production book. If there is a particularly long or complicated musical number involving choreography or musical staging, the production stage manager should insert those music pages and take notes on the manuscript. Reading music is a good skill for a production stage manager to develop.

Items 14 through 18 on the above list are products of the rehearsal process. As the director, music director, and choreographer are shaping a production, they will refer to props, lighting effects, sound effects, microphones, or costume pieces during rehearsals. The production stage manager should keep a list of all references to other departments and communicate these needs to the designers and crew chiefs of each crew.

THE CUE SCRIPT

The cue script is the production stage manager's complete documentation of the final lighting, set changes, and sound cues for the performance of a production. It is her job to assemble and maintain the complete cue script.

If the production stage manager's production book is neat and organized, it might be possible to add the final cues for lighting, set changes, and sound cues directly to the production book. If, however, the book is messy, it is better to start with a clean script and mark the cues and important notes in this second script. It is critical that the cue book be complete, accurate, neat, and easy to read if the show is to run smoothly.

The stage managers must be present when the director and designers are cueing a show. All stage managers should be taking notes during this process. The production stage manager should be recording all notes for every cue. Each assistant stage manager should be recording warnings and cues that apply to their specific assignment. For example, if an assistant stage manager is assigned to the cast stage right, that stage manager should understand and record all cues that occur on that side of the stage. If members of the cast have a stage right entrance at the beginning of scene three, but a large piece of scenery is being moved off-stage and stored stage right at the end of scene two, the assistant stage manager will have to hold the cast in a waiting area while the set change occurs, then move them quickly to places. Each assistant stage manager has to pay close attention to all cues and notes involving lights, set, props, costume changes, and microphone changes or placement.

The production stage manager records all the cues for the technical elements of the production. Lighting cues provide illumination for each scene and provide moments of transition from scene to scene. The production stage manager must understand how the director and designers set the pace and function of each cue. Calling cues correctly is an artistic ability; the timing of calling cues directly affects the experience of the audience and can impact the performance of the members of the cast and crew.

In a cue script, all the cues are written in the same column of the page. The types of cues the production stage manager should record and call are:

- Warning cues
- Lighting cues
- Sound cues
- Set change cues

Different types of cues should be written in different colors so that the production stage manager knows at a glance what the cue signifies. Lighting, sound, and set change cues are most frequently synchronized with one of three performance elements: the words, the music, or a specific action.

Text Cue
A text cue is called with a specific word (or syllable) in the spoken script or sung lyric of a song.

Music Cue
In calling a music cue, the production stage manager is either watching the musical conductor for a downbeat or cut-off, or is reading the musical score for a specific measure where a change in tempo occurs or a new musical theme is introduced. Again, reading music is a good skill for a production stage manager to develop.

Visual Cue

In calling a visual cue, the production stage manager is watching the stage for a specific action to occur (for example, when the actor touches the light switch, when the actress faints, when the actor exits, when the door slams). When the action happens, the cue is called.

The Role of the Production Stage Manager During Rehearsals

During most of the rehearsal process, the stage managers work with the cast and with three members of the creative staff: the director, the music director, and the choreographer. In rehearsal, the production stage manager records notes in his script and gains an understanding of the show as it develops from day to day. By participating in the daily rehearsal process, the stage managers learn to see the big picture (where each actor is placed on the stage, the purpose of each character's movement, how characters relate to one another) through balance or contrast of movement.

DAILY REHEARSAL RESPONSIBILITIES

The production stage manager is responsible for taking daily rehearsal attendance for the cast, props crew, and stage management team and keeping an accurate master attendance record. She should arrive at least fifteen minutes early for each rehearsal. Her prerehearsal checklist should include: unlocking the doors, switching on lights, presetting director's table, presetting set and props for the scheduled rehearsal, and checking for safety (no tools lying around, floors swept). This routine is the same for all rehearsals—blocking, music, and choreography. Before the cast arrives, she should preset her production book and prepare her personal workspace, setting out her rehearsal supplies. She should organize any new information that needs to be distributed to the company and prepare to collect paperwork from members of the cast as they arrive.

During *blocking rehearsals,* the production stage manager's primary responsibility is to work with the director, recording all the blocking for each scene of the show. He should record the blocking in his production script (including notes integrating props, set, lighting, sound, or costumes) as each new scene is developed. He should give blocking corrections when needed during subsequent rehearsals of the same scene. The production stage manager should assign an assistant stage manager to work with the props crew. This assistant stage manager should oversee and coordinate the inclusion of props in rehearsal as soon as the props are available for use.

During *off-book rehearsals,* the production stage manager should give line and blocking prompts as needed. She should continue to facilitate the integration of props, set, and minor costume pieces into each rehearsal, assigning specific tasks to the assistant stage managers as needed.

During *music rehearsals,* the production stage manager should learn the music, paying close attention to the melodies and structure of each song in the show. He should compare the lyrics printed in the music to those printed in the script. There are often many differences. When these differences occur, the production stage manager should amend the script to reflect accurate music lyrics. It has been my experience that when the script lyrics are highly inaccurate (missing verses, eliminating repeated lyrics, or omitting reference to music or dance breaks), it is best to type a new "correct" version of the song and substitute the new pages in the existing script. These new pages should be photocopied and distributed to all members of the cast, all members of the creative staff and all crew chiefs for inclusion in their scripts. Unfortunately, lyric errors in a musical script are very common. The production stage manager should assign an assistant stage manager the job of making rehearsal recordings of the music as requested by the director or choreographer. The assistant stage manager is also responsible for the setup and cleanup of the recording equipment needed for these sessions.

During *choreography rehearsals,* the production stage manager records general movement notes in her script for later reference during rehearsal and cue sessions. She should assign an assistant stage manager to assist the choreographer in each dance rehearsal. This assistant stage manager should coordinate all rehearsal tapes and run the sound playback for the choreographer. The assistant stage manager is also responsible for the setup and cleanup of sound equipment needed for the choreography rehearsals.

At the end of each rehearsal, the production stage manager is responsible for cleaning up the rehearsal space. The assistant stage managers and the cast should assist with this daily process. The postrehearsal checklist should include: all set pieces, props, and costume pieces properly stored; all lights turned out; every door locked and pulled shut.

TAKING BLOCKING NOTES

In every rehearsal, the stage manager takes notes *in pencil* about the blocking, choreography, use of props, reference to costumes and set, reference to microphones, and complete music notes. The production book reflects the complete realization of a production.

If a production book is to be useful, it must be neat, well organized, and complete. When taking notes in a rehearsal, it is very important to take them in an orderly manner. Blocking notes should reflect the movement and important actions of each actor in a scene. They should also reflect the movement of each prop, set piece, or costume item: where does each item start, who moves it, and where does it end up.

All staging directions reflect the actor's perspective when facing the audience. Here are the most common shorthand abbreviations for blocking terms:

COMMON SHORTHAND NOTATION FOR BLOCKING

SR = Stage Right	CS = Center Stage	SL = Stage Left
DR = Downstage Right	DC = Downstage Center	DL = Downstage Left
UR = Upstage Right	UC = Upstage Center	UL = Upstage Left
X = Cross	FZ = Freeze	/ = Beat
@ = At	w/ = With	w/o = Without
♪ = Music Cue		

The diagram below illustrates the easiest way to organize notes in a production stage manager's production book. In the right column of the text page, all the blocking should be clearly marked. In the left column, notes on props, set, and costumes should be marked. On the blank page (left side of the binder), special notes and choreography or blocking diagrams can be made without running out of space.

SAMPLE PAGE OF THE PRODUCTION STAGE MANAGER'S PRODUCTION BOOK

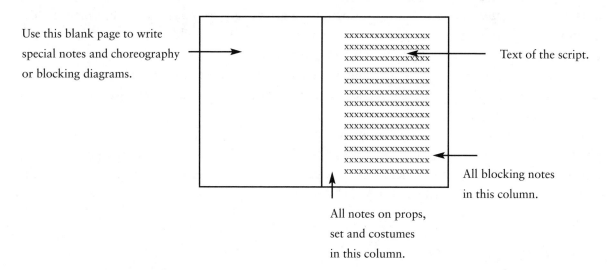

Use this blank page to write special notes and choreography or blocking diagrams.

Text of the script.

All blocking notes in this column.

All notes on props, set and costumes in this column.

THE PRODUCTION STAGE MANAGER'S REHEARSALS

As the rehearsal process progresses, the production stage manager should be expected to run parts of blocking rehearsals, starting and stopping the rehearsal as needed, making corrections, and giving notes. These rehearsals should be warm-up rehearsals before the cast demonstrates specific progress for the director. They should be woven into the normal rehearsal schedule. The cast should be aware of the production stage manager's rehearsal in advance and of the director's expectations from that rehearsal. These rehearsals should be short (fifteen to twenty minutes maximum) with clear goals. The production stage manager and cast should perform their scene for the director immediately following their brief rehearsal. Here are two strategies for a production stage manager's rehearsal:

Running a Mini-rehearsal for Blocking Accuracy
When the cast is faced with a particularly difficult scene and simply needs to run it over and over again to develop a flow of movement, the production stage manager can take over and run these rehearsals for the director, freeing the director to check in with the technical crews or paperwork.

Running a Mini-rehearsal for Memory Accuracy
When the cast is working on a scene from memory for the first time, it is good for the production stage manager to run the first off-book rehearsal, making corrections to lines and blocking as needed.

Once the cast discovers its off-book rhythm, it is time to perform for the director and continue the rehearsal.

During this rehearsal, the production stage manager should watch for accuracy in all areas: blocking, use of props, accuracy of lines, and pace of the scene. His production script should be complete; he should feel confident giving notes and making corrections as needed.

The Role of the Stage Management Team During Tech and Dress Rehearsals and Performances

It is important for the production stage manager to delegate responsibilities to the assistant stage managers once the production schedule moves into technical and dress rehearsals. The production stage manager has to give up many of the day-to-day duties and focus on his principal job: working with the director and designers to cue the show, then executing those cues in a consistent and artistic manner.

CUEING THE SHOW

During the process of cueing the show, the production stage manager joins the director's table and works with the director and lighting, set, and sound designers. As the creative team discusses and designs cues, the production stage manager accurately records them in his production book. If he does not understand the function of a cue, where to place it or how to call it, he should raise those questions as that cue is being discussed. At the end of the cueing session, the production stage manager should have a good understanding of each cue in the production, the personnel necessary to implement the cue, how and when to call the cue, and what the specific result of the cue should be. As scene changes occur during the cueing session, an assistant stage manager should be assigned the responsibility of working with the crew chiefs to help place all the parts of each set appropriately on the stage for spiking. Although the crew chiefs know which parts of the set are needed for each scene, they have not spent time in rehearsal to know where things are placed or how they are used. The assistant stage manager should provide this information to the run crew chiefs during the cueing session to facilitate the process.

If members of the cast are present for light walking during the cueing sessions, an assistant stage manager should be assigned the responsibility of directing the actors to the appropriate places onstage for each scene.

Once the production stage manager has recorded complete and accurate cues in her production book, she should schedule a meeting with all crew chiefs. At this meeting, cues should be synchronized between departments, and all crew chiefs should make appropriate notes in their scripts in preparation for the technical and dress rehearsals.

DELEGATING RESPONSIBILITIES TO THE ASSISTANT STAGE MANAGERS

There are many daily tasks and production responsibilities that should be delegated to the assistant stage managers. These include:

- Take daily attendance at all tech and dress rehearsals and at all performances
- Create multiple copies of large format of running order of show
  The running order should include:
  - Complete list of scenes and songs, including reprises
  - Complete list of all characters (including chorus or extras)
  - Where scene changes occur
  - Note time of day, season, or year
  - Note critical costume/props/sound reminders
  - Make any additional important notes, reminders or warnings
- Post large format running orders backstage right, backstage left, in dressing rooms and wherever else members of the cast and crew congregate
- Collect and process any paperwork or ticket orders from the cast or crew
- Assist artistic staff as needed
- Assist all crew chiefs as needed
- Maintain consistent discipline in cast and crew. Enforce the rules and regulations of the company (such as whether guests are allowed to visit during dress rehearsals, or actors are permitted to eat in costume, and when cast and crew are permitted breaks)

THE PRODUCTION STAGE MANAGER

By the time your production moves into tech and dress rehearsals, the production stage manager should be the student executive of the cast and crew. As the production leader, all crew chiefs and all assistant stage managers should be scheduled for a daily meeting with the production stage manager. At this meeting, the production stage manager should distribute any new information, review changes from previous rehearsals, and answer any questions posed by the assistant stage managers or crew chiefs. Following this meeting, each crew chief should have a meeting with the members of his crew.

The production stage manager actively assumes responsibility for the form and discipline of each technical and dress rehearsal. From the production meeting to the preshow checklist, the production stage manager must be focused, have a clear agenda, and must treat all members of the production with professional courtesy and respect.

Preshow Checklist
- Receives daily attendance reports from all assistant stage managers and crew chiefs at each tech and dress rehearsal and every performance

- Receives a report from each crew chief when their preset is complete
- Rehearses difficult technical elements with crew as needed
- Calls crew to places ten minutes prior to the start of each tech or dress rehearsal or performance
- Conducts the final headset check before starting the show to be certain all equipment is in good working order
- Runs the technical rehearsal, dress rehearsals, and performances, calling all cues
- Before each performance, communicates with the house staff and the run crew chiefs to determine when the house is ready to open
- Before each performance, communicates with the box office to confirm the start-of-show time

The production stage manager must rehearse his technique for calling the cues. It is critical that he calls cues in a consistent and measured tempo, and that his voice is calm and his diction precise. The production stage manager should continue to work closely with the director to perfect this technique and to discuss the details of the production.

Once the performances begin, the show belongs to the production stage manager. If he is well prepared, your show is guaranteed to be a success.

CHAPTER 4

BACKSTAGE CREWS, HOUSE STAFF, AND ORCHESTRA

Student Leadership and Crew Members

Many high school theater directors find their time absorbed by rehearsals with actors. Although working on blocking, choreography, character interpretation, and other acting issues are critical for bringing the play to life, attention to the physical needs of the production (set, lighting, and sound) are often not given equal planning time by the director. Even more often, the students working on these crews are given vague directions, little or no adult instruction, poor supervision, and few, if any, clearly stated standards.

Although good acting is critical to a good performance, it is important to keep all elements of the play balanced and equal. Students involved in the technical elements of a production should have the same intense experience during the process of building and creating a play as the student actors. Just as a student actor clearly knows what is expected of her during each part of the rehearsal process, a technical student should have the same standard of clearly stated expectations. This chapter defines the roles and responsibilities of the student members of the crew.

Student Leadership

The student leaders of each crew—set construction, run, sound, lighting, props, costume/makeup— are called crew chiefs; student leaders of the house staff and orchestra are called, respectively, house managers and orchestra managers. With the exception of the lighting crew, it works well to have two chiefs or managers for each crew. The two student leaders can then divide up responsibilities with the result that the production will run more smoothly.

Ideally, crew chiefs and managers are the most experienced members of their respective crews. Students chosen for these positions should possess good leadership, communication, and organizational skills. They should be students who have shown good judgment in past performances and are reliable and trustworthy. These students must be good, dependable collaborators and good role models for other members of their crew and staff. When possible, seniors should occupy these positions. All crew chiefs should have the following two items:

A complete script. The script should be in large print and kept in a three-ring binder. Dividers should separate each scene. Each crew chief should read the script several times to have a complete understanding of production requirements.

First-aid kit. This is necessary for basic safety.

In addition, the run, sound, lighting, props, and costume/makeup crew chiefs will need the following items:

Small personal flashlight. Crew chiefs should carry a small flashlight in case there is an emergency (either an accident or injury, locating a missing item, or making a quick repair).

Notepad, pencils, pens (black or blue and red), highlighter, ruler. Each crew chief needs these supplies to take notes and accurately mark his script. The marked script should serve as a complete record of all the requirements for his crew, such as lighting cues for the lighting crew and sound cues for the sound crew.

Responsibilities of the Backstage Crews

Students should learn the correct vocabulary for parts of the stage, equipment and tools, and tasks their crew performs. They should develop an understanding of how a crew is organized and the correct chain of command in assigning jobs and responsibilities. They should be respectful of their workspace, their equipment and supplies, and responsible for their upkeep and maintenance. Students should learn a good work ethic: how to carefully listen to and follow directions, how to complete every task they begin, how to ask for assistance when needed, and how to assist others when asked. If each crew is disciplined and focused, the whole production will run more smoothly.

Backstage crews should follow the behavior expectations and productions responsibilities listed on page 62 (see box).

Set Construction Crew

All members of the set construction crew work closely with and receive instruction from a professional set designer.

RESPONSIBILITIES OF THE CONSTRUCTION CREW CHIEFS

If possible, choose two crew chiefs: one for backstage right and one for backstage left. These students should possess basic skills in construction and painting. The responsibilities of the student crew chiefs include:

- Working closely with the set designer on all elements of the production
- Being a role model to the construction crew membership in meeting behavior expectations and production responsibilities (page 62)
- Working with set designer to create the construction crew work schedule
- Assigning student crew members to the construction work schedule
- Notifying the student crew members of work assignments and responsibilities
- Working with the director, set designer, and lighting designer to organize the run crews (This is discussed in further detail on page 77.)

CONSTRUCTION CREW MEMBERS

The set construction crew makes the greatest time commitment to the production next to the cast. Student crew members will learn how to do the following:

- Employ basic safety rules of construction
- Work with a set designer
- Work with a student crew chief
- Use basic construction techniques
- Correctly use construction tools and equipment
- Use a variety of techniques for set painting and set decoration
- Keep supplies clean and organized
- Keep their work space clean and organized
- Organize permanent storage and create an inventory list for all construction materials and tools owned by the school or theater program

The set construction crew should begin meeting at the same time that the actors begin the rehearsal process. Just as the first meeting of actors is customarily a read-through of the script, the first meeting of the set construction crew is customarily an organization and information meeting.

This first meeting should include the director/producer, the set designer, and all student members of the construction crew. The director begins by conducting a business meeting, giving the crew members a clear list of all their production responsibilities. This is a good time to distribute all necessary paperwork for the production. Once the business part of the meeting is concluded, the director focuses on the creative part of the production by presenting a brief synopsis of the plot of the play, including descriptions of the various settings as the story develops. When the director has concluded this presentation, the meeting is turned over to the set designer. At this meeting, it is customary for the set designer to:

- Describe the set concept
- Show and discuss the construction plans and drawings
- Describe the skills the students need to accomplish the project
- Announce the student crew chiefs and describe their roles
- Discuss how the crew work schedule will be constructed (number of days per week, number of hours per work session, specific kinds of tasks to be performed)
- Discuss how the crew membership will be assigned to positions in the work schedule
- Describe the behavior expectations and production responsibilities common to all crew members (see page 62)
- Address any special needs or concerns about the project

Run Crew

The run crew works closely with and receives instruction from the director and the set and lighting designers. Crew members facilitate all the scene changes in a production. In a musical, this is often a big job with many complicated elements; in a play, the job is often much simpler. As a member of the run crew, each student learns how to be a productive and equal member of a team; each is assigned a specific role in each scene change. Since scene changes need to be performed quickly and silently, members need to be well rehearsed and choreographed. The best crew members have good memory skills, possess the ability to concentrate under pressure, and are self-disciplined individuals. When a run crew is organized and cohesive, members share a tremendous feeling of accomplishment.

RESPONSIBILITIES OF THE RUN CREW CHIEFS

The student leaders of the run crew should be the crew chiefs from the construction crew. They are the students who were most responsible for construction of the set. Since they know its construction, they can assist with minor repairs and upkeep as needed. The crew chiefs also know all the student members of the construction crew very well. Since they were responsible for assigning student members of the construction crew to work positions during the construction process, the crew chiefs know the level of expertise of each individual crew member. This will allow them to divide the student membership into two equal teams: backstage right and backstage left. Each crew chief is then responsible for his own half of the run crew for the duration of the show. During the final rehearsals and performances, the props crew becomes part of the run crew. Members of the props crew are assigned to backstage right and left positions and are responsible to the crew chiefs for the duration of the production.

The run crew chiefs will collaborate closely with the director, the set designer, the lighting designer, and the production stage manager. They should be the primary contacts with these staff members and should relay all necessary information and instructions to the members of their crews.

The student crew chiefs will have a great deal of responsibility during the final dress rehearsals and performances of a show. The director and lighting and set designers should work closely with the crew chiefs as the production is assembled during the final rehearsals. The set designer should offer supervision and advice as the crew chiefs organize their crew members, their backstage spaces, incorporate the props crew and their supplies and materials, and coordinate the choreography of the set changes.

During the final rehearsals, crew chiefs may be asked to temporarily assign members of their crew to assist the set designer, the director, any member of the adult design staff, and any parent volunteer when needed. These accommodations should be made whenever possible.

To do her job correctly, each crew chief needs the following supplies, in addition to those listed on page 75:

Lit workspace backstage. Each crew chief needs a place to keep his script binder and personal supplies. This space can be as simple as a music stand with an orchestra light attached. If you have a lot of backstage space, a small table or student desk is another option.

Tape for spiking the stage. During the technical rehearsal, and continuing through the dress rehearsals, each set piece must be spiked in its exact location on the stage. If your budget allows, glow tape is a wonderful tool for spiking set pieces. If your budget does not allow for this luxury, masking tape works very well also.

Notepad for making diagrams and taking notes during the final rehearsals. During the technical rehearsal, the director, set designer, and crew chiefs are certain to notice elements of the set that need attention or dressing. The crew chief responsible for that set piece should keep a current work list for items that live in her domain so that the members of his crew can fix, adjust, or repaint items as needed. In addition, the crew chief should keep meticulous notes on specific student job assignments for each set change, problems that occur during the rehearsal, and a repair list.

Posterboard and heavy black markers. Once the set changes are coordinated and job assignments are finalized, each crew chief should make large poster boards that list each scene change and job assignment within that scene change. These posters should be prominently displayed backstage as a reference for all members of the run crew to see (see next page).

Two first-aid kits. There should be a complete kit backstage right *and* backstage left.

Checklists and Task Assignments

In addition to coordinating the run crew's work assignments during the production, the crew chiefs also coordinate the crew's responsibilities in the daily care and management of the performance space. The director and set designer should consult with the crew chiefs to be sure all expectations of facility care are carefully itemized and addressed. Once the crew chiefs are aware of their facilities responsibilities, it is their job to create the following checklists and assign personnel to specific tasks on those lists.

General Checklists
- Location of tools and supplies for quick minor repairs to set
- Location of nearest fire extinguishers

Daily List for Preshow Tasks
- Facilities care: sweep and damp mop stage space; clean/dust set pieces and furniture or props
- Exact preset for all set pieces and props (coordinate with the props crew chiefs)
- Location of first-aid kits (stage right and stage left)

Daily List for Intermission Tasks
- Sweep stage space
- Intermission set and props changes (coordinate with the props crew chiefs)

Daily List for Postshow Tasks (after all dress rehearsals and performances)
- Complete strike list for set pieces detailing where (and how) they should be stored overnight
- Complete strike list for all props detailing where (and how) they should be stored overnight. Pay special attention to food items, live plants, animals, expensive period pieces, and fragile items (coordinate with the props crew chiefs)

MARKING THE RUN CREW CHIEF'S SCRIPT

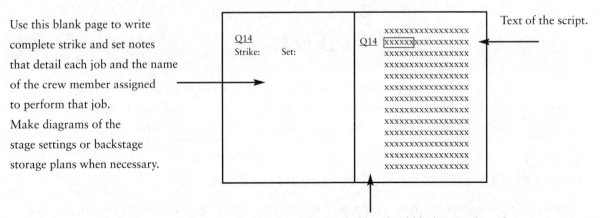

Use this blank page to write complete strike and set notes that detail each job and the name of the crew member assigned to perform that job. Make diagrams of the stage settings or backstage storage plans when necessary.

Q14
Strike: Set:

Q14

Text of the script.

All cue numbers should be kept in this column

The information on the blank left page of the run crew chief's script should be copied neatly onto large poster boards and posted backstage for all members of the crew to see.

THE RUN CREW MEMBERS

For most productions, the members of the run crew include students from the construction and props crews. If additional hands are needed for a large show, it is possible to enlist the services of members of the costume/makeup crew, the lighting crew, or members of the cast.

Students on the run crew will work closely with the set designer and run crew chiefs. The run crew should begin its process during the lighting cue rehearsals, continue through the technical rehearsal, run for time during the dress rehearsals and keep the show fluid during performances. The run crew members should be organized, well disciplined, and focused. When the run crew is preparing for or making a set change, each student is busy with specific assigned tasks. In between set changes, the crew members should review their next assignment as they sit quietly out of the way while the scene onstage is being played.

Another major responsibility of the run crew is facility management of the performance space. This includes the cleaning, care, and organization of the stage area and all set pieces. This responsibility begins during the lighting cue sessions and continues through the final show strike. The run crew responsibilities in this area include:

- Sweeping and damp mopping the stage before each performance
- Setting and checking a complete preset for all set pieces before each dress rehearsal and performance
- Setting and checking a complete preset for all props before each dress rehearsal and performance (coordinate with the props crew chiefs)
- Checking all spike marks before each dress rehearsal and performance; respike daily as needed
- Sweeping stage during intermission
- Storing all set pieces in a safe manner at the conclusion of each dress rehearsal and performance
- Storing all props in a safe manner at the conclusion of each dress rehearsal and performance (coordinate with the props crew chiefs)

Light Crew

Lighting crew members work closely with and receive instruction from a professional lighting designer. Students should learn the correct vocabulary for parts of the stage, lighting instruments and cables, lighting accessories, and the safety rules specific to theatrical lighting work.

RESPONSIBILITIES OF THE LIGHTING CREW CHIEF

In professional theater, this position is called assistant to the designer or master electrician. Since high school students do not have the proper training or professional licensing to hold these titles, it is better to call the student leader the crew chief. The lighting crew chief coordinates the student crew membership, facilitates the designers work style, yet bears no responsibility for design or facility decisions.

He initially works closely with the lighting designer. Once the load-in and hang are completed and the cueing and technical rehearsal process begins, the lighting crew chief will also collaborate with the director, the set designer, the run crew chiefs, and the production stage manager. The responsibilities of the lighting crew chief include:

- Working closely with the lighting designer on all elements of the production
- Being a role model to the lighting crew membership in meeting behavior expectations and production responsibilities (page 62).
- Working with the designer to create the lighting crew work schedule
- Assigning crew members to the lighting work schedule
- Notifying the crew members of work assignments and responsibilities
- Working with the director, lighting and set designers, and production stage manager during the technical rehearsal and dress rehearsals
- Performing the role of troubleshooter during all final dress rehearsals and performances

The lighting crew chief will have a great deal of responsibility during the final dress rehearsals and performances of a show. The director and lighting designer should work closely with the lighting crew chief as the production is assembled during the cueing sessions and the technical rehearsal. The lighting designer should offer supervision and advice as the lighting crew chief assumes responsibility for his crew.

The lighting crew chief, in addition to the supplies listed on page 75:, will need a copy of the magic sheet for the production and must be able to read and interpret it. The lighting crew chief must take careful notes during the cueing sessions, the technical rehearsal, and the dress rehearsal. These notes should include the location of the cue, the cue number, its speed and function, and any special details of that specific cue. When completed, the marked script serves as a complete record of the use of lighting in the production. The crew chief, along with the director and lighting designer, is certain to notice elements of lighting that need attention. She should keep a current work list for items that her crew members can fix, adjust, or refocus as needed.

Checklists and Task Assignments

In addition to coordinating the lighting crew's work assignments during the production, the crew chief also coordinates the crew's responsibilities in the daily care and management of the lighting equipment. The director and lighting designer should consult with the crew chief to be sure all expectations are carefully itemized and addressed. Once the crew chief is aware of his responsibilities, it is his job to create the following checklists and assign personnel to specific tasks on those lists.

General Checklists
- Location of tools for quick, emergency repairs; includes wrenches, ladders, genies, cherry pickers
- Location of supplies for quick, emergency repairs; includes gaff tape, duct tape, tie line, replacement lamps, gel frames, replacement gel, extra safety cables
- Location of magic sheet (and extra copies if available)

- Location of back-up disks with recorded show (if using a computerized lighting system)
- Location of nearest fire extinguishers
- Location of first-aid kit

Daily List for Preshow Tasks
- Procedure for full dimmer check
- Procedure for spotlight check

Daily List for Intermission Tasks
- Procedure for quick emergency repairs (if needed)

Daily List for Postshow Tasks(after all lighting work sessions, technical and dress rehearsals and performances)
- Procedure for shutting down the lighting system and lighting board
- Procedure for shutting down external dimmer/power sources
- Procedure for storing spotlights and lighting effects as needed for production

LIGHTING CREW MEMBERS

The first meeting of the lighting crew should be scheduled during the beginning of the rehearsal process. This meeting includes the director/producer, the lighting designer, and all student members of the lighting crew. The director begins by giving the crew members a list of all their production responsibilities and distributes all necessary paperwork for the production. Once the business part of the meeting is concluded, the director presents a synopsis of the plot of the play, including descriptions of the various settings as the story develops. When the director has concluded this presentation, the meeting is turned over to the lighting designer. At this meeting, it is customary for the lighting designer to:

- Describe the lighting concept
- Announce the student crew chief and describe his role
- Discuss how the crew work schedule will be constructed (number of days per week, number of hours per work session, specific kinds of tasks to be performed)
- Discuss how crew membership will be assigned positions in the work schedule
- Announce the dates of the cast rehearsals that members of the lighting crew are expected to attend as observers
- Describe the behavior expectations and production responsibilities common to all crew members (page 62)

The lighting crew will usually have a second meeting with the designer shortly before the load-in and hang. At this second meeting, it is customary for the designer to:

- Show and discuss the completed lighting plot
- Describe the skills the students need to accomplish the project
- Address any special needs or concerns about the project

For most productions, the lighting crew will not begin its official lighting work until two or three weeks before the show opens. Although members of the lighting crew make a shorter time commitment (in terms of weeks), they generally put in very long days once they begin. Through participation in the lighting crew, all student crew members should learn the skills necessary for lighting a theatrical production. They will learn how to do the following:

- Employ correct safety practices and procedures used by lighting crew members
- Load-in lighting equipment
- Read a lighting inventory
- Read a lighting shop order (if materials are rented for the production)
- Read a formal lighting plot
- Accomplish a hang according to the specifications of the design plot
- Troubleshoot and focus the plot once the hang is completed
- Cue a show: learn to record lighting cues (as directed by the lighting designer) for the specific lighting system in your theater
- Operate a lighting board
- Operate a spotlight
- Rehearse lighting cues during the technical and dress rehearsals
- Read a magic sheet
- Run a complete dimmer check
- Run cues during the performances
- Complete a full lighting strike
- Organize permanent storage and create an inventory list for all lighting instruments, cable, replacement lamps, lighting supplies and accessory items owned by the school or theater program

The most common assignment of positions on a lighting crew are:

Board Operator

The board operator runs the lighting board. The board controls each new lighting cue as it appears onstage. When using a manual board, it is often helpful to have two board operators who work together. Most schools have moved (or are quickly moving to) computerized lighting systems. When using a computerized lighting system, only one board operator is needed. During the run of the show, the board operator takes his cues directly from the production stage manager.

Spotlight Operators

The spotlight operators are very important people in a musical. Spotlights are rarely used in plays, but in musicals, they provide the dimension needed to support the intensity of the musical numbers. During the run of a show, spotlight operators take cues directly from the production stage manager.

Troubleshooter

The troubleshooter should be your lighting crew chief, the most experienced and responsible member of the lighting crew. She needs to remember how each lighting cue in the production appears, how it is used, and how it transitions. She should be knowledgeable about the intricacies of the lighting plot and functions of the hang and accomplished in using the lighting board for the production.

During the run of the show, the troubleshooter simply watches the performance. At all times, she should have her notepad ready to record small problems that appear throughout the production, such as a light that has moved, a burned-out lamp, or a gel that needs replacing. These are normal occurrences during the run of a show and are part of basic lighting maintenance.

If the troubleshooter possesses a good visual memory of the lighting cues, he will often be aware of a problem as it is occurs during a performance. Of course, everyone hopes for a smooth show, but for those times when emergencies happen, the troubleshooter is an indispensable person.

Backstage Light Crew Positions (repatching, special effects)

Some productions call for special effects or dramatic mood changes. These effects are often accomplished through lighting, thus special effects usually fall within the domain of the lighting crew to operate during the production.

Sound Crew

All sound crew members work closely with and receive instruction from a professional sound designer. Students should learn the correct vocabulary for parts of the stage, sound equipment, microphones, cables, and sound accessories.

RESPONSIBILITIES OF THE SOUND CREW CHIEFS

Choose two crew chiefs: One whose primary responsibility is coordinating body microphones and another whose primary responsibility is coordinating area microphones, the internal communication system (headsets), and supervising the sound board operators.

The sound crew chiefs work closely with the sound designer. Once the load-in and hang are completed, the sound crew chiefs will also collaborate with the director, the music director, the set designer, all student crew chiefs (run, lighting, and costume/makeup crews), and the production stage manager. The responsibilities of the sound crew chiefs include:

- Working closely with the sound designer on all elements of the production
- Being a role model to the lighting crew membership in meeting behavior expectations and production responsibilities (page 62)
- Working with the designer to create the sound crew work schedule
- Assigning crew members to the sound work schedule
- Notifying the crew members of work assignments and responsibilities
- Working with the director, lighting and set designers, and production stage manager during the technical rehearsal and dress rehearsals
- Performing the role of troubleshooter during all final dress rehearsals and performances

The sound crew chiefs will have a great deal of responsibility during the final dress rehearsals and performances of a show. The director and sound designer should work closely with the sound crew chiefs as the production is assembled during the technical and dress rehearsals. The sound designer should offer supervision and advice as the sound crew chiefs assume responsibility for their crew.

Crew chiefs will need to read the script several times and attend at least two final cast rehearsals to see how the actors move in their rehearsal space. During the technical rehearsal and the dress rehearsals, the director, music director, sound designer, costume designer, and sound crew chiefs are certain to notice elements of sound application that need attention. The crew chiefs should keep a current work list for items that their crew members can fix or adjust as needed.

As the show is being cued, the sound crew chiefs should take meticulous notes about the microphone assignments as they are decided. These notes should include the stage location, microphone number(s), character name(s), the cue's speed and function, effects needed, alternative sound sources, and any special details of that specific cue. The completed script should be as professional and organized as possible. When completed, the marked script serves as a complete record of the use of all sound and sound effects in the production.

Checklists and Task Assignments
In addition to coordinating the sound crew's work assignments during the production, the crew chiefs also coordinate the crew's responsibilities in the daily care and management of the sound equipment. The director and sound designer should consult with the crew chiefs to be sure all expectations are carefully itemized and addressed. Once the crew chiefs are aware of their responsibilities, it becomes their job to create the following checklists and assign personnel to specific tasks on those lists.

General Checklists
- Location of tools and supplies for quick, emergency repairs (electrician's tape, gaff tape, tie line)
- Location of replacement batteries for body mikes
- Location of first-aid kit

Daily List for Preshow Tasks

- Procedure for full sound check of all area mikes
- Procedure for full sound check of all body mikes
- Procedure for full sound check of all internal communication system
- Procedure for check of all sound effects and alternative sound sources

Daily List for Intermission Tasks

- Procedure for quick emergency repairs (if needed)
- Change batteries in all body mikes

Daily List for Postshow Tasks (after all dress rehearsals and performances)

- Procedure for collecting all body mikes and removing batteries for overnight storage
- Procedure for shutting down the sound system
- Procedure for shutting down all effects and alternative sound sources
- Procedure for shutting down internal communication system
- Procedure for storing all sound equipment in a safe manner

SOUND CREW MEMBERS

The first meeting of the sound crew should be scheduled during the beginning of the rehearsal process. This meeting should include the director/producer, the sound designer and all student members of the sound crew. The director begins by conducting a business meeting, giving the crew members a clear list of all of their production responsibilities, and distributes all necessary paperwork for the production. The director then presents a brief synopsis of the plot of the play. When the director has concluded, the meeting is turned over to the sound designer. At this meeting, it is customary for the sound designer to:

- Describe the sound concept of the production
- Announce the student crew chiefs and describe their roles
- Discuss how the crew work schedule will be constructed (number of days per week, number of hours per work session, specific kinds of tasks to be performed)
- Discuss how crew membership will be assigned positions in the work schedule
- Announce the dates of the cast rehearsals that members of the sound crew are expected to attend as observers
- Describe the behavior expectations and production responsibilities common to all crew members (page 62)
- Address any special needs or concerns about the project

The sound crew will usually have a second meeting with the designer before the sound load-in. At the second meeting, it is customary for the designer to:

- Show and discuss the completed sound plot
- Describe the skills the students need to accomplish the project
- Address any special needs or concerns about the project

For most productions, the sound crew's responsibilities fall into two distinct categories: creating special effects (or music samples) and providing microphones and sound support. During the first weeks of rehearsal, the sound crew should create all the necessary sound effects (or music samples) needed for the production. This will allow the director to incorporate the sound effects into the early play rehearsals and will give the cast ample opportunity to become comfortable with the effects. Providing microphones and sound support for a production usually occurs at the end of the rehearsal process during the technical and dress rehearsals.

Through participation in the sound crew, all student crew members should learn the skills necessary for providing sound support and sound enhancement for a theatrical production. They will learn how to do the following:

- Create sound effects specific to the needs of your production (If your school [or individual students within your school] have the technological resources, the final package of sound effects and music samples should be stored in sound files on a computer and/or burned onto a CD.)
- Read a sound inventory
- Read a sound shop order (if equipment is rented for the production)
- Read a formal sound design plot
- Load-in sound equipment, including control boards, mixers, amplifiers, effects boards, speakers, computer sound files, a variety of types of microphones, an internal communication (headset) system
- Troubleshoot the sound design once installation is complete
- Cue a show: learn to record basic sound cues for your production (as directed by the sound designer, director, and production stage manager)
- Operate a mixing board
- Operate an effects board
- Equalize an amplifier for the performance space
- Operate and troubleshoot a variety of microphones (body mikes, handheld wireless, wired handheld, booms, shotgun) as appropriate for the production needs
- Rehearse the sound cues during the technical and dress rehearsals
- Run sound cues during the performances
- Run a complete sound check
- Complete a full sound strike

- Organize permanent storage and create an inventory list for all sound equipment, cable, replacement parts and batteries, sound supplies, and accessory items owned by the school or theater program

The following are common positions for sound crew members:

Sound Board Operators

The board operator mixes the show during the technical rehearsal, dress rehearsals, and performances. For a play, one person is usually more than enough for this job. For a musical, I highly recommend having two students share this position: one whose primary responsibility is to operate the body mikes and one whose primary responsibility is to operate area mikes. If the show also requires the use of special effects and/or alternative sound sources, a separate person should be assigned to that role. During the run of the show, the board operator may take his cues directly from the production stage manager or from an assistant stage manager. (See chapter 3 for more specific options.)

Body Mike Manager

One member of the sound crew should be assigned a permanent position backstage for any show using body mikes. This crew member should be responsible for:

- Daily distribution and collection of body mikes
- Battery replacement (use new batteries at the start of the first act and again at intermission for each dress rehearsal and performance of a musical)
- Daily removal of the batteries before overnight storage of the body mikes
- Daily inspection of body mike receivers
- Troubleshooting minor body mike problems

Troubleshooter

The troubleshooter should be one of your sound crew chiefs, the most experienced and responsible member of the sound crew. If you are using two chiefs, each might be assigned the position of troubleshooter for one act of a musical and might be assigned to oversee the board operators for the other act. The troubleshooter needs to have a good memory of how each sound cue in the production is used. He should be knowledgeable about the intricacies of the sound design, the functions of each piece of equipment, and accomplished in using the sound board for the production.

During the run of the show, the troubleshooter simply listens to the performance. At all times, he should have his notepad ready to record small problems that occur throughout the production, such as a microphone that has moved position, a windscreen that is missing, or a cable that has come loose from the set piece it is attached to. These are normal occurrences during the run of a show and are part of basic sound maintenance.

If the troubleshooter possesses a good sound memory of the cues and a good visual memory of how the sound equipment appears on the stage, often he will be aware of a problem as it is occurs during a performance. Like the lighting troubleshooter, the sound troubleshooter is an indispensable person.

Properties Crew

All members of the properties crew work closely with and receive instruction from the director and the properties coordinator of the play. Although the props crew works backstage during the performances, this crew should be thought of as an extension of the cast and should be completely involved in the rehearsal process from day one.

RESPONSIBILITIES OF THE PROPS CREW CHIEFS

Choose two crew chiefs: The first props crew chief is responsible for all props and perishable items coming from stage right; the second props chief is responsible for all props and perishable items coming from stage left.

The props crew chiefs will work closely with the properties coordinator, the director, and an assistant stage manager. It is helpful if your crew chiefs are experienced in some area of production, but this is a great training-ground position for eager and interested younger members of your program. During the rehearsal process, the props crew chiefs will work primarily with the properties coordinator, an assistant stage manager, and the members of the cast. Once the production moves to the technical and dress rehearsals and the performances, the props crew chiefs will coordinate with the set designer and run crew chiefs. The responsibilities of the props crew chiefs include:

- Working closely with the director, the properties coordinator, and the assistant stage manager during the rehearsal process
- Working closely with all cast members during all rehearsals and performances
- Working closely with the set designer and run crew chiefs during the technical and dress rehearsals and the performances
- Being a role model to the props crew membership in meeting behavior expectations and production responsibilities (page 62).
- Notifying the crew members of work assignments and responsibilities
- Keeping all properties paperwork organized and up-to-date (this is discussed later under checklist on page 90)
- Researching the appropriate style of props for the production (correct period, authentic colors, proper use of items)
- Contacting members of the cast, members of other crews, parents, community members and local businesses to borrow specific prop items
- Creating props from scratch as needed
- Organizing the day-to-day storage of props during the rehearsal process
- Facilitating the use of props during each rehearsal, the technical and dress rehearsals, and performances
- Performing the role of troubleshooter during all final dress rehearsals and performances

To do his job correctly, each properties crew chief needs the following supplies, in addition to those listed on page 75:

A notepad for taking notes during the technical and dress rehearsals and performances. During each technical rehearsal and dress rehearsal, the director, the properties coordinator, the assistant stage manager, and props crew chiefs are certain to notice props that need attention. Each crew chief should keep a current work list for items that his crew members can repair, replace, or adjust as needed.

Storage containers. Each crew chief will need several storage containers as the props collection for your production grows. Props should be stored by act and scene and by location (stage right, stage left). Any kind of storage that allows for safe keeping of small and fragile items will work: plastic tubs and containers, cardboard boxes, shelving. It might be necessary to have a place to lock valuable or prized prop items to keep them safe and out of reach.

A lit workspace backstage right and left. There should be two tables designated for prop items: one backstage right and one backstage left. The tables should be dimly lit so that props, the checklists, and the crew chief's show scripts can be easily seen. If you have extra orchestra lights, they work well for the purpose of lighting small backstage areas.

Checklists and Task Assignments

In addition to coordinating the props crew members during the production, the crew chiefs also coordinate the crew's responsibilities in the daily care and management of all prop supplies and equipment. The director should consult with the props crew chiefs to be sure all expectations are itemized and carefully addressed. Once the crew chiefs are aware of their responsibilities, it becomes their job to create the following checklists and assign personnel to specific tasks on those lists.

General Checklists
- Location of props storage area and supplies
- How to store perishable items (food, beverages, flowers, or plants)

Daily List for Preshow Tasks (before all rehearsals and performances)
- Preset list for stage right, organized by act
- Preset list for stage left, organized by act
- Food or beverages: getting the food or beverage items needed, preparing food or beverages correctly according to directions

Daily List for Intermission Tasks
- Preset Act II props stage right
- Preset Act II props stage left
- Strike and store valuable or fragile items from Act I

Daily List for Postshow Tasks (after all rehearsals and performances)
- Clean all plates, cups, glasses

- Store all food and beverage items safely according to food directions
- Check inventory of perishable items. Make a shopping list to replace supplies as needed.
- Collect all props from the set or backstage areas and store safely
- Check props for breaks or stains that need immediate attention

THE PROPS CREW MEMBERS

Students who are members of the props crew will make a time commitment equal to that of a leading cast member. Members of the props crew should be expected to attend every cast rehearsal, first to observe and take notes on how the blocking is executed and which props are required, then to procure the necessary props and integrate them into the rehearsal process.

The first meeting of the props crew should be combined with the first meeting of the cast. The director conducts this meeting, giving both the cast members and props crew a list of all their production responsibilities and describes the behavior expectations of the props crew members at work sessions (see page 62). This is a good time to distribute all necessary paperwork for the production. The director then presents a brief synopsis of the plot of the play, including descriptions of the various settings as the story develops and specialty props that will be needed. The director concludes by addressing any special needs or concerns about the project

Through participation in the properties crew, all student crew members should learn the skills necessary for providing props, both permanent and perishable, for a theatrical production. They will learn how to do the following:

- Work with a director and properties coordinator
- Interpret the use and importance of props when reading a script
- Mark a script for props application
- Shop for prop supplies and accessories
- Create specialty props as needed for the production
- Create a scene-by-scene prop breakdown
- Create an inventory and checklist for production props
- Organize an entire prop collection for a production
- Keep an accurate record of rented or borrowed prop items
- Keep an accurate record of personal props supplied by the cast members
- Keep props clean, organized, and properly stored during rehearsals and performances
- Troubleshoot problems involving props during dress rehearsals and performances

MARKING THE PROPS CREW CHIEF'S SCRIPT

The props crew chief's script is marked in a similar manner to the stage manager's and run crew chief's script, that is, on the blank left pages of the script book are written a complete list of all props for the scene, which character needs the prop, and how it is used during the scene. Diagrams of the stage settings or backstage storage plans are also drawn when necessary. In the text of the script, the props crew chief highlights all stage directions and references to the presence and use of props.

Costume/Makeup Crew

All members of the costume/makeup crew work closely with and receive instruction from a professional costume designer.

RESPONSIBILITIES OF THE STUDENT CREW CHIEFS

Assign two students as crew chiefs: One whose primary responsibility is costumes and costume accessories and another whose primary responsibility is makeup, hairstyling, and hair accessories. The costume/makeup crew chiefs work closely with the costume designer and members of the designer's staff. The responsibilities of the costume/makeup crew chiefs should include:

- Working closely with the costume designer on all elements of the production
- Being a role model to the costume/makeup crew membership in meeting behavior expectations and production responsibilities (page 62)
- Working with the designer to create the costume/makeup crew work schedule
- Assigning costume/makeup crew members to the work schedule
- Assisting the designer with assigning costume/makeup crew members as dressers for specific cast members
- Notifying the crew members of work assignments and responsibilities
- Keeping all costume paperwork organized and up-to-date (this is discussed later under supplies)
- Assisting the designer with shopping for costume pieces, accessory items, and makeup supplies
- Assisting the designer whenever possible in sewing, fabric painting, and other creative tasks
- Working closely with all cast members
- Working closely with the sound designer and sound crew chief
- Performing the role of troubleshooter during all final dress rehearsals and performances

To do her job correctly, each costume/makeup crew chief needs the following supplies, in addition to those listed on page 75:

A notepad for taking notes during fittings, dress rehearsals, and performances. During each costume work session and dress rehearsal, the director, costume designer, and costume/makeup crew chiefs are certain to notice elements of wardrobe, hair, and makeup that need attention. Each crew chief should keep a current work list of items that the members of his crew can repair or adjust as needed.

Wardrobe, hair and makeup forms, and research materials. The wardrobe, hair and makeup forms include: women's measurement forms, men's measurement forms, complete character wardrobe assessment, and scene-by-scene costume breakdown by actor. Although the costume designer should keep the master copies of all these records, each crew chief should have a copy of each form in her show binder. When completed, each costume/makeup crew chief's show binder should include the script, all wardrobe paperwork, all measurement forms, all hair and makeup design notes and sketches, and any research materials related to the production or the time period of the show. The completed binder should be as professional and organized as possible. When finished, each binder serves as a complete record of the use of wardrobe, hair and makeup in this production. (See the sample wardrobe forms beginning on page 96.)

Complete body mike chart. The complete body mike chart should be provided to the costume designer and the costume crew chiefs by the sound designer. Since body mikes are traditionally incorporated into a character's costume or hair design and often complicate costume changes during the show, this information should be made available as soon as possible in the production schedule.

Ironing boards and irons. These items are necessary for daily care and maintenance of the costumes.

Complete sewing kit. These items are necessary for daily care and maintenance of the costumes.

Checklists and Task Assignments

In addition to coordinating the members of the costume/makeup crew during the production, the crew chiefs also coordinate the crew's responsibilities in the daily care and management of all wardrobe, hair and makeup supplies, and equipment. The director and costume designer should consult with the costume/makeup crew chiefs to be sure all expectations are itemized and carefully addressed. Once the crew chiefs are aware of their responsibilities, it becomes their job to create the following checklists and assign personnel to specific tasks on those lists.

General Checklists
- Location of ironing boards, irons and necessary extension cords
- Location of sewing kit
- Location of first-aid kit

Daily List for Preshow Tasks
- Iron costumes as needed
- Check preset for all costume pieces and accessories stored in dressing room
- Check preset for all costume pieces and accessories needed on the set or backstage for Act I
- Plug in all hair items to preheat, such as curling irons, electric rollers
- Prep all makeup and hair supplies

Daily List for Intermission Tasks
- Costume changes as needed for production
- Retouch hair and makeup for all cast
- Check preset for all costume pieces and accessories needed on the set or backstage for Act II

Daily List for Postshow Tasks (after all dress rehearsals and performances)
- Hang or fold all costume pieces and accessories
- Clean and store all hair and makeup supplies (empty water containers, be sure all lids and covers are in tact)
- Check hair and makeup supply inventory. Make a shopping list to replace supplies as needed.
- Collect all costume pieces and accessories from the set or backstage areas
- Unplug all electrical items, such as irons, curling irons, electric curlers
- Check costumes for tears or stains that need immediate attention
- Sweep floor of the dressing room

THE COSTUME/MAKEUP CREW MEMBERS

The first meeting of the costume/makeup crew should be scheduled during the beginning of the rehearsal process. This meeting should include the director/producer, the costume designer, adult members (or volunteers) of the designer's staff, and all student members of the costume/makeup crew. The director begins by giving the crew members a list of all their production responsibilities and distributes all necessary paperwork for the production. The director presents a brief synopsis of the plot of the play. When the director has concluded, the meeting is turned over to the costume designer. At this meeting, it is customary for the costume designer to:

- Describe the visual concept of the production: color palate, style, period
- Show and discuss specific costume needs, including description of shoes, hats, gloves, jewelry, other costume accessories
- Show and discuss specific requirements for hair and makeup design
- Describe the skills the students need to accomplish this project
- Announce the student crew chiefs and describe their roles
- Discuss how the crew work schedule will be constructed (number of days per week, number of hours per work session, specific kinds of tasks to be performed)
- Discuss how members of the crew will be assigned positions in the work schedule
- Announce the dates of the cast rehearsals that members of the costume crew are expected to attend as observers
- Describe the behavior expectations of the crew members at work sessions and the production responsibilities common to all students in the play (page 62)
- Address any special needs or concerns about the project

Members of the costume/makeup crew have an uneven work schedule during the rehearsal process. During the first week of rehearsals, crew members will be busy assisting the costume designer by taking measurements of each cast member, creating a needs assessment for each character in the show, and reviewing current inventory of your school's costume collection to see what materials you already have on hand. Once these tasks are completed, the designer works with the director to determine which costumes will be rented, which costumes will be custom built for your production, and which costumes, supplies, and accessories will be purchased. From that point, the designer will notify the costume crew chiefs when students are next needed.

Once your show is ready to begin final costume fittings and hair and makeup design sessions, it is time to organize your costume crew into dresser assignments. Each member of the costume crew should be assigned as a dresser to specific actors. Every crew member must learn the show from each individual actor's point of view: every costume change, details of hair style or makeup requirements, and microphone changes as needed. Careful consideration should be given to creating the dresser assignments, being certain to divide the actors with similar costume-changing patterns among several different dressers. If possible, each costume/makeup crew chief should be assigned only one or two characters as dressers to enables the chiefs to oversee the members of their crew and keep a sharp eye for disparity between style of dressers and consistency from performance to performance.

Through participation in the costume/makeup crew, all student crew members should learn the skills necessary for providing wardrobe and hair and makeup design for a theatrical production. They will learn how to do the following:

- Measure all cast members at the start of the rehearsal period
- Record each character's complete wardrobe assessment
- Create a scene-by-scene costume breakdown by actor
- Organize an entire costume collection for a production
- Keep an accurate record of rented costume items
- Keep an accurate record of personal costume items supplied by the cast members
- Create appropriate hair and makeup designs for a variety of characters
- Shop for costume supplies and accessories and hair and makeup supplies
- Organize the dressing room areas, providing appropriate space for each actor and all his costume needs
- Organize hair and makeup supplies for each dress rehearsal and performance
- Execute a variety of hair-styling techniques
- Execute a variety of theatrical makeup applications
- Iron costumes and properly care for different fabrics
- Make emergency repairs to costumes and to master basic sewing skills
- Check that each actor is dressed correctly and completely before going onstage for each dress rehearsal or performance
- Assist with quick costume changes during the production as needed
- Clean and organize dressing rooms following each dress rehearsal and performance
- Organize permanent storage and create an inventory list for costumes, costume supplies and accessories (including hats, bags, gloves, parasols, jewelry, period items), and hair and makeup supplies owned by your school or theater program

COSTUME MEASUREMENTS: WOMEN

Name of Actress:_____

Name(s) of Character(s):_____

_____   Height
_____   Weight
_____   Head (measure around head above ears)
_____   Bust (measure at fullest part)
_____   Shoulders (measure across back from shoulder joint to shoulder joint)
_____   Waist (measurement should be taken at the actual waist and should be comfortably
            tight)
_____   Hips (measure at fullest part)
_____   Back: neck-waist (measure from neck bone to waist)
_____   Sleeve: neck bone-wrist bone, over bent elbow (measure from neck bone to the wrist
            bone over the bent elbow)
_____   Waist-knee cap (measure from the waist to the top of the kneecap)
_____   Waist-ankle (measure from the side, over hip, from waist to ankle)

COSTUME MEASUREMENTS: MEN

Name of Actor: _____

Name(s) of Character(s): _____

_____   Height
_____   Weight
_____   Head (measure around head above ears)
_____   Neck (measure around base of neck)
_____   Chest (measure at fullest part, taking a deep breath)
_____   Shoulders (measure across back from shoulder joint to shoulder joint)
_____   Back: neck-waist (measure from neck bone to waist)
_____   Sleeve: neck bone-wrist bone, over bent elbow (measure from neck bone to the wrist
            bone over the bent elbow)
_____   Waist (measurement should be taken at the actual waist and should be comfortably
            tight)
_____   Inseam (measure from crotch to desired trouser length with shoes on)
_____   Outseam (measure from the side, taken from natural waistline to desired trouser length with shoes on)

COMPLETE CHARACTER WARDROBE ASSESSMENT (ORGANIZED BY ACTOR)

Name of Show: _____ Director: _____

Costume Designer: _____

Name of Actor	Name of Character	Description of Character (e.g., king, husband)	Act/Scene	Costume #	Costume Description	Rent	Buy	Build

The table below shows an overview of costumes both by actor and by scene. It is often helpful when organizing the costume needs of a musical or other large-scale production.

COMPLETE SHOW COSTUME PLOT (OVERVIEW BY CHARACTER)

Name of Show: _____ Director: _____

Costume Designer: _____

CHARACTER	ACT I						
	Scene 1	Scene 2	Scene 3	Scene 4	Scene 5	Scene 6	Scene 7

In the Character Costume Breakdown table, a complete and detailed description of each costume should appear the first time the costume is listed in the "Complete Costume Description" column. After that, only changes to the original description should be recorded. A complete costume description should include footwear, special undergarments, socks or stockings, each piece of clothing, headgear, jewelry, and hair ornamentation. All costume accessories (or costume pieces used as props) should also be listed. Under the "Notes" column, information regarding the care, use, storage, or preset of the costume (or any part of the costume) should be listed. Reminders and instructions about quick or difficult costume changes, including special assistance required, should also be documented here.

CHARACTER COSTUME BREAKDOWN (SCENE BY SCENE)

Name of Show: _____ Director: _____

Costume Designer: _____

Character(s): _____

Costume #	Act/Scene	Complete Costume Description	Notes

ORGANIZING THE MAKEUP TABLE

If you have one general makeup table with supplies for members of the cast to share, organizing the makeup in a convenient and understandable way is a challenge. You will need a large table (the type you might find in your cafeteria or library), a large roll of craft paper, masking tape, and a thick black magic marker. Position the table away from the wall so that it can be accessed on all four sides. Cover it completely with the craft paper. Use the masking tape to secure the paper to the underside of the table. Arrange your makeup on the table in categories that reflect the needs of your show and your cast: men's foundation, women's foundation, men's blush, women's blush, men's eye shadow, women's eye shadow, fight scene blood, beard supplies, clown greasepaint, and so on. After all your supplies are carefully laid out on the table, use the marker to outline and clearly label each separate area. When anyone needs a specific makeup supply, it will be easily accessible. All supplies should be returned to their proper places after use. This system also makes the process of taking a daily supply inventory after each dress rehearsal or show fast and simple.

The diagram below is an example of how to organize a makeup table. Modify this concept to fit your production.

MAKEUP TABLE OVERVIEW

Men's Foundations	Women's Foundations		Women's Eye Shadow
Men's Blush	Beard Supplies	Tissues, Paper Towels	Mascara and Eyeliner
Men's Eye Shadow	Men's Lipstick	Baby Wipes	Women's Lipstick
		Bobby Pins, Hair Clips	

House Staff

The members of the student crew who meet and greet the audience as they arrive for your show are called the house staff. The student members of the house staff are the first ambassadors of your theater program to greet the public. The house staff has a multitude of jobs: ushers, house managers, refreshment servers—in general, they act as hosts for all the paying customers. All members of the house staff work closely with and receive instruction from the director. Their conduct and demeanor should be well rehearsed and of the same high quality as the production they represent.

RESPONSIBILITIES OF THE STUDENT HOUSE MANAGERS

Choose two students to be house managers: one whose primary responsibility is the house right side of the theater and another whose primary responsibility is the house left side. The house managers work closely with director and the production stage manager and should be experienced members of your program. The responsibilities of the house managers include:

- Recruiting ushers as needed
- Coordinating with the adults responsible for ticket sales and refreshment sales
- Making the preshow and intermission house announcements

Checklists and Task Assignments

House managers are responsible for assigning members of the house staff specific jobs for pre- and postshow, during the show, and intermission. The following are the most common job assignments.

Preshow
- Set up ticket sales and refreshment sales tables
- Post signs and notices as needed
- Fold playbills if needed; insert addendum into playbills when necessary
- Set the call-board
- Seat the audience
- Monitor the ticket sales table for the first thirty minutes of the show for late-arriving patrons

During the Show
- Monitor the doors to the theater
- Before Act I, close the doors with house announcement
- Before intermission, open the doors when act curtain closes
- After intermission, close the doors with house announcement
- At end of Act I, open when the company bows
- Assist any late-arriving patrons

During Intermission
- Assist the parent volunteers with the refreshment sales
- Reseat audience members as they return to their seats

Postshow
- Strike ticket sales and refreshment sales tables; store refreshments safely between performances
- Strike the call-board

BEHAVIOR EXPECTATIONS AND PRODUCTION RESPONSIBILITIES

In addition to the guidelines listed on page 62, the staff house should do the following:

- Wear the official show T-shirt with black pants, socks, and shoes during performances
- Do not leave post to talk with friends
- Do not go backstage or in the dressing room before or during the dress rehearsals or performances
- Order a show T-shirt by the stated deadline
- Sell sponsor subscriptions or advertisements for the production
- Report for a call-board photo on the assigned day and time
- Create the call-board
- Assist the parent audience on parent photo night

Student Orchestra

All student members of the pit orchestra work closely with and receive instruction from the music director and/or conductor of the production. Through participation in the orchestra, student musicians should learn how music supports a story, defines each character, and adds to the artistic value of the play. Students should learn correct musical theater vocabulary, techniques for marking an orchestra book, and performance etiquette for a pit orchestra.

Through participation in the orchestra, all student musicians should learn the skills necessary for providing musical support and underscoring for a musical theatrical production. They will learn how to do the following:

- Work with a director, music director and conductor
- Interpret the use and importance of the music when reading a score

- Mark a score for cues, cuts and special production needs
- Create an inventory and checklist for necessary orchestral supplies
- Set up and organize an orchestra pit
- Keep an accurate record of rented music and borrowed equipment
- Keep the orchestra pit clean and properly organized during rehearsals and performances
- Troubleshoot problems involving music during dress rehearsals and performances

RESPONSIBILITIES OF THE STUDENT ORCHESTRA MANAGER

The student leader of the pit orchestra is called the orchestra manager. If your pit orchestra is large, you might want to have two or more students share this position.

The orchestra manager works closely with the music director/conductor and the lighting crew chief. He should be an experienced member of your student orchestra. The responsibilities of the orchestra manager include:

- Working closely with the musical director/conductor during the rehearsal process
- Being a role model to the orchestra membership in meeting behavior expectations and production responsibilities (page 62)
- Notifying the orchestra members of scheduled rehearsals
- Working with the music director/conductor to set up the pit for rehearsals and performances
- Working with the lighting crew chiefs to set up adequate orchestra lighting for the musicians in the pit for all dress rehearsals and performances
- Organizing the day-to-day storage of musical equipment during the dress rehearsals and performances

THE STUDENT MUSICIANS

The first meeting of the pit orchestra should be scheduled as soon as the rented orchestra parts arrive. This meeting should include the director/producer, the music director/conductor and all student members of the orchestra.

The director begins by giving the student musicians a list of all their production responsibilities and distributes all necessary paperwork and orchestra music for the production. The director then presents a brief synopsis of the plot of the play. When the director has concluded, the meeting is turned over to the music director/conductor. At this meeting, it is customary for the music director/conductor to:

- Announce the orchestra manager
- Discuss how the orchestra rehearsal schedule will be constructed (number of days per week, number of hours per session, specific rehearsal goals)

- Describe the behavior expectations of the student orchestra members at rehearsals and performances and the production responsibilities common to all students in the play (page 62 and below).
- Address any special needs or concerns about the project

The student orchestra member responsibilities include:

- Attendance at all scheduled orchestra rehearsals and performances
- Practicing their music at home
- Bringing their music and a pencil to all rehearsals
- Assist the orchestra manager with setting up the orchestra pit before dress rehearsals and performances
- Striking the orchestra pit immediately following the final performance of the show
- Erasing all marks in their orchestra book at the conclusion of the show

Behavior Expectations of the Student Musicians

In addition to the behavior guidelines listed on page 62, the student musicians should observe the following:

- Student musicians should not leave the pit orchestra to talk with friends. Friends are not permitted to visit during rehearsals. Friends are not permitted in the pit at any time.
- No eating or drinking during the orchestra rehearsals, dress rehearsals, or performances. No food or drinks should ever be permitted in the orchestra rehearsal room or orchestra pit. Just as in professional theater, the music director will call a break for everyone at an appropriate time.
- Orchestra members are not allowed backstage or in the dressing room before or during the dress rehearsals or performances.
- Student musicians should be willing to assist the music director/conductor whenever needed.

CHAPTER 5

THE AUDITION

From Preaudition to Casting

The audition process is a part of the educational experience of the student actor; it is a part of the educational responsibility of the director and creative staff. Through the audition, the director and staff teach audition skills, performance skills, and personal evaluation skills. The audition provides an opportunity for each student to experiment with new skills, challenge his natural abilities, and take performance risks. The audition requires the director to create an environment that is exciting, creative, and nonthreatening.

The audition process can be stressful for the student actors, the director, and the members of the creative staff. During the audition process, everyone feels the pressure of needing to be at his best: to give the best performance, to create the best impression, to provide the best audition opportunity. Since a successful audition is critical to all the parties involved, it is important to structure the process in a way that reduces stress and allows everyone's best to emerge.

A successful audition requires careful planning, clear and constant communication, and thoughtful evaluation. There are many ways to facilitate the structure of the audition process. The purpose of this chapter is to define each part of the audition structure and clarify the roles of the personnel involved in the audition process.

Philosophy and Standards

PHILOSOPHY

It is important to state clearly your philosophy for a student audition. If you have never given a lot of thought to your audition philosophy, here are a few questions to ponder.

1. Do you think of the audition as part of the educational structure of your theater program or something that happens before the play begins rehearsal?
2. Do you think of the audition process as exclusive or inclusive? Do you use it to weed out students with less natural ability or do you use it to include as many students as possible in the casting of your play or musical?
3. Do you think of the audition as a test that students can pass or fail?
4. Do you structure your audition differently for each play or musical, or is your audition always the same?

These are a few questions that every director should consider when discussing the value and purpose of a student audition. Here are my responses to these issues:

1. The audition should be a part of the educational structure of your theater program. Most often, the high school director is the first person to teach a young actor how to audition. This instruction is invaluable. It is important for the director to be clear, organized, unbiased, and professional when introducing and executing the audition process. It is imperative to have clear educational goals for all the students involved. Each student should be able to successfully complete the audition if the process is well defined and well structured.
2. The director should always think of the audition process as a tool to include as many students as possible in the casting of your production. This is easier to accomplish when the property is a musical where secondary and minor characters offer opportunities to cast developing talent and a chorus allows the inclusion of every student who successfully completes the audition process. When the property is a play, however, there is much less flexibility in casting roles, and it is often impossible to include all the students who perform a successful audition. The director can lessen the exclusionary parameters of a play with a few "creative casting" decisions. These are discussed in on page 120.
3. The audition is a test that every student can pass or fail. But the pass/fail should not be based on talent; it should be based on the ability of each student to follow the directions for the audition, complete all the assigned audition tasks, be prompt for audition appointments, and make the best use of her talent and experience when performing her audition material. The most experienced student and the newest member of your program both have an equal chance to pass or fail standards such as these.
4. The structure of your audition is very important. If you believe that your role as a high school director is to teach a student *how* to audition, then you will want your audition to be both familiar (having elements in common for every show) and challenging (introducing something new that has specific relevance to the play being produced). Think of the structure of a professional audition or a college audition. Almost every standard audition has the same requirements: two contrasting monologues under two minutes and/or two contrasting songs, sixteen measures each. Part of your school audition should be standard, so your students learn the objective routine of the audition process and can measure their own progress from audition to audition. In addition, introduce a new element for each show, either in the first audition or the callback audition, that requires the students to experiment and challenges

their comfort zone. This can include solo or group improvisation, pantomime, dance, creative movement, cold readings—anything that is included in the property you are producing.

Once you have developed a philosophy for the audition with a clear educational goal, then it is possible to detail the performance standards by which all student actors will be evaluated.

STANDARDS

Like all educational standards, the audition standards for every play or musical should be objective and measurable. The audition standards should apply equally to all students. They should be clearly stated in your audition meetings. The standards should include both minimum and maximum expectations.

- Each student must attend all required preaudition meetings and audition appointments.
- Each student must be prompt for all scheduled audition appointments.
- Each student must meet the minimum requirement of selected audition material. (Selecting audition material is discussed in detail on page 114.)
- Any student seeking a leading role must complete the maximum requirement of selected audition material.
- Each student must wear appropriate attire for the audition.

Although these standards seem obvious and simple, stating them as minimum expectations for all students will immediately raise the level of performance in your student actors. The newest member will feel empowered to meet these standards; the most experienced member will feel challenged to strive for excellence and not rely on past performance to secure his position in your cast. Students will know what you deem important and what you expect of them. The "mystery" of the audition will disappear. Students know the standards by which they are being evaluated, and every student has a greater chance to successfully complete the audition process.

Staffing the Audition

It is important to decide which members of your creative staff should participate in the audition process. It is even more important to define the role of each staff member who will be involved with the audition: what you expect of them, when and how they should interact with the student actors, and how to record their specific observations of each student performer.

Although many of your staff members might volunteer to help with the audition, it is not a place for casual observers. Since the audition is part of the educational process for the student actor, you need to keep the audition environment as professional as possible. The following criteria are important to consider when assembling your audition staff:

1. Only the most critical members of your creative staff should be part of your audition team. These staff members should include:

   • Director/producer
   • Adjunct staff: dialect coach, production specialists (mime, fencing, magic instructors)
   • Music staff: music director, conductor, vocal coach, pianist
   • Choreographer

   The staff members who will be working directly with the cast on a regular basis should be invited to participate in the audition process. The number of creative staff members will vary with each production. A contemporary play might have a smaller staff than a period piece. A big musical with many production numbers (*Hello, Dolly!* or *Barnum*) may have a larger staff than a more intimate piece (*You're a Good Man, Charlie Brown* or *Godspell*).

2. Each member of the audition team should be present for the audition of every student actor. If your audition staff is not consistent from day to day, your students may see the audition process as unfair or biased from the start. Since you want to promote equity for all students and want each student to feel that her audition has equal consideration with that of her peers, it is important to have the full audition team present for all parts of the audition process.

   Additionally, from a casting perspective, it is important for each staff member to see every part of the student audition. If your audition is structured by specialty area (Day 1: Acting, Day 2: Singing, Day 3: Choreography), each staff member should attend all audition sessions—not just the session dedicated to his specialty. A great dancer might be a weak actor. A great actor might not be able to carry a tune, or might have a nice voice but with a very limited range. In any case, most high school students are not triple threats, and casting is usually a matter of compromise. Each staff member needs to see the strengths and weaknesses each actor exhibits during every part of his audition.

3. Each member of the audition team should have a specific role during the audition process. It is very important to allow each member of your audition team to run a part of the student audition. In doing this, each staff member and each student has an opportunity to interact with one another. Students tend to relax during the audition when they have an opportunity to interact with the adult staff rather than just perform for them. If the staff is able to promote a comfortable interactive audition environment (similar to a normal rehearsal environment), the student actor will be able to give an audition performance that better reflects her natural talents, performance skill level, and degree of preparation. Each staff member will also see a more accurate and realistic picture of each student's attitudes, behavior patterns, and interpersonal skills.

4. Each member of the audition team should use a common standard to evaluate each student actor. I highly recommend creating a standard form for the audition staff to use for each student. This form should reflect every element of performance required of the student during the audition process. A common form that addresses specific performance standards will promote more professional and accurate discussion during your casting meetings.

Specific comments on the evaluation sheets and all discussion during the casting meetings should remain confidential between members of the audition team. However, the information garnered from the collective observations of the professional staff can be synthesized and those results shared privately through the director in the student postaudition conferences. These conferences are addressed on page 121.

SAMPLE AUDITION EVALUATION SHEETS

Name of Show:

Staff Member:

Actor's Name: Actor's Grade: Audition Date and Time:

	EVALUATION	COMMENTS

Singing	Musical Selection: _____
	   (High) 1 2 3 4 5 (Low)
	
	Musical Selection: _____
	   (High) 1 2 3 4 5 (Low)	

Acting	Monologue or Scene Selection: _____
	   (High) 1 2 3 4 5 (Low)
	
	Monologue or Scene Selection:_____
	   (High) 1 2 3 4 5 (Low)	

Dancing	Tap: (High) 1 2 3 4 5 (Low) Ballet: (High) 1 2 3 4 5 (Low) Jazz: (High) 1 2 3 4 5 (Low) Modern: (High) 1 2 3 4 5 (Low)	
Other Skills:		
General Observations:		

Preaudition Meetings

The director's preparation is the key ingredient to having a successful audition. The director provides the artistic vision for the production, the collaborative forum for the creative staff, the organization and materials for the audition process, and an equal and fair opportunity for all student actors to showcase their talents. All these elements should be addressed in preaudition meetings with each group participating in the audition process: the creative staff, the student stage managers, and the student actors.

MEETING WITH THE CREATIVE STAFF

The Director's Vision

Most casting requirements are detailed in the script of a play or musical, but there are often areas left open for interpretation. When a production calls for extras, such as townspeople or a chorus, the director must construct definitions for these groups. Can actors be double-cast to form the extra groups or chorus? Can actors playing minor roles appear in the chorus? How many scenes require extra actors? How many costumes will each extra or chorus member need and how will that affect the production budget? Only the director can answer these questions, and they should be addressed before meeting with the creative staff and starting the audition discussion.

When meeting with the creative staff, the director should provide the following information:

- Total size of the production: minimum and maximum casting goals
- Complete breakdown of cast requirements: principals, minor roles, chorus/extra
- Complete descriptions of the characters, their ages and relationships

Discussion of Audition Goals, Priorities, and Structure

When meeting with the creative staff, the director should create a collaborative environment allowing each staff member to clearly state his own views of the character requirements. This discussion should evolve into a description of the specific skills needed for this production by the student actors. Some of the most common skills or requirements needed are listed below.

Acting Requirements
- Are there a lot of monologues (*Amadeus, Our Town, I Never Sang for My Father*)?
- Do most scenes involve many characters?
- Does one character carry the show?
- Are actors onstage for uninterrupted long periods of time?
- Does the play feature heavy, dramatic roles?
- Does the play use physical comedy?
- Does the play require physical skills (such as running, fighting, falling down)?

Special Skills
- Does the play require improvisation?
- Does the play require pantomime (*Our Town*)?
- Does the play require speaking in a dialect or with an accent?
- Does the play require an actor to speak in a character voice?
- Does the play require actors who have special talents (juggling, painting, knitting)?

Music Requirements
- Does the play require actors to sing?
- Does the play require actors to play an instrument?
- What are the specific vocal ranges for each role in a musical?
- Which parts in a musical are most demanding in stamina?
- Which parts in a musical are most demanding in range?
- Are there voices that must blend together in a musical?
- Are character voices necessary when singing?
- Can you use a good actor with a terrible singing voice in a musical?

Movement or Dance Requirements
- Does the play require much physical movement from specific actors?
- Does the play require limited movement from a specific actor (*The Man Who Came to Dinner*)?
- What are the dance requirements of the leading parts in a musical?
- What are the dance requirements of the chorus in a musical?
- Can students with weak movement or dance skills be used in a specific musical?

Setting Audition Goals and Priorities

Once the creative staff has detailed the skills necessary for the production, it is possible to answer the following questions:

1. What do you want to see from a student auditioning for a major role?
2. What do you want to see from a student auditioning for a small part?
3. What do you want to see from a student auditioning for a chorus part?
4. Which parts do you expect to be most difficult to cast?
5. In a musical, can you define the type of performer needed for each specific role, such as a actor/singer/dancer or a singer/dancer/actor or a singer/actor/dancer?

Choosing an Audition Structure

The members of the audition team should determine the best structure for the audition. The structure you select should meet the goals and priorities established by the audition team for the specific show under consideration. In general, for all productions, select two to four official audition dates and publicly announce them. On the audition days, break up each hour into twenty- to thirty-minute segments and plan to see six to eight students during each block of time. It is further recommended to separate the student audition groups by age, with the more experienced upperclassmen auditioning first. This gives the younger, less-experienced students a little more preparation time. For some productions, particularly musicals, it might be helpful to see groups of all men and all women for the first round of auditions. During the audition, each group of six to eight students performs its prepared audition material for audition staff members.

Model 1: A Play. Plan to see six students during each twenty-minute segment on two or three audition days. For a play, the prepared audition usually includes a choice of character monologues and possibly a scene reading or improvisation exercise.

Model 2: A Musical with Movement (No Choreography). Allow more audition time for a musical: three to four days broken into twenty- to thirty-minute segments during which six to eight students audition. For a musical, the prepared audition usually includes a choice of character monologues and eight to sixteen measures of one or two songs. Usually one of the songs is performed by the entire company, and a choice of songs is performed by a leading character. Depending on the specific requirements of the musical, it might be possible to include a brief scene reading or improvisation exercise. If the musical requires any unified movement of the cast, that movement can be taught in either the small audition groups or by bringing all auditionees together on one of the scheduled audition days.

Model 3: A Musical with Choreography. Auditioning time should be the same as for a musical: six to eight students seen during each twenty- to thirty-minute segment over the course of three to four days. For a musical with choreography, the prepared audition usually includes a choice of character monologues and eight to sixteen measures of one or two songs, usually one of the songs performed by the entire company and a choice of songs performed by a leading character.

If there is a heavy dance requirement, one full day should be devoted to the choreographer. Students should wear appropriate clothing and shoes to the dance audition. During this audition, the choreographer will teach dance combinations to the whole group and then to a variety of subdivisions of that large group. If choreography is important to your show, this audition day is a must.

SAMPLE SCHEDULE FOR AUDITION MODELS		
Day 1 March 12 Monday	Group 1 3:00–3:20 P.M. *Senior Women*	1. 2. 3. 4. 5. 6.
	Group 2 3:20–3:40 P.M. *Senior Men*	1. 2. 3. 4. 5. 6.
	Group 3 3:40–4:00 P.M. *Junior Women*	1. 2. 3. 4. 5. 6.
	Group 4 4:00–4:20 P.M. *Junior Men*	1. 2. 3. 4. 5. 6.

Schedule Requirements and Physical Needs

The producer/director is responsible for coordinating the exact schedule and physical requirements of the audition. All members of the audition staff should be certain their needs are clearly stated to the director and that the time allotted for their specialty is adequate.

The audition team should agree on:

- Number of audition days
- Length of each audition day
- Content and structure of each audition day

- Physical and equipment needs for each audition day
  - A large open space for choreography, movement, or pantomime
  - Cassette or CD player for choreography or movement
  - A piano for musical accompaniment
  - Chairs for actors as needed in the acting audition
- Adequate lighting for the audition space
- Procedure for determining callback auditions
- Time and place of callback auditions
- Schedule for casting meetings
- Specific date to post the cast list

MEETING WITH STUDENT STAGE MANAGERS

The stage managers are necessary for a smooth, professional audition. They act as a liaison between the director and the student actors, handling scheduling, miscellaneous paperwork, and answering basic questions that can often monopolize a busy director's time. When having a preaudition meeting with the stage managers, it is important to clearly communicate the expectations you have of them. They usually fall into the following four categories: (1) preaudition responsibilities; (2) expectations for meeting with student actors; (3) expectations for audition days; and (4) expectations for callbacks.

For a complete description of the stage managers' responsibilities, see chapter 3, page 63, "The Role of the Stage Managers During Auditions."

MEETING WITH STUDENT ACTORS

The energy level of student actors attending a preaudition meeting is indescribable. This is the time when every student believes she has the ability to do whatever you, the director, need her to do to be cast in your production. It is, therefore, critical that you provide clear instructions, specific expectations, and ample written materials for each student. The written instructions and printed audition materials should be assembled in an audition packet.

The audition packet should include the following written information:

- The title and author/composer/lyricist of the play or musical
- All performances dates and times
- All technical and dress rehearsal dates and times
- Dates and times for daily rehearsals

- Dates and times for all auditions and callbacks
- Any audition dress requirements
- Required monologues or scenes to prepare
- Required songs to prepare
- Minimum performance standards

During the preaudition meeting with the student actors, the director should be prepared to present the following:

- The title of the play and a summary of the plot.
- A brief description of the characters, including their relationships to one another and any special acting requirements needed for a specific role.
- The audition process. Dates for the auditions; time structure for each day; how audition groups will be formed; which members of the creative staff will be present at the audition.
- Specific audition requirements. Acting (monologues or scenes to be prepared, improvisational exercises, cold readings); singing (How many songs to be performed? Will each student sing a whole song or just sixteen to thirty-two measures?); dancing (What are the styles of dance needed for the show?).
- Distribute and discuss the specific audition materials. This is discussed on the next page, "Choosing Audition Materials."
- Clearly state *minimum* performance standards. It is obvious to students that an actor with a leading role should be able to perform all the audition requirements well. But the minimum performance requirements should be clearly stated for an actor who is auditioning for his first play or is hoping to be just good enough to be included in the chorus.
- Appropriate dress. Be sure to address the subject of audition clothing. If you do not state any expectations, the students will not even give a thought to their physical appearance. What is important to you in this area? Do you want your students to present themselves casually? Do you want them to treat your audition as a "professional" audition and wear specific attire? Do you need the women to wear heels to see how they move? Or the men to wear dress shoes for the same reason? What should students wear for the dance audition? The audition dress is usually dictated by the choice of play. Sometimes it makes a big difference; other times dress is not a factor at auditions.
- Procedure for callback auditions. The dates and times of callback auditions; how a student will be notified if he/she is needed at the callback; what each student might be asked to do at the callback audition
- Procedure for posting the cast. When and where will the cast list be posted? If a student is not cast in the play, can she still be involved in the production in some way? If so, how does she express that interest to you?

Choosing Audition Materials

Students do not come to an audition with equal backgrounds. Some students take acting classes, while others take singing or dance lessons. Some students have experience participating in other productions, while others have none. Some are born with a greater level of natural ability than others. There are students whose parents help and support their love of theater, and others whose parents are barely aware of their interest in theater. Because of all these factors, it is important for the director to make the playing field as level as possible during the audition process.

The most common mistake school directors make is allowing their students to choose their own monologue and/or song for an audition. This is a wonderful opportunity for the student with a private singing teacher or acting coach, but for the inexperienced student, it is often the factor that makes him question his decision to audition and sometimes quit before he has even begun.

Instead, the director should provide *all* the audition materials for each student. This is a lot more work for the director, but the benefits are incredible:

- All students have equal access to the audition materials.
- All students have equal time to prepare the audition materials.
- The materials are of equal length and difficulty for all students.
- The materials reflect the skills most necessary for success in this production.

CHOOSING MONOLOGUES

Every student should be required to perform a monologue when auditioning for a play or musical. In a monologue performance, each student is completely in control of her own progress and success. She does not need to coordinate time or effort with another student. She has the opportunity to use as much preparation time as she needs, consult with any personal resources she requires, and demonstrate her true level of commitment and ability through her performance. Her success will be her own; any lack of success cannot be blamed on anyone else.

Whenever possible, try to select audition monologues from the play you are producing. If the play does not have suitable monologues, then select monologues from other sources that reflect the needs of the roles in the play under consideration.

The director should offer several monologue selections for women and several selections for men. The monologues can vary slightly in length and acting content; some may be labeled as difficult and others as easy. Students auditioning for principal parts should be required to learn a more difficult monologue; students who do not want to be considered for a leading role might be encouraged to learn a shorter and easier monologue.

All students should be required to memorize their audition monologue. First of all, if a student is unable (or unwilling) to memorize a short monologue in several days, it is unlikely he will meet your off-book deadlines during the rehearsal process. Second, unless the student has the monologue memorized, you will not get a sense of his interpretive skills: how he judges his volume and inflection, how he uses space on the stage, and how he interprets the words of the monologue.

CHOOSING SONGS

General Guidelines

Every student should be required to sing at a musical audition, even students auditioning for a non-singing role. It is also important to require all students to memorize their audition music for the same reasons stated for the monologues earlier.

When selecting the music to be performed at the music audition, it is best to think in professional audition terms and choose sixteen to thirty-two measures of each song you select. It is not necessary to hear each student sing a full song to determine her ability to learn music, assess her vocal timbre, and evaluate her ability to interpret musical material. Sixteen to thirty-two measures of a song is enough for a first audition. Students who return for callback auditions should be asked to demonstrate greater ability, and you can then have the opportunity to hear full songs.

When determining which sixteen to thirty-two measures of a song to use, choose the part of the song that is most difficult. The most difficult material rarely occurs in the opening measures; usually, the bridge or the ending of a number features the climax. Your goal is to find the material that will most challenge the ability of the student, either in range, tessitura, speed, or volume.

Students auditioning for a leading role should be able to sing the music for that character in the key it was originally written. *If a student cannot sing in the range required for a role, they should not be considered for that role.* Unless your music director is willing (and able) to transpose and rewrite the rehearsal piano score and all the orchestral parts for your show, it is important for the actor to meet the musical requirements specific for each character.

Keep in mind that the material written for a Broadway musical was not conceived with high school voices in mind. Broadway solos are written for professional, highly trained singers with a big vocal range and strong vocal technique. If a high school student struggles with the tessitura of a role, that is normal. If a student has the physical vocal ability and a strong work ethic, your music director should be able to help a talented student expand his range and grow into a role. If a student does not have the physical ability or musical foundation for a specific role, you will do a great disservice to him if you miscast her in a role unsuited for her talents. And finally, if you are unable to correctly cast the vocal requirements for a musical, *change course and choose another show!* It is better to change your mind and choose another property that is within the range of your students' talents than to pursue a show that might harm their voices, discourage them, and stifle the growth of your educational program.

Selecting Audition Songs for the Company

In most musicals, there is at least one big number for the full company. This song often appears at the end of the second act or at the curtain call. Every student auditioning should be required to sing the sixteen to thirty-two measures selected from this song as a mandatory part of his musical audition. This could be the *only* music required of students auditioning for the chorus.

Selecting Audition Songs for Leading Characters

Students auditioning for leading roles in a musical should have their audition selections memorized. Their audition goal should be to show their ability to interpret the music and sing "in character." This is possible when the sixteen to thirty-two measures of music selected by the director or music director is chosen wisely. In the structure of a musical, a song is usually placed where words no longer suffice to express the emotion of the moment. Most musical-comedy songs are filled with passionate feelings and require a high level of energy in performance. These musical moments are usually the most memorable parts of each character's role. Your students will enjoy performing these highlight moments for you during their audition.

The Audition and Callback

The audition process takes place over several days and should be conducted in as professional a manner as possible. The first audition and the dance audition involve the greatest number of student actors. These two auditions are traditionally the most difficult to manage and evaluate due to the large number of student participants. The large group audition usually involves a more select group of students with special talents and abilities. Finally, the callback audition is an invitation only event and has the smallest number of student participants. All parts of the audition process are necessary to fully evaluate student performance and successfully cast a show.

THE FIRST AUDITION

Signing In

When the student actors arrive for their audition appointments, they should report to the stage manager's table, sign-in, and receive the required paperwork. The stage manager will give each actor an audition profile form and a student contact information form to complete before his scheduled audition begins. Each actor should complete these forms, return the completed pages to the stage manager, and then warm up while waiting for his audition appointment (see page 119).

At the appointed time, the stage manager should escort the audition group (six to eight actors who will be auditioning in the same time block) into the audition space and give the completed audition profile forms for that group to the director. The stage manager then leaves the room before the audition begins and returns to his post to sign-in the next group of actors. All student contact information forms should be filed alphabetically and held by the stage manager.

Getting Started

Each audition group should begin with introductions. Do not assume that each student knows all the members of the creative team that are present at the audition or that the members of the creative staff know all the students. The director should begin by welcoming the student actors and introducing (or reintroducing) each staff member present by name and position.

Students are often so nervous when they walk into an audition that they are not breathing regularly or thinking clearly. It's helpful to combine the student introductions with a short icebreaker activity to refocus their energies. For example, after students introduce themselves, have them state their favorite actor or favorite book, food, movie, or TV show. This simple activity only takes a few moments, but it releases tension and can improve students' audition performances.

Monologues and Songs

Each member of the audition group should have several opportunities to perform.

Round One. have each student perform his prepared monologue.

Round two. students perform any required music.

Round three. students auditioning for leading roles perform additional songs or monologues as stated in the audition requirements.

At the conclusion of this process, students should be given an opportunity to reperform one element of the audition if they feel their original performance did not reflect their best ability.

After the audition, tell students how they will be notified for callback auditions. Then staff members should thank the students for attending the audition, and the stage manager brings in the next group.

LARGE GROUP AUDITIONS

Audition sessions for large groups of performers often address specific skills, like improvisation, pantomime, juggling, magic, gymnastics, or tumbling. A large group audition can be a required part of the audition process (all actors participate in an improv audition) or can be a select open call (any actor who can juggle, who has gymnastic skills). Dance auditions also often involve large groups. It is important to take accurate attendance as students arrive.

When the student actors arrive, they should report to the stage managers' table and sign-in. Then the performers should enter the audition space, change into appropriate dance clothing and footwear, and begin stretching.

Dance Audition

Although all members of the creative staff are present, the dance audition is conducted by the choreographer. If the dance audition is performed to recorded music, one of the stage managers should assist the choreographer with the music playback, running the cassette or CD as instructed. If the dance audition is performed to live music, the rehearsal pianist or music director should be present to play for the choreographer.

During a dance audition, the choreographer teaches several different dance combinations to the entire company, then divides the group into small ensembles, giving each small group several opportunities to perform each combination.

At the conclusion of the dance audition, the choreographer should meet with the other members of the creative staff to compare and discuss the students' audition performance.

Special Skills Audition

Although all members of the creative staff are present, this audition session should be conducted by the specialist in that area. During the audition, students should have the opportunity to perform in large groups, small groups, and individually. At the conclusion of the audition, the members of the creative staff should meet to compare and discuss the students' audition performance.

THE CALLBACK AUDITION

When all the audition groups have completed their first audition, the director and members of the creative staff meet to discuss the students' strengths and weaknesses. At this time, make a list of all possible candidates for each role in the production. If there are several equally strong candidates for one or more roles in the play, you will need a callback audition.

Notifying Students for Callbacks

The production stage manager should telephone each student invited to the callback audition. This call should be rehearsed with the director so it is businesslike and professional. The production stage manager should give the same information to each candidate:

- The time, day, and place of the callback audition
- A summary of what each candidate will be expected to do (such as cold readings, repeat prepared monologues, learn new monologues, sing a complete song, dance)
- Appropriate dress requirements (dance clothing, special footwear)

After students have been notified, the director should also post a complete list of students invited to the callback audition.

Audition Protocol

When the students arrive for their callback appointment, they should report to the audition space and sign-in with the production stage manager. Once all the actors are present, the production stage manager will escort the performers into the audition space. The director should welcome the student actors and reintroduce each staff member present by name and position. Then it is time to start!

The structure of the callback audition is usually more relaxed and flexible than that of a first audition. In a callback, there are fewer students to see and more time to devote to them. The callback audition should provide an opportunity for the director and members of the creative team to assess the talent ability and work style of each student. Every member of the audition group should have several opportunities to perform each element of the callback audition.

At the conclusion of this process, all students should feel they have had the opportunity to showcase their talents in an equal forum. The director and all members of the creative staff should feel that they have given equal opportunity to each student and have a better understanding of the strengths and abilities of each individual actor. The director and members of the creative staff should thank the students for attending the callback audition and clearly state the date when the cast list will be posted.

Now it's time to cast the show!

SAMPLE AUDITION PROFILE FORM
(To be completed by all students auditioning for the cast)

Title of Show

Audition Profile

Student Name: _____   Student Phone Number: _____

Grade: _____   Student E-mail: _____

Height:

Please list all after school activities, lessons, job and family commitments:

Specific Role(s) for which you are auditioning:

Will you accept a role in the chorus?

SAMPLE STUDENT CONTACT INFORMATION FORM
(To be completed by all members of the cast and crew)

Title of Show

Student Contact Information Form

Student Name: _____   Student Phone Number: _____

Grade: _____   Student E-mail: _____

Mailing Address: _____

_____

Parent Name(s): _____   Parent Phone Number: _____

Parent E-mail: _____   Parent Cell Phone: _____

Student Cast or Crew Position: _____

Casting and Postaudition Responsibilities

CASTING THE PRODUCTION

Every high school director I know hates the prospect of casting a show. Theoretically, it seems an easy thing to do following a well-run audition. But practically, when you are considering real students, it is the most difficult part of the entire process of producing a show.

Each member of your audition team will offer her insights and reactions to the performances of each actor who auditioned. Your job, as the director, is to weigh all the facts and assign the best actors possible to the roles available.

In a musical, casting is often easier because of the huge demands of principal roles: singing and acting and dancing. Many students excel in one or two of these disciplines, but few are equally skilled in all these areas. For this reason, casting principals, secondary, and minor roles in a musical is often self-evident. Additionally, a musical is usually a big production with enough roles to distribute to many talented students, offering both beginning opportunities to younger students and showcase roles to experienced performers. The chorus opens the door for all students who want an educational theater experience to have the opportunity to participate in a production.

In a play, casting is often more difficult. The structure of a play determines the number of characters needed. Some plays allow for flexible casting of "townspeople" or include minor roles that might have been double-cast when the play was originally produced. When working with a property such as this, it is best to determine both the minimum number of actors needed and the maximum number possible to use before casting the show. If you have enough qualified actors, cast the largest number of students the property can support. This gives many students the opportunity to participate in rehearsals and gain stage experience in front of an audience.

When considering ways to involve a larger number of student actors, the director might consider double-casting a role. Double-casting should only be used when student actors have performed equally well in the all parts of the audition and there is no discernable difference in their ability to perform the role. Double-casting does not work well for a principal role, but for a supporting character, it has merits. When double casting a role, the director determines which performance dates will be assigned to each actor. Both actors must be present at every rehearsal for their character.

I do not favor the tradition of understudies in educational theater. There is little motivation for a student actor to learn a role if he has no guaranteed chance of performing it. If you like the concept of understudies and allow them ample rehearsal time to prepare, you might consider assigning each understudy one of the performance dates.

Finally, the director should never view casting as a permanent decision. If a student actor gave a beautiful audition and won a leading role, but continually fails to deliver acceptable performances in rehearsal and regularly misses deadlines for off-book scenes, the director should recast that role in fairness to the rest of the cast.

POSTAUDITION MEETINGS WITH STUDENTS

As a theater educator, it is important to offer the opportunity for students to have a postaudition meeting with you. Many students will want your personal feedback on their audition performances. For students who plan to audition for future shows, they will want to know how to improve their performances. For students interested in auditioning for professional, college, or community productions, they will want to know about the specific strengths and weaknesses you see in their work. In all cases, your opinions will be valued and carefully considered.

When meeting privately with students following an audition, it is helpful to give specific reactions to their performance. You should never discuss the performance of another student nor should you feel any need to discuss your casting decisions. Restrict the discussion to the audition performance of that student *only*. Comments should include compliments on areas of the student performance that met the established standards and constructive criticisms for future audition situations.

The beneficial areas to discuss with each student are:

1. Did the student meet the basic audition standards? (attend all required meetings on time, wearing appropriate attire for the audition)
2. Did the student meet the minimum or maximum requirement of audition materials? (monologue or song well prepared, memorized, and executed without error)
3. How did the student use his or her voice performing the monologue? (volume, diction, pace)
4. How did the student use his or her voice performing the song? (volume, diction, vocal range, breathing)
5. Did the student's performance demonstrate an understanding of interpretive skills? (vocal quality, emotional structure, contrasting moments, use of facial expression, use of gesture, use of space [blocking], appropriate use of body posture)
6. Did the student demonstrate the ability to understand structured movement in a dance audition? (ability to follow basic choreography, awareness of the people around him or her, appropriate use of space)

When addressing areas such as these with an individual student, applaud the student's strengths and encourage the continued development of weak areas. This overall assessment should leave the student with a feeling of accomplishment and inspiration that promotes future growth and development.

CHAPTER 6

THE CAST

Rehearsal Expectations, Responsibilities, and Performance Goals

The cast spends most of its rehearsal time working with the director of the production. The director's daily example and careful instruction create the environment necessary for careful study of the play and the artistic growth of each member of the ensemble. Throughout the rehearsal process, the actors should learn about the craft and technique of the art of theater. The director should provide instruction in theatrical vocabulary and terminology, creating a character through vocal development and physical interpretation, and the parameters of working with a script.

During the rehearsal process, it is important to discover and rehearse a "good" performance from every actor, but that alone is not enough. Each actor should also gain an understanding of theater technology and profit from the rehearsal experiences of the technical and dress rehearsals. It is essential for young artists to recognize how each production department contributes to the success of the whole. This chapter defines specific rehearsal expectations, responsibilities, and performance goals for actors of every level in any production.

The Early Rehearsals

During the read-through and early rehearsals of a production, the actor experiences the process of learning a play. This process includes individual study and group rehearsal of the script. It requires each actor to be a responsible individual and a cooperative member of an ensemble.

It is during the early rehearsals of a play that the greatest student learning takes place. Each actor begins the rehearsal process studying an unfamiliar property with a newly formed group of people who possess different talents and abilities. Throughout the early rehearsals, the students move through the process of becoming a cast, growing as individual performers, and developing an artistic understanding of the play.

PREREHEARSAL RESPONSIBILITIES

It is the actor's job to meet all the requirements and responsibilities outlined by the director. The director should clearly state her expectations of the actors and provide each performer with all necessary printed material and instructions.

Once an actor receives his production packet, his first responsibility is to read all printed materials and instructions for the show. He should pay special attention to the rehearsal schedule, carefully marking all rehearsals on his personal calendar. The actor's rehearsal schedule should also be marked on his family's calendar to avoid scheduling medical or social appointments that conflict with a rehearsal. All paperwork included in the production packet should be completed neatly and returned promptly to the director. If the actor's production packet includes a rehearsal script, that script should be placed in a three-ring binder with dividers separating each scene.

The actor should read the script several times before the read-through or first rehearsal of a play. The actor's initial reading of a script should be relaxed and enjoyable. She should read for an understanding of plot, general character relationships, and overall structure of the play. During the second reading of the script, the actor should try to understand the play from her character's point of view. A third read-through should be for a technical understanding of the role—personal props and costumes needed, special physical demands of the part, and so on.

Once the actor has recorded the rehearsal schedule, completed all paperwork, and has a basic understanding of the script, he is ready to attend the read-through or first rehearsal with the cast and begin creating the play.

BASIC REHEARSAL ETIQUETTE

There are basic rules of rehearsal etiquette that apply to all actors in all productions.

Be Prompt. The actor should be on time for every rehearsal. Lateness shows disrespect to the director and other members of the cast.

Be Prepared. The actor should be prepared with all necessary materials for every rehearsal. An actor should bring his script and his music to every rehearsal, including off-book, technical, and dress rehearsals. He needs several sharpened pencils for taking notes. He often needs special shoes or other attire for choreography rehearsals and personal props for blocking rehearsals. If the director supplied the cast with a complete and detailed schedule of rehearsals, the actor should arrive at each rehearsal with his lines and music prepared for the day's work.

Be Respect and Cooperative. The actor should be attentive in rehearsal, carefully listening to the instructions of the director, music director, and choreographer. The actor should be respectful of the stage management team and cooperate with any requests or instructions given by a stage manager. Each actor should be respectful and courteous toward all other members of the cast, regardless of their position or the size of their role.

VOCABULARY

All members of the cast should learn and use correct theatrical vocabulary during every rehearsal and in all discussions about the production. The director should teach the correct terminology for movement, parts of the stage, theatrical equipment and supplies, soft goods, masking, parts of the set, and so on. Members of the cast should use this vocabulary throughout the rehearsal process.

PRINCIPLES OF INTERPRETATION

The actor has two tools to develop and use in the process of creating a character: her voice and her body. The director should give specific instruction in each of these areas and encourage the performer to develop her full artistic potential.

Creating a character results from the vocal and physical choices an actor makes during the rehearsal process. When vocal interpretation is combined with physical performance, a character emerges and an actor is born. The director should provide instruction and fundamental technique in the following areas of vocal interpretation:

Pronunciation. Are all the words of the script pronounced correctly? Does the actor have a speech problem that affects his pronunciation of specific vowels, consonants, or combinations of sound? Does the actor have an accent that affects his pronunciation of certain words or sounds?

Diction. Does the actor pronounce all the sounds of each word? Does her speech sound natural? Are all her words clear at all times? Does the actor speak words as written or does she change short phrases into colloquial contractions (substituting "it's" for "it is" or "wud'ya mean" for "what do you mean")?

Breathing. Does the actor use proper breathing technique? Does he breathe at appropriate places in the script? Is the actor able to perform long sentences? Is he able to use breath interpretively to show fright, sadness, frustration, excitement?

Projection. Can the actor be heard? Does her voice balance the other members of the ensemble?

Volume. Is the actor able to control the volume of his voice and vary it as needed? What is the actor's normal speech volume? What is his maximum volume? Minimum volume? Can he be heard in the theater when speaking softly? Can he perform a stage whisper?

Pitch. Is the actor able to control the pitch of her voice and vary it as needed? What is the actor's normal spoken pitch? How does that vary when expressing different emotions (fear, anger, or surprise)?

Pace. How quickly does the actor speak? Is the pace of his speech appropriate for the play or the character? Does his pace balance the other actors in the scene? Does the actor's pace affect his diction? His volume? His breathing?

Accent or Dialect. Does the character require an accent? Does the character speak in dialect? Does the character use words or phrases in a foreign language?

The director should provide instruction and fundamental technique in the following areas of physical interpretation:

Posture. Does the actor have good physical posture while standing, sitting or walking? Does her posture reflect the intention or qualities of the character (strength or weakness, boldness or shyness, good health or physical ailment)? Does the actor's interpretation of the character's posture balance the physical interpretations of the other actors in the scene?

Pace. Does the actor move at the correct pace for the character? Are his movements gentle and fluid or sharp and distinctive? Does the pace of the actor's movements balance those of the other actors in the scene?

Gesture. How does the actor use her arms and hands in daily conversation? How does she use her arms and hands while interpreting a character? Is the actor able to make small movements? Large movements? Are her gestures natural or contrived? Do they reinforce or distract from the intent of the script? Are there too many gestures? Too few? How does the actor's use of gestures balance with the other actors in the scene?

Facial Expression. How does the actor's face reflect expression in daily conversation? How flexible is his face? Is the actor able to control the parts of his face and vary them at will? How does the actor use his eyes? His eyebrows? Forehead? Mouth? Does the actor's face reflect any physical tensions? Does he demonstrate a performance understanding of basic emotions (happiness, contentment, anger, sadness, fear, excitement, and surprise)?

WORKING WITH A SCRIPT

Working with a script is often the most complicated and detailed task an actor faces during the early rehearsal process. During script rehearsals, the director is creating the play, or putting it on its feet. Directions for blocking and the use of props, and set and costume pieces are all communicated during rehearsals with the script. It is important for the actor to reap the greatest benefit possible during these rehearsal hours.

All actors should be expected to take accurate personal notes in their scripts during each rehearsal. The actor's notes should include personal blocking, personal use of the set, and personal use of props and costumes. All entrances and exits should be clearly indicated. Each actor's script should be a complete reflection of the play from his point of view. No actor, no matter how small his role, should be excused from this process.

The director should teach the members of the cast how to take blocking notes in their scripts and should periodically check scripts to be sure actors are taking notes correctly. When all the members of the cast take accurate rehearsal notes and practice their parts at home, the entire production is more focused and progresses to a higher level of artistic achievement. When members of the cast do not take accurate rehearsal notes, they are unable to rehearse effectively at home, and the entire rehearsal process becomes slow and rudimentary. In these instances, the play rarely achieves a high level of artistic realization.

The same principle of taking complete and accurate rehearsal notes is true for music rehearsals. When the music director assigns parts within an ensemble, divides harmonies between members of a company, or gives instruction in breathing, diction, and other musical matters, all members of the cast should be expected to make the appropriate notes in their scores.

Some novice actors find it difficult to be expressive while holding a script in rehearsal. It is important for the director to require actors to show vocal and physical interpretation while rehearsing with a script. Since most actors spend more time rehearsing with a script than without one, too much valuable rehearsal time is wasted if character interpretation is delayed. Actors need to move out of their comfort zones and become the character as early as possible in the rehearsal process.

Technical and Dress Rehearsals

Technical and dress rehearsals are exciting and stressful occasions for the cast of any show. These rehearsals provide clear evidence of the achievements of the ensemble and the areas where improvements must still be made. It is often hard for the cast to share the attention of their director during these critical, final rehearsals. It is a challenge for the director to oversee and coordinate the total efforts of all members of the production while keeping cast members focused on their goals and confident about their ability to achieve them.

Before the technical and dress rehearsals occur, the director must instruct the cast on appropriate etiquette. The director should clarify how the technical and dress rehearsals are structured, who has authority to give instruction in any area of the backstage theater spaces, how to follow instructions from those in authority, and the general expectations for each of the technical and dress rehearsals.

LIGHT WALKING

All members of the cast should participate in light walking during the cueing sessions for the show. During the light-walking sessions, cast members should become familiar with the general principals of lighting, sound, set, and space as they apply to the current production. This knowledge will help the technical rehearsal run more smoothly and quickly. When cast members can identify the technical elements of a production, understand how the technical elements affect the use of stage space, and recognize how the technical elements are integrated into the staging and design of the production, they become collaborators in the technical rehearsal. Each actor becomes a more intelligent performer possessing a greater awareness of the contribution and significance of each department of the production.

THE TECHNICAL REHEARSAL

The director should make the purpose of the tech rehearsal clear to the cast, which is to combine all the separate technical elements of the show into one fluid production. The director will *not* devote her attention to specific performances of individual members of the cast during this rehearsal. This does not mean, however, that cast members can perform less than their best. In fact, it is critical that the cast be as perfect as possible so the technical elements can be easily assimilated during the rehearsal. Since significant mistakes from any member of the cast can affect the progress of the tech rehearsal, an assistant stage manager should be assigned the job of watching for line and blocking errors. The goals of the cast should include correct blocking and choreography (especially all entrances and exits), accurate delivery of all lines, and focused and interpretive performances.

If a member of the cast has a question during the tech rehearsal, he should consult a stage manager for advice. If the stage manager is unable to answer his question, she will approach the appropriate staff member or director at a convenient time, and then return to the cast member with the response. Although there will be many stops and starts during the tech rehearsal, they should be the result of technical need rather than cast performance error.

During the technical rehearsal, an actor might receive instruction from the lighting, set, or sound designers. These instructions generally have to do with safety, correct use of technical equipment, or specific stage placement during a lighting cue or special effect. Actors should be respectful to all members of the design staff and cooperate fully with their directions and safety instructions.

THE DRESS REHEARSAL

The director should be clear that all members of the staff, cast, and crew understand the purpose of a dress rehearsal, which is to run the show without stopping. The dress rehearsal provides the opportunity to experience the show under performance conditions but without an audience. All technical cues, all costumes and props, all set changes should happen as called by the production stage manager. If it becomes necessary to stop the rehearsal, the director will make that call. There are only two reasons a dress rehearsal should be stopped: if something dangerous occurs and personal safety is jeopardized or if a mistake occurs that is so great the rehearsal cannot continue. The director will then stop the rehearsal, clear the stage until it is safe to continue, and identify the point to restart the show.

During the dress rehearsal, the goals of the cast should include correct blocking and choreography, accurate delivery of all lines, and interpretive performances. Each member of the cast should focus exclusively on giving his personal best performance. If a member of the cast has a question during the dress rehearsal, she should consult a stage manager for advice. If the stage manager is unable to answer her question, he will approach the director at a convenient time and then return to the cast member with the response.

During the dress rehearsals, each crew chief assumes complete responsibility for her domain: his crew, a specific stage area, and any personnel in that area. An actor might receive instruction from a crew chief during a dress rehearsal. These instructions generally have to do with safety, correct use of technical equipment, or specific stage placement during a lighting cue or special effect. Actors should be respectful to all crew chiefs and all members of their crews and cooperate fully with their directions and safety instructions. It is not appropriate for any member of the cast to offer suggestions or corrections to any crew chief or member of a crew. That is the exclusive right of the director or the production designers.

During the dress rehearsals, all costumes, costume accessories, and costume changes are finalized. All designs for makeup application and hairstyling will be viewed under the stage lights and modified as needed. All cast members should cooperate fully with the costume designer, costume crew chiefs and members during this process. Additionally, each actor will be assigned a dresser to assist him during the dress rehearsals and performances. It is important for every member of the cast to understand the role of the dresser. The dresser is not responsible to the actor; she is responsible to the costume designer. The dresser's job is to assist the actor *only if necessary*, to check the actor's costume, hair, and makeup before he leaves the dressing room, and to report any problems or needed repairs to the designer. It is not the dresser's responsibility to find the actor's costume, hang and store it properly, or pick up after the actor. Each performer is entirely responsible for his own costumes and accessories. The actor should treat his dresser and all members of the costume crew with respect and cooperation.

Performance Practice and Strike

The cast has spent weeks and weeks of rehearsal addressing details of blocking, nuances of gesture and movement, and specific characteristics of props and costumes. Once it is performance time, however, most young actors simply think of their product as "the show" and forget all the meticulous decisions that led to the final product.

It is, therefore, *critical* for the director to clearly state performance goals before every performance for both individual members of the cast and the ensemble as a whole. The director must furnish a list of general do's and don'ts, friendly performance reminders, and safety and technical warnings for all members of the cast and crew before each show.

THE PRESHOW COMPANY MEETING

The energy level for all students is very high on performance days. As the members of the cast and crew arrive at the theater at their specified call times and go about their assigned preshow preparations, the energy level continues to rise. After the technical crews have completed their preshow work lists, the actors have completed their costume, hair, and makeup, and the chorus has completed its vocal warm-up with the music director, excitement surpasses reason in the hearts and minds of all members of the company. It is at this point that the director must hold a company meeting before each production to focus all members of the company on the task at hand by providing them with concrete and specific reminders and warnings.

If the members of the cast are young and inexperienced, the biggest concern facing the director is the timing of the show. Too much untamed energy and excitement can destroy even the best performances. When inexperienced performers feel the rush of adrenaline, all sense of pacing, timing, and restraint disappear. After dismissing the crew from the general company meeting, the director should have cast members perform several warm-up activities before they are called to places. A few of the warm-up activities should be familiar to the cast. These warm-ups allow cast members to discover their normal volume, tempo, and intensity. If they are able to accomplish this task, it is a good sign that they will most likely find their familiar performance tempo for the play. The director should also have a few new warm-up exercises that require the cast to be alert, respond to directions, and execute a thoughtful response. These exercises should be structured toward the director's goals for the cast's performances. For example, if the director is concerned with maintaining volume, the warm-up exercises should address volume; if the director is concerned with maintaining a physical presence, the warm-up exercise should address that concern. When the director ends the preshow meeting and the cast is called to places, all actors should focus on giving their best possible performance.

SETTING PERFORMANCE GOALS

During the hours before each show, it is wise for the director to spend a few minutes with each leading player to discuss her goals for that evening's performance. If a principal player is asked "What are your specific goals for tonight's performance?," she typically has a thoughtful and detailed response. Remember, every actor wants to be good, wants to perform at her best, and wants to deserve the audience's applause. Once a performer shares her personal goals with the director, those goals are intensified for the performer. If an actor is unable to respond to the question of personal goals, the director should review the performer's most recent goals during a dress rehearsal. This is often enough to refocus the actor to the detail and nuance of her character. When a director makes the time to speak to all leading players and new performers about their goals, a more thoughtful, and often better, performance results. The increased attention of a few actors will positively affect the concentration of many.

When working with a large ensemble in a musical, it is wise for the director to give many reminders about personal backstage conduct, even though it might not be a problem for most members of the cast. It is better to give a reminder unnecessarily than regret the lost opportunity after a minor mishap occurs. The director's comments should serve as a reminder that the success of the show does not rely exclusively on the performance presented to the audience. Success is also reflected through the support and cooperation that each member of the cast and crew offers one another throughout the performance.

POINTS OF ETIQUETTE

Once your show opens to rave reviews, it is not uncommon for a member of the cast or crew to become a self-proclaimed expert, offering tips and advice on acting and job performance to other members of the company. This is never acceptable. A well-intentioned comment suggesting any alteration to a well-rehearsed line or event can begin a domino effect of small, unpredictable changes to the show. The result of many small, unrehearsed changes is a new and foreign performance that does not reflect the intention of the director and, sometimes, the playwright. No student should offer comments or suggestions to improve the show once the show has opened.

If anyone makes a mistake during a performance, the mistake should *never* be acknowledged and the person responsible *never* ridiculed. Part of the excitement of live theater is the human element. Every person involved in a production is doing his best job to get his part right. If every person is successful, you have a perfect show. But we all know that perfect shows rarely happen. Even in the world of professional theater, even at the Broadway level, perfect shows are rare. If each person is doing his best and offering 100 percent of his talent to the production, mistakes should be forgiven. There is another performance tomorrow. Try again.

Coach your performers to say thank you! It is impossible for any actor to say thank you enough times. Actors hear a resounding thank you in the applause from the audience following each performance. Every actor feels the exultation that accompanies the burst of applause. It is a unique feeling. Every actor should feel responsible to offer his own personal thanks to all members of the company who do not receive and bow to the audience's applause. A personal thank you should be offered to all crew chiefs, crew members, parent volunteers, and staff members.

THE STRIKE

Since actors rarely assist with the physical creation of a show, they sometimes (mistakenly) believe they are not responsible for the strike. Nothing could be further from the truth!

During the light-walking sessions and the technical rehearsal, all members of the cast should become familiar with the production elements that support their stage performances. Each cast member should develop an understanding of the complexity of the set and the equipment needed to execute the lighting and sound designs. In addition, every cast member has personal experience with the costume and prop departments. It should come as no surprise, then, that all members of the cast should be expected and required to assist in the strike. During the strike, the responsibilities of the cast include:

- Striking all personal props and costume pieces
- Assisting the costume designer and members of the costume crew with the strike of all show costumes
- Assisting the costume crew with cleaning and restoring all dressing room areas
- Assisting the lighting designer and members of the lighting crew as requested, with coiling cable, sorting gels, and counting and sorting rented equipment
- Assisting the set designer and construction crew as requested, with striking set pieces and cleaning the stage
- Assisting the director as requested with any general strike needs

CHAPTER 7

PRODUCTION HIGHLIGHTS

From Show Logo to Parent Photo Night

T his chapter identifies specific production elements that can help your show reach a higher level of professional achievement. The production highlights discussed in the following pages address strategies for increasing the art design elements of a production, implementing specific types of rehearsal schedules, developing better communication techniques, and establishing an attainable set of professional goals for student members of the cast and crew.

Show Logo and T-Shirt Design

CREATING A SHOW LOGO

It is fun to create a personal show logo. A logo gives your production a visual signature. It should appear on all your print materials from parent letters to rehearsal schedules to ticket order forms to the playbill. A logo unifies your banners, signs, advertisements, and promotional materials. It creates a strong and unique impression of your show. Don't use an original Broadway show logo without permission. Logos bear copyright protection and are the property of their creator.

If you have a student who is a graphic or computer artist, consider giving him an opportunity to design your logo. But you must give the student specific art direction. Here are some design parameters for your young artist.

- How many lines should the title be? If all the words must fit on one line, that will affect the size and style of font choice (for example, *Gypsy* versus *On a Clear Day You Can See Forever*).

- What mood or emotion do you want the font to evoke? The font chosen can suggest tradition, horror, carnival, fun, frenzied—the list is endless.

- What color do you have in mind for your logo? For the principal font? For the background? Color makes a strong impression on the viewer; the color of your logo should reflect the spirit and energy of your production.

- Does your logo include text only or do you want to include graphics?

- Do you want any text beyond the name of the show? You can include the name of the school or theatrical company, the dates of the production, or any other specific information that is important to your membership or community.

Once you've chosen a font and designed a logo, use it whenever possible: on clothing, formal letterhead, company announcements, rehearsal schedules, parent letters, promotional materials, publicity articles, banners and posters, and, of course, your playbill.

CREATING A PRODUCTION T-SHIRT

Another easy and fun way to both promote your show to the public and build a sense of community within is to create a production T-shirt or sweatshirt. Most Broadway shows and major feature films create shirts or jackets emblazoned with their logo. These shirts and jackets are worn by members of the cast and crew and are often sold retail.

It is easy to create a T-shirt for your show. First, complete your logo design. Second, choose a shirt color that will become your show color. The shirt color should compliment the logo design and reflect the mood or energy of your show. Do a little investigating when choosing the color to see if paper stock is available in the same or similar shade. If so, coordinate the playbill cover and poster stock to match the T-shirt color. This will give your whole production a more finished and professional appearance.

Once you've designed the T-shirt, take your completed artwork to your local T-shirt printer and print enough shirts for all members of your cast and crews. When a student wears the T-shirt, it identifies her as a member of the theater program and gives her a feeling of pride and ownership of the final product. And when the show is over, the shirts become personal momentoes. Creating production T-shirts is a good tradition to establish in your theater program.

The Playbill

The playbill serves multiple purposes for every production. It helps the audience follow the show, provides a complete record of the structure and personnel of the show, and recognizes the accomplishments of the students in the production. Finally, the playbill provides an opportunity to identify and tap additional sources of revenue in the form of community support through personal and business advertisements.

Creating a playbill is a big job. It requires assembling information from a wide variety of sources, hours of computer data entry, creative page layout design, scanning and manipulating advertising graphics, and endless hours of proofreading. Although this sounds daunting, it is well worth all the effort. The final playbill will be as complete and professional as all the other elements of your production.

Start creating your playbill early. You can begin creating the first pages of your publication before the rehearsals begin. As soon as you have chosen the show and confirmed the staff, you are ready to create the playbill cover, title page, staff list, breakdown of acts and scenes, and list of musical numbers. As soon as the student membership of the cast and crews are finalized, additional playbill pages can be designed: the cast of characters, the student staff list, and cast and crew bios. It is wise to begin the thank you page as early as possible and update it often. If you wait until the last minute to create a list of acknowledgments, you may forget someone special who made an early contribution to your production.

PRODUCING PLAYBILL PAGES

If you want to produce a professional-looking playbill on a budget, you will have to do all the page design work in-house and bring camera-ready pages or a disk to your printer.

Design the playbill to use standard $8^1/_2$-by-11-inch-size sheets, folded in half, so that each page measures $5^1/_2$ inches wide by $8^1/_2$ inches long. Since each $8^1/_2$-by-11-inch-size sheet will be printed back to back to make four pages, total page count for the playbill must be divisible by four (for example, sixteen, twenty, or twenty-four pages long).

When formatting the playbill in your computer, select landscape page orientation. A suggested margin width for for the top, bottom, and right and left sides of the page is $1/_2$ inch. A suggested page layout is a two-column design with a $1/_4$-inch space between the columns; two columns will enable you to put more text on each page.

ESSENTIAL PARTS OF THE PLAYBILL

The Cover
The playbill cover should include the name of your school or organization, the name of your theater group, the show logo, and the dates of the production.

- Name of school
- Name of theater group or club
- Name of show (use logo)
- List of performance dates

The Title Page
The title page *must* include the specific information required by your licensing agreement. It should also include information about your creative team. The following should appear on the title page:

- Name of school
- Name of theater group or club
- Name of show (use logo)
- Show creators: playwright, composer, lyricist
- Original production credits (as required by your licensing agreement)
- Your creative staff members:
  - Director
  - Producer
  - Production stage manager
  - Set designer
  - Costume designer
  - Lighting designer
  - Sound designer
  - Music director
  - Choreographer
- Dates of all performances
- "Produced by special arrangement with . . ." (as required by your licensing agreement)

Cast of Characters

The cast of characters is traditionally listed in order of appearance in the production.

Act/Scene Breakdown

This page identifies the structure of the play or musical for the audience. The act breakdown identifies location of each scene, the passage of time, and where the intermission occurs. In a play, the act/scene breakdown is usually quite short.

ACT I
Scene 1: The Dining Room, 6:00 P.M.
Scene 2: The Porch, two hours later

Intermission

ACT II
Scene 1: The Porch, the next day
Scene 2: The Kitchen, at noon
Scene 3: The Dining Room, 6:00 P.M.

In a musical, however, the listing of scenes in each act is usually quite long and detailed and often includes the list of musical numbers.

List of Musical Numbers

The list of musical numbers details all the music in the production. It includes the overture, entr'acte, each major song or dance number, and any reprises. Traditionally, the list states the music title in the left column and the character(s) performing that number on the right.

It is often easiest to include the list of musical numbers in the act/scene breakdown. Here is a brief example of how to combine these elements:

ACT I

Overture . . . . Orchestra

Scene 1: The Dining Room, 6:00 P.M.
Opening Song . . . . Company
Second Song . . . . Character Name

Scene 2: The Porch, two hours later
Third Song . . . . Character Name

Adult Staff List

This is a complete list of all the adult staff positions, both hired staff members and adult volunteers. The most common staff positions for a musical are listed here in playbill order:

- Producer
- Director
- Music director
- Choreographer
- Set designer
- Lighting designer
- Costume designer
- Sound designer
- Props coordinator
- Publicity coordinator
- Ticket manager
- Refreshment coordinator
- Parent volunteer coordinator

Student Staff List

This is a complete list of all the student staff positions including all crew chiefs and crew members. The most common student staff positions for a musical are listed here in playbill order:

- Production stage manager
- Assistant stage managers
- Set construction crew chiefs
- Set construction crew
- Lighting crew chief
- Lighting crew
- Costume/makeup crew chiefs
- Costume/makeup crew
- Sound crew chiefs
- Sound crew
- Props crew chiefs
- Props crew
- House managers
- House staff
- Special student credits (logo design, playbill design, photographer, orchestra manager)

Orchestra Membership List

This list includes the conductor and all members of the orchestra, both student and professional musicians. Traditionally, the musician's name appears in the left column and the instrument(s) played in the right column.

Cast, Crew, and Orchestra Bios

All students members of your production should have a bio printed in the playbill. The professional model for this is a Broadway playbill. In a Broadway playbill, each actor is recognized with a bio that lists his previous accomplishments. Members of the crew and orchestra should also have bios with the same format as the cast bios.

The bio begins with the student's name, often set in boldface capital letters, followed by his cast role, crew position, or instrument set in italics in parentheses. The bio lists the student's past productions in your school, including the role or position held in each. This list should start with the most recent show and go backward. If this show is the student's first, the bio should say "is making his debut in this production" or "joins the company for his first show." Other theatrical credits should follow school productions and can include community shows and summer camp or summer stock productions. Professional work (theater, modeling, TV, radio spots, film) should appear next. The bio should end with a list of the student's additional school activities (newspaper, yearbook, service organization, various clubs and athletic teams) and his grade in school (senior, junior, sophomore, freshman). A senior bio can include future college plans once the student has received his acceptance letter.

This sample can be modified to accommodate the needs of your show or limitations of your playbill space. The general principle, however, is to keep the overall form of each student bio the same. Experienced students will have a longer bio; inexperienced students a shorter bio. Creating all student bios on a computer allows easy updating from show to show. Be sure to make a back-up disk.

Thank You

The thank you list should include any individual, group, or business that provides support and assistance for your production. This list might include special members of your school staff and administration, the school custodial staff, other schools or theater groups who loaned set pieces, costumes or supplies to your production, and individuals who provided props, furniture, set dressings, or accessories for the show. This list should also include the names of individuals who donated their time to assist with the production in special ways: running errands, assisting the director, assisting a designer, or providing any other unique service.

Advertisements

Many theater groups use the playbill as a means of raising revenue by selling personal sponsorships or advertisements. This can be a lucrative practice. Although it is possible to raise additional funds by selling playbill space, it is first important to put aside enough money to pay the costs of publishing a nice playbill.

When selling personal sponsorships, it is customary for private sponsors to have their names listed as donors in the playbill. Keep a very accurate record of these donations as they come in. Be certain to spell every sponsor's name correctly. If someone makes an unexpectedly large donation, be sure to follow up with a personal handwritten thank you note.

When selling advertisements, be certain the name, address, and phone number of the company is accurate. If the company provides graphics or a logo, use the art they supply. Scan the graphics into your computer, adjust the size, and incorporate the art into the ad layout. Personal service of this quality often encourages local businesses and private advertisers to become repeat customers and continue to offer support for many years to come.

Addendum

The addendum is not a part of the printed playbill. It is a separate sheet of paper that is inserted into the playbill before each performance. The addendum includes any information that was unavailable by the playbill print deadline. The addendum is created by the producer or director and inserted into the playbill by the house staff before each performance. The addendum can include:

- Additional personal sponsors
- Additional advertisers
- Additional thank you's
- Cast or crew changes
- Bios of new cast and crew members

PUBLISHING THE PLAYBILL

Before bringing your playbill to the printer, proofread it many times over. You can *never* proof a playbill enough. Enlist the aid of your best English students. Once you are sure the playbill is perfect, it is time to take the pages to the printer.

At the printer, you will be asked to choose the paper stock for the cover and the interior pages and the ink color for the print. If possible, the color of the playbill cover should coordinate with the color of the show T-shirts. If using colored stock is cost prohibitive, experiment with using a colored background behind the logo only. This is often much more affordable.

If you've sold many sponsorships and advertisements, be sure to spend enough of that revenue having your playbill professionally printed. If you have not sold sponsorships and advertisements, you might choose to photocopy your playbill to save on the cost. If you need a large number of playbills, however, the difference between bulk photocopying and printing might not be great. Price both options before making a commitment.

The Call-board

The call-board is a display of photographs located in the lobby of the theater. The call-board traditionally features headshots of the actors in a production, but it can also include character photos of the actors in costume, actual rehearsal shots from a dress rehearsal, and photos of the orchestra members and backstage crews. The call-board is used by most college, community, summer stock, regional, and off-Broadway theater companies. As the audience enters the lobby, the call-board acts as an appetizer and immediately involves the audience in the spirit of the play.

In an educational setting, it is important that the call-board include all members of a production. Creating a beautiful and all-inclusive call-board takes planning and cooperation from the members of the production staff and the student members of the cast and crews. If you are preparing a large production (a big musical), the call-board can become expensive. Be sure the costs of film, developing, enlarging, mounting, and so on are reflected in your production budget.

TAKING HEADSHOTS OF ALL CAST AND CREW

I am a firm believer in taking a traditional headshot of all members of the cast and crew. A headshot is the industry standard in the theater profession. Every professional actor uses a headshot as her calling card. Every professional director and designer has a headshot available on request for promotion or publicity purposes. It is good to require all members of the cast and crew to sit for a headshot photo and to display that photo on the call-board. Here are a few recommendations about taking student headshots:

- Headshots should be taken during production week 6 (see chapter 8, "Completing Act I").

- Announce the date of the headshots well in advance so students are able to think about their clothing and hairstyle for the event.

- No hats. Each student should be required to take a professional headshot.

- Schedule the cast and crew photos on separate days.

- Use the same photographer, the same framing, the same location, the same lighting, and the same setting for all of the headshots in a production. I favor using a student photographer. Few student photographers get to take headshots. You can provide this wonderful opportunity for a student interested in professional photography.

- An assistant stage manager should assist the photographer during the photo call. The stage manager should have a master list of all cast and crew members. As each student takes his required photo, the stage manager should check that student's name off the master list, thus keeping an accurate record of each student's participation. The stage manager should also keep the pace of the photo shoot moving at a consistent speed, making sure that the photographer is never waiting for a subject and that all students behave cooperatively.

- Take two shots of each student.

- Take the photographs quickly. This should not be a long process.

- Either color or black-and-white photos will suffice. Black-and-white 8-by10-inch photos are the industry standard, but they are very costly to develop. Five-by-seven-inch shots are a good substitute. If you are on a limited budget or have limited call-board space available, standard four-by-six-inch developing will do. Whatever size you choose, all headshots should be the same size.

OTHER CALL-BOARD PHOTO IDEAS

If you have time to be creative and have a lot of space available, it is fun to display a wide variety of photos on your call-board. Here are some suggestions:

- Photos of each crew, such the sound, props, costume, run, lighting, and house staff

- Photos of cast members in character in groups (by show relationship, wearing hairstyles, and appropriate costumes and accessories)

- Photos of cast members in specific poses using show blocking (these photos should be taken on the set)

- Production photos of the set in appropriate lighting

- Photos of crew members at work (calling cues, rehearsing set changes, on ladders hanging lights, painting the set, styling hair, fitting costumes)

- Photos of varying sizes; enlarge some of the character shots and group photos. Most office supply chains provide color copying and enlarging services at a very reasonable cost.

ASSEMBLING THE CALL-BOARD

The call-board should be the responsibility of the house staff. During production weeks 5 and 4 (see chapter 8, Completing the Playbill), the house staff should begin designing the call-board.

The first step is taking inventory of all the headshots. Be certain all student members of the cast and crew have an attractive photo. If any student was absent during the original headshot photo shoot or has an unusable photo, retakes should be scheduled.

Every photo needs a caption. For the headshots, the caption should be two lines: the first line is the student's name, the second his role in the play. For character shots, the photo should be captioned with the character names of the actors pictured. Ensemble crew shots should be labeled with the crew name: lighting, sound, and so on. The captions should be in similar printing or calligraphy. Computer design can help give all your captions a uniformed, professional appearance.

Although the headshots can be mounted weeks before the performances, mounting and captioning the costumed shots and character photos will need to be done during the final days before the performance.

STRIKING THE CALL-BOARD

Save all your pictures and reuse them. If you keep portfolios for your theater students, their headshots should be included in their individual portfolios. Incorporate the group and production photos into a collage commemorating the play. Creating a collage is fun and establishes a permanent and public memento of a show. Along with the photos, include logo artwork, a ticket from the production, and the playbill cover. Mount the photos and other items on posterboard cut to fit a standard-size frame. The framed collage can then be displayed near the call-board in your lobby during future productions. It's a wonderful way to remind your audience and your students of past theatrical productions.

The Orchestra Rehearsal

The orchestra rehearsal is an important part of tech week for a musical. This rehearsal takes place during production week 2 (see chapter 8, "Week 2: Teching the Show").

Although this event is called the orchestra rehearsal, it is not a rehearsal for the orchestra alone! This is a special rehearsal conducted by the music director for the purpose of joining the full cast and the orchestra together focusing on creating a strong musical ensemble. This rehearsal focuses on the music *only*. It does not include any dialogue, acting, staging, choreography, movement, or sound amplification. The singular goal is to sing through the score in performance order focusing *exclusively* on the ensemble nature of the music.

The typical length of the orchestra rehearsal is two or three hours depending on the length and complexity of the show. It is a good idea to have extra adult supervision present throughout this rehearsal to ensure that the personal needs of the students are met (injury, illness) without distracting the music director and interrupting the flow of the rehearsal.

ORGANIZING THE REHEARSAL SPACE

- Use a rehearsal room, such as a regular band, choir, or multipurpose room for the orchestra rehearsal. It is much more effective to have all the personnel (cast and orchestra members) on one level floor than on the multiple levels of a stage and orchestra pit. It simplifies rehearsal movement (standing, sitting, and approaching the conductor) and allows for better eye contact between all parties.

- The orchestra should be set up in the front of the rehearsal room. The members of the orchestra should be facing the cast; the music director stands between the cast and orchestra (see diagram below).

- Every cast member should have a chair and an assigned seat. The leading players should be seated in the first row nearest the conductor and the orchestra; the second leads should be seated in the second row. Members of the chorus should be seated behind the leads and in order of singing part assignment: sopranos together, altos together, tenors together, and basses together.

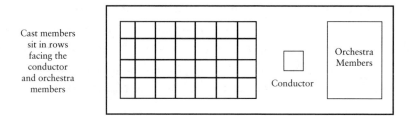

THE REHEARSAL PLAN

- Play and sing through the show in score order. This means that every member of the cast needs to be present for the entire rehearsal. This is very important for several reasons.
  - When playing through the score in order, the instrumentalists and music director have a better chance to see any inconsistencies that appear in the printed orchestra books. This could save valuable time in future dress rehearsals.
  - Singing through the score in order allows each singer to better assess his personal vocal strength and endurance ability. For leading players, this is a critical assessment point. For chorus members, it allows them to experience the pace of their musical numbers in the overall structure of the show.

- The orchestra rehearsal should start with the overture. Do not delete this from the rehearsal.

- During the rehearsal, when a principal player sings, she stands and moves to the front of the room near the conductor.

- During this rehearsal, when the chorus sings, each performer stands at his place and faces the conductor and the orchestra.

ADDITIONAL HINTS FOR A BETTER REHEARSAL

- All students should be required to bring bottled water to the rehearsal. This eliminates the distraction of students leaving the room for a quick drink.

- All students should be required to bring homework, or a book to this rehearsal. The orchestra rehearsal should be modeled on a professional rehearsal with high expectations for each student's personal behavior. There should be no talking or whispering. Everyone should have something to do to occupy their time when they are not singing.

- The stage managers should be present during this entire rehearsal. Their responsibilities include:
    - Taking attendance when cast arrives
    - Assisting the music director by keeping the cast on task
    - Assisting the director or volunteer parent chaperones as requested
    - Assisting the music director or orchestra members as requested
    - Taking notes about the music and conducting cues in their stage manager rehearsal scripts. These notes will be valuable during the lighting cue sessions

REHEARSAL ETIQUETTE

At the beginning of the rehearsal, it is appropriate for the music director or the director to introduce the cast and orchestra to one another. At this time, the music director should clearly state (or restate) the rehearsal process and goals to all present. It is customary to take an intermission break between acts of the rehearsal.

At the conclusion of the rehearsal, cast members should show their appreciation to the orchestra with applause. The stage managers and members of the cast (especially the leading players) should offer their assistance to the music director and members of the orchestra to restore the rehearsal room to its proper order. This usually includes moving instruments and chairs or packing equipment.

The Costume Parade

The costume parade is an exciting part of tech week. It takes place before the big technical rehearsal at the end of production week 2 (chapter 8, "Week 2: Teching the Show"). The costume parade is a pageant where each actor dresses in full costume and stands before the costume designer, director, and producer for critical assessment. The costume parade provides an opportunity for the costume designer to see every actor in full costume, hair, makeup, and accessories without the distractions that exist during a dress rehearsal. The costume designer is able to study the full effect created by each character and look for elements of balance and/or contrast between characters. Creating time for this studied, detailed look at each character often results in a final product that truly reflects the intent of both the costume designer and the director.

PREPARATIONS FOR A SUCCESSFUL COSTUME PARADE

Several things need to happen before the scheduled day of the costume parade.

- All rented costumes must arrive and be fitted to the actors.
- All other costumes (from the school costume collection or from the actor's personal clothing) must be clean, at the theater, and fitted.
- All costume accessories (gloves, scarves, hats) must be at the theater.
- All actors must have required footwear, leg wear, and undergarments.
- All actors should be coiffed in appropriate hairstyles.
- If wigs are needed, all wigs must be present and styled for the actor wearing the wig.
- All actors should be wearing makeup appropriate for their character.
- The costume crew should have finalized their dresser assignments.
- The dressing room areas should be clean and properly arranged with sufficient storage for all costumes and accessories, with enough mirrors for styling makeup and hair, and with appropriate areas for making costume changes.
- Sufficient copies of the scene-by-scene character costume breakdown (see page 98) should be made. Each dresser should complete the preliminary information on each actor's separate page. The remaining information will be completed during the costume parade.

THE COSTUME PARADE

If advance preparations have been successfully completed, the costume parade should last approximately two hours for a fully produced musical. There should be a large number of personnel present during the parade. These include:

- The director and producer
- The stage managers
- The entire cast
- The costume designer
- The costume/makeup crew chiefs and crew
- A parent volunteer who can assist by taking notes on missing items and then shop for them in a timely manner

The costume parade should follow the structure of the show. The dressers should assist their actors as they dress in their first costume, first hairstyle, and first makeup design. The actors should be called before the costume designer, director, and producer in scene order. Characters who are near one another onstage should stand near one another when they appear before the costume designer. Each dresser should be prepared with notebook and pen to take notes from the designer. The stage managers and costume/makeup chiefs should keep the costume parade moving at a pace that is comfortable for the costume designer.

At the conclusion of the costume parade, each actor should have a clear understanding of his costume, hair, and makeup for each scene of the show. Each dresser should have completed the scene-by-scene character costume breakdown and should have a complete set of additional notes about the actors for whom she is responsible. The costume designer and the director should have realized their vision for each character in the play.

Light Walking

The term *light walking* refers to the actor's role during the lighting cue sessions. Light walking is part of the process for creating the lighting cues for a production and should take place before the big technical rehearsal at the end of production week 2 (see chapter 8, "Week 2: Teching the Show"). In the process of light walking, the actors create a live tableau onstage. The actors assume their positions on the stage for each scene of a show beginning with act I, scene 1. The actors remain stationary in their positions while the lighting designer creates and records the lighting cue for that scene. When the designer completes one cue, the actors move to their next stage positions.

Light walking provides an opportunity for the lighting designer to create effective and appropriate stage lighting for the exact areas occupied by the actors. Light walking removes the rehearsal distractions of acting, sound, and movement and simplifies the picture for the designer. This process allows the designer to focus exclusively on space, dimension, and transition. The lighting cues will be more specific and accurate and will better support the staging created by the director.

Additionally, light walking serves as a tutorial about basic lighting equipment and general principals of stage lighting for members of the cast. There is no other time in the production schedule for actors to have this invaluable educational opportunity. Light walking allows the actors to experience a technical discipline as an artistic and creative force. For your most interested and talented students, understanding a new production dimension enhances their performances and enriches their understanding of the art of theater.

LIGHTING CUE PERSONNEL

The most effective lighting cue sessions require participation from many members of the staff, cast, and crew. Here is a brief description of the responsibilities of each department.

Lighting
The lighting designer, lighting crew chief, and full lighting crew should be present for every lighting cue session. Their job is to critically evaluate the lighting hang while creating cues. The designer and crew chief will take notes, create a work list, and make adjustments to the lighting plot while the cue sessions are in progress.

Director

The director should sit with the lighting designer during every lighting cue session. She should be prepared to offer the lighting designer summary ideas about each scene of the play. When the actors have assumed their tableau positions, the director should be able to clarify the mood or emotion of the scene, the time of day, and the dramatic focus of the moment. This information allows the designer to create specific lighting effects that support the dramatic action of the play.

Set

The set designer, run crew chiefs, and full run crew should be present for every lighting cue session. Their job is to move the sets into position for each scene. Once the set and lighting designers are satisfied with the set positions, the crew chiefs should spike the set pieces to exact stage positions. The set designer and run crew chiefs will take notes, create a work list, and make minor adjustments to the set while the cue sessions are in progress.

Cast

All members of the cast should participate as light walkers during the lighting cue sessions. The leading players should be required to attend all of the cue sessions. They should bring their rehearsal scripts with all blocking clearly marked. Each actor should refer to his script often throughout the cue session and add lighting notes that are specific to his stage movement. If the lighting design includes special effects, leading actors might receive specific stage placement for the key moment of a scene or song. The lighting crew chief will spike specific stage positions for actors as requested by the designer.

Members of the company of a musical should be assigned shifts during the lighting cue sessions. It is important for every actor to learn to light walk. During these sessions, actors become familiar with the function of light in a theatrical production. This knowledge can help them to be better performers. For the most effective light-walking session, actors should be required to wear clothing that is close to the color of their costume.

Stage Managers

The production stage manager should be with the director and lighting designer during every cue session. The production stage manager's job is to record each cue (and notes about the basic function of each cue) in his script. Once the show is cued, he acquires the job of calling the show. His book must be accurate.

The assistant stage managers should be on the stage with the actors. Each actor knows the show from her perspective, but each assistant stage manager should have the blocking of all actors in each scene in his script notes. During the light-walking sessions, the assistant stage managers should be certain that all the cast members are in the correct stage places for each scene. For full company scenes or major production numbers, the assistant stage managers should be certain that the members of the cast who are present spread out and reflect the total stage space required when all the actors in that scene are present. The assistant stage managers should keep accurate attendance records of cast members during light-walking sessions.

LIGHT-WALKING ETIQUETTE

- All principal cast members should be present for all light-walking sessions.
- All company members should be scheduled for light walking in equal shifts during the cue session.
- Cast members should wear comfortable rehearsal clothing in colors that approximate their costume colors.
- Cast members should bring their scripts to every light-walking session and should be prepared to take notes as needed.
- All members of the cast should bring water and snacks to light-walking sessions. This eliminates most of the personal interruptions.
- Lighting cue sessions are quiet. All members of the cast should bring homework or a book to each session to occupy their time while in tableau position onstage. Talking disrupts the process.

The process of light walking during lighting cue sessions allows the lighting designer, the director, the set designer, and the actor to collaborate on the final visual elements of a show. All parties are able to study the full effect created by each moment of the play and evaluate the effectiveness of those moments. Creating time for this studied, detailed look at a production usually results in a final product that unifies the intent of the director, the designers, and the actors.

The Technical Rehearsal

The technical rehearsal, or tech rehearsal, is a milestone in the production process. It is the first rehearsal where all the members of the production company are present and working together. This is the moment where each separate department contributes its completed part of the production. The job of the creative staff is to take all the separate production elements and combine them into a well-balanced, unified whole.

ELEMENTS OF THE TECH REHEARSAL

If a tech rehearsal is to be successful, each department must enter the rehearsal with its part of the project completed. Here is a departmental list of where your production should be on the morning of your tech rehearsal:

Set Construction and Run Crews
- All set pieces complete and stored backstage or onstage in proper positions for the start of the show.
- The backstage areas have been thoroughly cleaned. All unnecessary materials stored away.
- The stage has been swept and damp-mopped.

- All set spike marks on the stage are in good condition and easy to see.
- The run crew has been assigned to stage right or stage left positions.
- The set designer and run crew chiefs have assigned specific strike and set jobs to each member of the crew for every set change.
- The run crew chiefs have made poster-size signs of all strike/set job assignments, and these are clearly posed backstage right and left for all crew members to see.
- All soft and hard masking is in place.
- All backstage lighting (running lights) are in place and working.
- All extension cords, and sound and lighting cables are securely taped.
- Backstage sight lines are clearly marked.

Lighting Crew
- The lighting hang is complete. Run complete dimmer check to be sure all is in working order before the rehearsal begins.
- The backstage areas have been thoroughly cleaned and all unnecessary lighting materials are stored away.
- All lighting spike marks on the stage are in good condition and easy to see.
- The lighting crew members have been assigned to specific positions.
- All extension cords and lighting cables are securely taped.
- Assist with backstage running lights as needed.
- Assist with orchestra lighting as needed.

Sound Crew
- The sound load-in is complete. Run complete mike check to be sure all equipment is in working order before the rehearsal begins.
- All unused sound equipment is stored away.
- The sound crew members have been assigned to specific positions.
- The sound crew chiefs have made poster-size signs of all body mike assignments, and these are clearly posed backstage right and left for all cast and crew to see.
- Any extension cords and sound cables are securely taped.

Props Crew
- All props are present and stored backstage or onstage in proper positions for the start of the show.

Costume/Makeup Crew

- Dressing rooms are cleaned and organized.
- All dresser assignments are finalized.
- All hair and makeup designs are complete.
- All costumes are organized by actor, then show order.
- Any backstage costume changing areas are cleaned and well-lit.
- Any costume pieces needed on the set or backstage are preset.

Cast

- Hair and makeup styling is complete.
- All costumes are complete.
- Body mike assignments are complete.

Orchestra

- The orchestra pit is completely set with appropriate chairs and stands.
- All large instruments and amplifiers are preset in the orchestra pit.
- All orchestra lights are installed and in good working order.

COMMUNICATION HIERARCHY OF THE TECH REHEARSAL

There is a traditional professional communication order that is used for all technical and dress rehearsals. The purpose of this communication order is to direct all questions through the appropriate chain of command and provide as few interruptions as possible for the principal members of the creative team. This is the model for professional communication during these final rehearsal days.

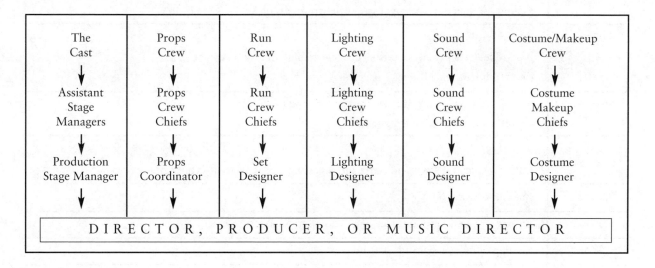

The Cast	Props Crew	Run Crew	Lighting Crew	Sound Crew	Costume/Makeup Crew
↓	↓	↓	↓	↓	↓
Assistant Stage Managers	Props Crew Chiefs	Run Crew Chiefs	Lighting Crew Chiefs	Sound Crew Chiefs	Costume Makeup Chiefs
↓	↓	↓	↓	↓	↓
Production Stage Manager	Props Coordinator	Set Designer	Lighting Designer	Sound Designer	Costume Designer
↓	↓	↓	↓	↓	↓

DIRECTOR, PRODUCER, OR MUSIC DIRECTOR

STRUCTURING A TECH REHEARSAL

Devote a generous amount of time to any tech rehearsals. Because so many different constituencies need to be addressed equally, a tech rehearsal is cumbersome and moves slowly. It is wise to build extra time into your planned rehearsal schedule.

For a fully produced musical, I recommend scheduling one long ten- to twelve-hour marathon rehearsal on a Saturday or Sunday. If this rehearsal is well planned and executed, 90 percent of all your problems will be solved on a single day. All the student members of the cast and crew will gain a global understanding of the various production elements from each department. All members of the production will have the appropriate time to collaborate effectively. Your future dress rehearsals will be smooth; you should be able to establish a true running time by your second dress rehearsal.

SAMPLE MARATHON TECH REHEARSAL SCHEDULE
10:00 A.M.–10:00 P.M.

10:00 A.M	• All members of the cast and crew arrive • Cast report for hair and makeup styling, then dress in costumes for final approval of costume designer • Members of each crew report to their designer and begin final preparations and preset
11:30 A.M	Cast to vocal warm-up
12:00 P.M.	General meeting in the theater for full company. At this meeting, each designer addresses the full company and shares safety warnings and final directions for the tech rehearsal. The director and music director address the full company. The rehearsal begins.
12:30 P.M.	Run Act I (Allow 3 hours for stops and starts and repeating scenes as needed for technical reasons)
3:30 P.M.	• End Act I • Cast change to rehearsal clothes • Each crew has short meeting with its designer • Short meeting of full company to review progress of Act I
4:00 P.M.	Dinner break for all. If possible, have parent volunteers provide a dinner for all on campus (see "Tech Rehearsal Dinner," page 54)
5:00 P.M.	• Cast to change into costumes, freshen hair and makeup • Each crew meets with its designer
5:30 P.M.	Run Act II (Allow 3 hours for stops and starts and repeating scenes as needed for technical reasons)
8:30 P.M.	Cue and rehearse bow
9:00 P.M.	All cast and crew clean up stage and dressing room areas
9:30 P.M.	Meeting of full company of cast and crew
10:00 P.M.	Rehearsal Ends

THE GOALS OF A TECH REHEARSAL

Of course, the obvious goal of the tech rehearsal is to combine all the elements of a production, but there are more specific goals for all the cast and crew that deserve attention during this important rehearsal. These include:

- Physical orientation of backstage areas (Where are the set pieces and props stored? Is there enough light to safely move backstage? How many people are entering or exiting from backstage right or left at any one time? Are set pieces interfering with the entrances or exits of the actors? Are actors interfering with the setting or striking of the set pieces? Are the props easy to access?)

- Physical orientation of onstage areas

- Adjustment to levels of lighting and sound

- Transitions between scenes (Are scene changes well choreographed? Is there enough personnel to facilitate rapid scene changes? Is there enough lighting on the stage during the scene changes to accurately see the spike marks? Is the scene change music long enough to cover the entire scene change? Is there enough space/light/time for fast costume changes between scenes?)

The tech rehearsal should not focus on the actors. It is not about missing lines or making small mistakes in blocking or about creating the finest moments in acting. The tech rehearsal should focus on the big picture. Does every department have an equal place in the production? Do all the members of the cast and crew work in a creative, collaborative, and professional manner with one another? If you are able to answer yes to these two questions at the end of your tech rehearsal, you and the members of your creative team have achieved a remarkable goal. You are on your way to a wonderful week of dress rehearsals and performances.

Dress Rehearsals

Dress rehearsals provide the opportunity to teach professional behavior and personal time management to all members of the cast and crew. The structure of each dress rehearsal should be modeled after the tech rehearsal. The communications model should continue through all the remaining rehearsals and performances. An exact timetable should be posted for each remaining rehearsal and for all performances so all members of the staff, cast, and crew can assess the company progress each step of the way.

I have always favored scheduling three dress rehearsals following the tech rehearsal. The greatest degree of progress is felt the night of the first dress rehearsal when the twelve-hour marathon rehearsal is reduced by half to six hours.

HELPFUL HINTS FOR A BETTER DRESS REHEARSAL

- Schedule all your dress rehearsals at night if your performances are at night. It is important for the students to adjust their internal clocks to a performer's evening schedule.

- Dress rehearsals should not be open to the public. Only members of the cast, crew, and parent volunteers should be permitted to attend. Additional viewers become a distraction for both the cast and crew who naturally fall into the performance mode of trying to please the audience. Unfortunately, this prematurely stops the rehearsal process.

- All students and staff should be reminded to eat dinner before reporting to the dress rehearsal. Too often, students skip meals. You must remind both the cast and crew to eat regularly and nutritiously during production week.

- Create a specific location for students to bring drinks and snacks to consume during the dress rehearsal hours. Both the cast and crew will be expending a lot of energy during the dress rehearsals and might need to refuel during these long rehearsal periods.

- Post specific call times for the cast and each separate crew.

- Post a complete timetable for each dress rehearsal and performance. This enables all members of the staff, cast, and crew to assess rehearsal progress.

- Schedule stage time to pre-rehearse rough spots before the dress rehearsal begins. The rough spots might include problematic set changes, intricate lighting cues or special effects, problem scenes, or fast costume changes. Rehearsing small problems with limited cast or crew before the full run begins can save an enormous amount of time during the dress rehearsal.

- Always require all members of the cast and crew to attend a full company meeting before beginning Act I of every dress rehearsal and performance.

- Always require all members of the cast and crew to attend a full company meeting following the final cleanup of every dress rehearsal and performance.

SAMPLE DRESS REHEARSAL SCHEDULE

5:00 P.M.	• Call for run crew; complete preset; sweep and clean stage • Call for lighting crew; complete dimmer check • Call for costume/makeup crew; assist principal cast • Call for principal actors; principals report for hair and makeup styling only; no costumes
5:30 P.M	• Call for all cast • Call for props crew; check preset • Call for sound crew; check equipment, replace batteries • Principal cast, run and light crews to stage for rehearsal of problem scenes
6:00 P.M	• Principal cast to wardrobe • Sound crew complete sound check • Run and lighting crews preset for start of show

6:30 P.M.	• Call for orchestra members • Cast to vocal warm-up • All crew members report for joint crew meeting
6:45 P.M.	• Full company meeting • Call to places for all crew members • Call to places for all cast
7:00 P.M.	Run Act I
9:00 P.M.	Run Act II
10:15 P.M.	• Complete clean-up • Full company meeting of all cast and crew
11:00 P.M.	Rehearsal Ends

Parent Photo Night and the Performances

Every parent wants pictures of his or her child in the school play; every director dreads the intrusion of the camera flash during a theatrical performance. These opposing views can be reconciled in a manner beneficial for all: The solution is establishing a parent photo night as a tradition in your school or community.

Parent photo night should coincide with your final dress rehearsal. The cast and crew will be well prepared and well rehearsed. The students will feel ready for a trial audience. Their parents will be pleased to be the invited audience and will be grateful for the opportunity to take photos of their children. The cast and crew should follow a normal dress rehearsal schedule on parent photo night. Parents should not be permitted backstage or in the dressing rooms for pictures, good luck wishes, or any other reason. Students should adhere to the posted schedule of the night.

At the full company meeting before Act I, give the cast and crew performance notes on how to react before an audience. These notes should include how to respond to mistakes from a member of the cast or crew, how to respond to laughter from the audience, and how to respond to applause, either unexpected or following a big musical production number.

When parents arrive for the dress rehearsal, the student house staff should be there to greet them, help them choose appropriate seats, and answer any questions the parents might have. Once the members of the cast and crew have been called to places, the director should address the parent audience, thank them for coming, introduce the members of the creative staff, and offer a reminder that this is still a dress rehearsal, not a finished performance, and that some minor changes and adjustments may occur before the opening night. Then, the final dress rehearsal should proceed on schedule.

Following the final bow of the night, the director should call all student members of the crew onstage to join with the entire cast for a company photo. Parents should be permitted to take many pictures at this time. After the photo session ends, thank all the parents for coming, then send the cast and crew to their normal evening routine of cleaning up the stage and dressing rooms and attending the full company meeting.

If you or any member of the creative staff feel the need to make any last minute changes to any part of the show, those changes should happen *now!* Once those changes are made, it is time to *freeze the show*. It is critical to define the moment when the director freezes the show. That single decision declares that the rehearsal work has been completed, every attainable goal has been reached, and the company has been successful in creating a show worthy of live performance.

After months of planning and rehearsal, the performance dates for your production finally arrive. This now becomes the time to teach a new mode of thinking to the students: re-creating a perfect show every night for each separate audience. This is the thought process of the working professional.

In the world of professional theater, re-creating a perfect show every night is a challenging goal. Imagine the effort, concentration, and discipline necessary from each actor who graces a Broadway stage eight times a week. And imagine that same goal existing in each professional crew member who runs the lighting, set, sound, and costume departments in each of those Broadway houses. This should be the goal the students strive for during the run of their performances—to give their best to each other and to the audience each time they hear the words "Places, please!"

CHAPTER 8

TIMELINE

Countdown to Opening Night

Many directors, producers, and designers consistently find themselves running out of rehearsal time show after show after show. They dread the final rehearsal days. Their most-repeated expression becomes "if only I had one more week!"

But that does not have to be the case. If you have a well-organized timeline that addresses all the requirements and special needs of each department of your production, you should rarely find yourself short of time. It takes a lot of careful planning, but it is possible to create and stay on a scheduled course when rehearsing and producing your show.

It is important to state that the *best* way to create and organize any rehearsal schedule is to work backwards. Begin with the performances, move through the dress rehearsals, and end at the beginning with the preproduction schedule. This chapter clarifies the production timeline. In the pages that follow, each element of the production is detailed for the creative and professional staff, the parent volunteers, the cast, and the members of the student crews. This timeline includes all the preparation and organizational work done by members of the professional staff, the audition period, a typical eight-to-nine week rehearsal period, and a strike plan.

Preparation: The Director's Creative Vision

The director's creative vision is not a mysterious inspiration. Instead, creative vision is the result of a series of carefully considered decisions that evolve in a logical and methodical manner. In total, these decisions provide a vision and shape for each production.

The director often works with the producer in determining priorities for a production. The collaboration between the director and the producer is the most important partnership of the creative staff. In many high school productions, the director and producer are the same person. When that is the case, it is important for this individual to examine every decision from both the director's and the producer's perspective.

GOALS

During the initial stages of preparation, your primary goal, as the director/producer, is to examine the chosen property through the eyes of each production department. Try to anticipate which challenges will be greatest, which expenses are unavoidable, and which production elements are most within your grasp. Each show has a unique blend of talent requirements, technical elements, and spatial needs. If you are able to visualize the show from the point of view of each production department (the set designer, lighting designer, choreographer, music director, sound designer, costume designer, cast member, stage manager, and so) and meet the needs of each of those separate interests, the show is probably the right choice for your group.

Your next major goal is assembling a good creative staff. Of course, you want designers that are talented individuals who enjoy working with young people. But more important, you want the members of your staff to share a similar work ethic and be strong and willing collaborators. The more your creative, professional staff is unified in thought and purpose, the better your production will be.

STEPS FOR PREPARING THE PRODUCTION

1. Choose a show.
2. Make a preliminary budget.
3. Outline show requirements:
   - List all required costumes
   - List all required sets
   - List all required props
   - List all required lighting effects
   - List all required special effects, sound effects or music needed
   - List all required sound amplification
4. Determine total personnel needed for this production: adult staff, student staff, minimum number of cast and crew needed, maximum number of cast and crew possible to include.
5. Hire production staff; write contracts as needed.
6. Coordinate chair positions for parent volunteers.
7. Create a complete schedule of the rehearsal period that includes deadlines and expectations for each department (when the set should be ready to use, when the costumes should be completed, when props should be available for use, etc.). Be sure it is possible to meet the needs of each department in the time you have available for your production.
8. Create and photocopy all standard production paperwork.

Week 13: Going Public

Now that all the early planning for the production is underway, it is time to announce the show and begin involving the students. It is important to promote the show well within your school community. Students should be encouraged to sign up for participation in the cast or crew during this week. Information about the upcoming auditions should be clearly posted.

GOALS

The critical goal for the you, as director/producer, during this week is to consult with the music director and choreographer about the upcoming auditions. Careful planning of the audition process and selecting appropriately difficult audition material will lay the groundwork for successful student auditions. Once the audition material is selected and the creative team agrees on an audition schedule, an audition packet should be made for each student actor. These packets will be distributed next week at the preaudition meeting and should include a complete audition schedule, an overview of rehearsal dates and times, all performance dates and times, an overview of the audition requirements, audition monologues and/or scenes to prepare, and audition music to prepare.

HIGHLIGHTS

- Announce the show.
- Post sign-up lists for all students interested in the cast or crew.
- Select the student audition materials.
- Prepare the student audition packets.

PROFESSIONAL STAFF	STUDENT STAFF

PRODUCER
- Announce show.
- Post sign-up sheets for all students interested in being a part of cast or crew.
- Meet with set designer, costume designer, and director to create initial design concept.
- Meet with music director; establish budget for orchestra.

DIRECTOR
- Post show information: brief act/scene description, song list, character list.
- Meet with music director to select audition music.
- Meet with choreographer to discuss and plan dance/movement audition.
- Prepare and photocopy audition packets for students.
- Meet with set designer and producer to create initial set concept.
- Meet with costume designer to create initial costume concept.

MUSIC DIRECTOR
- Meet with producer to discuss orchestra budget.
- Meet with director to choose materials for music auditions.

CHOREOGRAPHER
- Meet with director to plan dance/movement audition.

SET DESIGNER
- Meet with producer and director to create initial set concept.

COSTUME DESIGNER
- Meet with director and producer to create initial costume concept: choose color palette and style; identify priorities.

STAGE MANAGERS
Assist director with preparing student audition packets.

CAST
Interested students sign up on the posted audition list.

CREWS
Interested students sign up on the posted crew lists.

The Preaudition Meeting

The preaudition meeting for the student actors is a very important element of your production. At this meeting, expectations for both the quality of the audition and the overall quality of the production are established. You should use this opportunity to give a clear overview of the plot and characters of the show. Additionally, you should clearly state any special challenges this property presents to the performers.

GOALS

The goals of the preaudition meeting are very specific. All students should leave this meeting with a general understanding of the production and a specific understanding of the audition requirements and expectations. The rehearsal and production schedules should be outlined and attendance policies clearly defined. Students who have multiple conflicts with the schedule should not be permitted to audition for the show. At the preaudition meeting, the director and music director should present the audition materials, teach the audition music, and explain the standards by which all students will be measured. At the conclusion of this meeting, all students should be assigned a specific audition time.

HIGHLIGHTS

- Hold a general preaudition meeting with all student actors to introduce the show, distribute audition materials, and explain the audition process.
- Assign a specific audition time to all students.

PROFESSIONAL STAFF	STUDENT STAFF
PRODUCER • Assist director with the preaudition meeting. • Meet with set designer, costume designer, and director to finalize design concept. **DIRECTOR** Conduct a preaudition meeting with all students auditioning for the show. At this meeting: • Introduce the show giving a brief plot summary and general character descriptions. • Define all audition requirements for both leading players and chorus parts. • Create a schedule for the first auditions. • Assign students to a specific audition time. **MUSIC DIRECTOR** Attend preaudition meeting and teach any musical selections from show that will be used for first audition. **CHOREOGRAPHER** If there are specific dance requirements for dance audition, address students at preaudition meeting and state expectations of dress and movement abilities. **SET DESIGNER** • Meet with director and producer to finalize the set design. • Begin drafting blueprints and/or creating a model of set design. **COSTUME DESIGNER** Meet with director and producer to finalize the costume plot.	**STAGE MANAGERS** • Attend preaudition meeting. • Assist director in distributing audition packets and scheduling actors for first auditions • Type and post final audition schedule. **CAST** • Attend preaudition meeting for all student actors. • Prepare audition. **CREWS** Interested students continue to sign up on posted crew lists.

Week 11: Audition Week

This is the week of auditions! The producer, director, music director, choreographer, and other members of the creative staff should be present for all parts of the audition process. The stage managers will be instrumental in running a smooth and on-time audition schedule. All the student actors will present themselves at a first audition. Callback auditions should also take place this week. By the end of the week, the final cast list should be posted.

GOALS

Your biggest goal this week is to cast the show. If auditions go well and the student actors have the right talents for the play or musical you've selected, your goal will be easy to reach. You will be able to cast all the roles in your production from the leading players to the chorus parts. If, however, the student talent pool is less than you hoped for and you are unable to cast all the roles in your announced show, look more closely at the abilities of the student actors you have and choose a different property that better suits their abilities.

This is also the best week to gather student contact information for all members of the cast and crew (see page 119 for sample form). Student actors should complete this form before or after their scheduled first-audition appointment. All crew members should stop by the stage managers' table during the auditions to complete the form on any of the scheduled audition days.

HIGHLIGHTS

- Auditions and callbacks for the cast.
- Casting and posting the final cast of characters.
- Final student crew sign-ups.
- Gathering all cast and crew information for company contact list.

PROFESSIONAL STAFF	STUDENT STAFF
PRODUCER, DIRECTOR, MUSIC DIRECTOR, CHOREOGRAPHER • Conduct all scheduled first auditions. • Conduct the callback auditions. • Cast the show. • Post final cast list.	**STAGE MANAGERS** • Arrive early for each audition day: set up a stage managers' table near the stage door. • Have the audition schedule available to check-in the actors as they arrive. • Have extra copies of the required audition materials and extra pens and pencils. • Have the student audition profile forms ready for actors to complete before their auditions begins. • Have each actor and crew member complete a student contact information form on audition days. • Have a complete checklist of students who have signed up for the various crews. • Keep the audition area quiet. **CAST** • Arrive at audition early; check in with stage managers. • Complete audition profile form before audition begins. • Complete student contact information form either before or after scheduled audition. • Observe all audition etiquette: be well prepared, be on time, wear appropriate clothing. • Attend callback audition if needed. **CREW** Stop by the stage managers' table during any audition day to complete student contact information form.

Week 10: Getting Organized

This is the final week to get all paperwork in order and photocopied for the staff and student members of your production. This is also a good week to touch base with each member of your adult staff to be sure all his needs have been articulated and are being addressed.

All student crew chiefs should assist in preparing the production packets for the members of their crew. Student crew chiefs should also begin acting as a liaison between you (the director/producer), the adult staff members, and the student members of their crews.

GOALS

Make your lists and check them twice—or even three times! At this time, your production should be as well documented as possible. Finalize the cast rehearsal schedule and crew work schedule; check your personnel lists; update your anticipated production budget. The producer should have a complete sense of what each department is contributing to the production; the director should feel her vision is being supported by the plans of the designers. The crew is finalized; the cast is in place. It's time to kick off the show with an opening meeting for all members of the company: the staff and all cast and crew members.

HIGHLIGHTS

- Final planning meeting with stage managers.
- Prep and photocopy all show materials (schedules, contact sheets, order forms, job descriptions, all miscellaneous paperwork).
- Make a production packet for each student and staff member in the production.
- Company meeting for all members of the cast and crew.
- Distribute production packets to all staff and student members of the production.
- All students complete bio forms for the playbill.

PROFESSIONAL STAFF	STUDENT STAFF
PRODUCER • Create master contact list of all students in production; distribute to all members of creative staff, stage managers, crew chiefs, and parent volunteers. • Complete all paperwork and assemble a production packet for all staff and each student member of the production. The production packet should include: – Ticket order forms – T-shirt order form – Complete cast rehearsal or crew work schedule – Contact sheet for all members of cast and crew – Written rules that clearly state the expectations and requirements for all students, including policy statements addressing attendance, lateness, illness, personal behavior, etc. – Written description of the specific responsibilities of each separate crew – Written description of the specific responsibilities of all cast members – Conflict sheet – Parent volunteer form – A complete script for all members of the cast, stage managers, props crew, and all crew chiefs – All music for the show (if the production is a musical) • Collect completed playbill bio forms from each student. **DIRECTOR** • Work closely with producer to complete all paperwork and assemble production packets for all staff and student members of production • Conduct the opening meeting for all members of staff, cast, and crew. Distribute production packets to everyone.	• Stage managers work closely with the producer and director to assemble the production packets. • All student members of the cast and crew attend and the opening meeting for the full company. • All students complete a playbill bio form and submit it to the producer.

Week 9: Let the Rehearsals Begin

Rehearsals begin! If you are producing a play, rehearsals might begin with a read-through, then move to blocking Act I. If you are producing a musical, intensive music rehearsals should take precedence. It is a good idea to phase in your crew starting dates. Set construction is usually the most time-consuming process, so the construction crew should start when the cast rehearsals begin. Props and costumes should also begin their work at that time.

Most important, start promoting your production right now! The publicity committee should be active from the first day of rehearsal. Begin aggressive ticket sales. The advance sales revenue helps keep an accurate and realistic view of the production budget.

The first month of production requires a lot of paperwork. There are forms for everything: bios, tickets, T-shirts, costume measurements, and so on. Spend as much time as possible training your student stage managers to collect and organize all the forms and documents for your production.

GOALS

As the director/producer, you should be omnipresent and optimistic during this week. Although the first rehearsal week is very exciting, it can also be overwhelming to inexperienced students and their parents. If you express confidence and enthusiasm for all elements of the project, that energy will be contagious.

HIGHLIGHTS

- Cast rehearsals begin.
- Set construction, costume, props, and publicity crews begin.
- Ticket sales, sponsor subscriptions, and playbill advertisement sales begin.
- Begin playbill.

PROFESSIONAL STAFF	STUDENT STAFF
PRODUCER • Approve completed bio forms from all students; have students correct bio information as needed. • Approve logo design. • Oversee playbill design. **DIRECTOR** Begin scene rehearsal with principal actors. **MUSIC DIRECTOR** • Begin intensive music rehearsals with full company. • Begin working with principals on their music. **SET DESIGNER** Set construction begins. **PROPS COORDINATOR** Approve lists of props by act/scene created by the props crew. **COSTUME DESIGNER** • Measure all cast. • Approve master list of costume accessories created by the costume crew. **PUBLICITY COORDINATOR** • Begin typing all available information for playbill (title page, staff list, student staff list, cast list, act/scene breakdown, musical numbers). • Design logo for show; incorporate in T-shirt design, playbill cover, and posters. **TICKET MANAGER** • Ticket sales begin. • Sponsor subscription sales begin. • Process incoming ticket orders weekly; keep an accurate accounting of ticket sale revenues as prepaid orders arrive. **PARENT VOLUNTEER COORDINATORS** Work with director to determine the volunteer needs of production.	• All students order show T-shirts. • All students begin selling tickets, sponsor subscriptions, and playbill advertisements. **STAGE MANAGERS** • Create a master list of all cast members. • Create and post weekly rehearsal schedule that includes the time of each rehearsal and personnel needed for each day. • Create an official attendance book; use it daily to record cast attendance. • Assist producer in collecting student paperwork: ticket order forms, T-shirt order forms, parent volunteer forms, and student bios from all cast and crew members. • Work closely with director and music director; be aware of their expectations for student staff members. • Attend all music rehearsals. • Attend all scene rehearsals with principal cast members. **CREW CHIEFS (CONSTRUCTION, PROPS, AND COSTUME/ MAKEUP)** • Create a master list of all crew members. • Create and post weekly work schedule that includes the time of each work session and personnel needed each day. • Record crew attendance. • Work closely with designers (set and costume); be aware of their expectations for crew members. **CONSTRUCTION AND RUN CREWS** Set construction begins. **PROPS CREW** • Attend all read-through and blocking rehearsals. • Begin making lists of required props by act/scene. **COSTUME/MAKEUP CREW** • Measure actors for costumes. • Create master list of all costume accessories needed for each character. **CAST** Rehearsals begin for all actors. *For a Play* • Read-through for full company. • Begin blocking Act I. *For a Musical* • Intensive music rehearsals for all members of the company; learn the full company songs first. • Principals begin music rehearsals on their numbers. • Read-through of scenes with principals; begin work on character development.

Week 8: Building the Show

Music rehearsals continue for the company and blocking scenes begin for principal characters. Work on the set, props, costumes, publicity, and playbill continues. Begin collecting furniture and set dressings as needed: furniture pieces, lamps, rugs, artwork, and so on.

GOALS

Both the company and principal cast should be required to have a good portion of their music memorized by the end of this week. In scene rehearsals, try to incorporate as many elements as possible. Use props and furniture pieces from the beginning so all members of the cast and crew become familiar with the complete requirements of each scene. Provide constant reminders to all cast and crew to complete paperwork in a timely manner and to continue selling tickets, sponsor subscriptions, and playbill advertisements. Stay in communication with your design team. Be certain that all set and costume developments are proceeding according to schedule and that all designers are meeting the goals defined by the show concept.

HIGHLIGHTS

- Record music rehearsals for choreographer.
- Assemble orchestra personnel.
- Begin scene rehearsal with principal characters.

PROFESSIONAL STAFF	STUDENT STAFF

PRODUCER
- Oversee progress of playbill.
- Approve all publicity materials.
- Determine budget allowance for professional orchestra musicians.
- Compare projected budget with current total ticket revenue; if necessary, make budget adjustments.

DIRECTOR

Continue scene rehearsal and character development with principal cast.

MUSIC DIRECTOR
- Continue music rehearsal with full company.
- Continue working with principals on their music.
- Begin assembling personnel for orchestra; recruit student musicians; hire professional musicians.
- Make rehearsal recordings of company numbers to use in choreography rehearsals next week.

CHOREOGRAPHER
- Get rehearsal recordings of company numbers from music director.
- Consult with costume designer to discuss movement needs and costume concerns.

SET DESIGNER
- Construction continues.
- Consult with costume designer to discuss set/costume concerns (period costumes, extra room needed for hoop skirts, etc.).

PROPS COORDINATOR
- Approve master list of required props by act/scene created by the props crew.
- Coordinate the organization and use of rehearsal props.

All students continue selling tickets, sponsor subscriptions, and playbill advertisements.

STAGE MANAGERS
- Create and post weekly rehearsal schedule that includes time of each rehearsal and personnel needed for each day.
- Take attendance of cast at all rehearsals.
- Assist the producer in collecting student paperwork: ticket order forms, T-shirt order forms, and parent volunteer forms.
- Attend all music rehearsals.
- Attend all scene rehearsals; record blocking and props in rehearsal script.

CONSTRUCTION AND PROPS CHIEFS
- Create and post weekly work schedule that includes the time of each work session and personnel needed each day.
- Take attendance at all crew work sessions.
- Keep a record of any responsibilities assigned to a specific crew member.

CONSTRUCTION AND RUN CREWS
- Set construction continues.
- Begin acquiring furniture pieces as needed (chairs, occasional tables, etc.).

PROPS CREW
- Attend all blocking rehearsals
- Acquire rehearsal set pieces as needed (chairs, tables, benches, etc.).
- Continue making lists of required props by act/scene.
- Begin using props in scene rehearsals.

PROFESSIONAL STAFF	STUDENT STAFF

COSTUME DESIGNER
- Identify rental sources for costumes.
- Create designs as needed for costumes to be built for production.
- Oversee research and shopping assigned to crew members.
- Consult with choreographer to discuss movement needs and costume concerns.
- Consult with set designer to discuss set/costume concerns (period costumes, extra room needed for hoop skirts, etc).

PUBLICITY COORDINATOR
- Continue typing all available information for the playbill; begin two sections of student bios: cast and crew.
- Write press release for school or community paper.
- Design publicity posters using logo design.

TICKET MANAGER
- Continue processing incoming ticket orders on weekly basis.
- Begin a master list of names of subscription sponsors.
- Total the current ticket revenues; make that information available to the producer.

PARENT VOLUNTEER COORDINATOR
Contact parents of all cast and crew members to fill needed volunteer positions.

COSTUME/MAKEUP CREW CHIEFS
Working with the costume designer, assign specific jobs to crew members:
- Research and/or shop for appropriate costume accessories.
- Research appropriate styles of hair, makeup and ornamentation for the production.

COSTUME/MAKEUP CREW
- Begin shopping for costume accessories.
- Research appropriate styles of hair, makeup, and ornamentation for the production.

STUDENT MUSICIANS
Apply to music director for orchestra membership.

CAST
For a Play
- Continue blocking Act I

For a Musical
- Continue music rehearsal for full company.
- Make rehearsal recordings of company numbers to use in choreography rehearsals next week.
- Continue music rehearsal for principals.
- Begin blocking scenes with principals.

Week 7: Adding Choreography

Choreography begins for all cast members! Music and blocking rehearsals are also scheduled through the week. Continue work on the set, props, costumes, publicity, and playbill. Continue to collect furniture and set dressings as needed and incorporate these items in the blocking and movement rehearsals.

GOALS

All members of the company begin choreography this week. Be certain they are dressed appropriately for dance. If your costume designer has determined the style of footwear, students should wear their performance shoes in all choreography rehearsals. It is critical that all members of the cast have their music memorized for the choreography sessions. Students should be encouraged to combine singing and dancing as early as possible. In scene rehearsal, continue to incorporate as many elements as possible. Use props and furniture pieces from the beginning so all members of the cast and crew become familiar with the complete requirements of each scene.

Provide constant reminders to all cast and crew to complete paperwork in a timely manner and to continue selling tickets, sponsor subscriptions, and playbill advertisements. Stay in communication with your design team.

HIGHLIGHTS

- Choreography of major production numbers begins.
- All cast members receive list of required personal costume items.
- Block Act I scenes that include company members.
- Producer schedules production meeting of complete design team for next week.

PROFESSIONAL STAFF	STUDENT STAFF
PRODUCER • Compare projected budget with updated total ticket revenue; if necessary, make budget adjustments. • Oversee playbill and publicity materials. • Schedule production meeting for all creative and design staff for next week. **DIRECTOR** • Continue scene rehearsal with principal cast. • Block Act I scenes that include company members. • Approve set construction as it develops; be sure set works for staging and choreography. **MUSIC DIRECTOR** • Continue working with the cast on music. • Begin incorporating music in scene rehearsals. • Finalize orchestra membership and orchestra rehearsal schedule. • Continue making rehearsal recordings as needed for the choreographer. **CHOREOGRAPHER** Choreography begins with major production numbers involving the company. **SET DESIGNER** • Construction continues. • Lighting designer will need final measurements to begin lighting plot. **LIGHTING DESIGNER** Meet with set designer for updated measurements of set construction and use of space. **PROPS COORDINATOR** Continue to supervise and coordinate props as required.	**STUDENT STAFF** All students continue selling tickets, sponsor subscriptions, and playbill advertisements. **STAGE MANAGERS** • Create and post weekly rehearsal schedule that includes time and location of each rehearsal; agenda (music, blocking, choreography, etc.); and personnel needed for each day. • Take attendance of cast at all rehearsals. • Assist the producer in collecting student paperwork. • Continue to attend all music rehearsals. • Attend all scene rehearsals; carefully record blocking and props in rehearsal script. • Attend choreography rehearsals; take note of stage positions, entrances and exits, and all significant movement. • Run the sound playback for the choreographer at dance rehearsals. **CREW CHIEFS (CONSTRUCTION, RUN, SOUND, PROPS, AND COSTUME/MAKEUP)** • Create and post weekly work schedule that includes the time of each work session and personnel needed each day. • Take attendance at all crew work sessions. • Keep a record of any responsibilities assigned to a specific crew member. • Continue to work closely with designers. **CONSTRUCTION AND RUN CREWS** • Construction continues. • Continue acquiring furniture as needed. **SOUND CREW** • Meet with director to discuss use of music and special effects cues. • Make a master sound cue list. • Attend rehearsals to see how the sound cues are incorporated into the blocking. • Begin researching special effects cues. • Begin researching music as needed.

PROFESSIONAL STAFF	STUDENT STAFF

COSTUME DESIGNER
- Create list of personal costume items required for each cast member.
- Continue designing, building, renting costumes as needed.
- Oversee crew as they collect and organize personal items of cast.

PUBLICITY COORDINATOR
- Continue to create and proof playbill pages; add two new sections: orchestra membership list and student orchestra bios. Begin design of playbill cover.
- Finalize all press releases for school and community papers.
- Take publicity photographs of principal actors.
- Mail all publicity materials to press.
- Finalize design of publicity posters; have posters printed.
- Finalize T-shirt art.

TICKET MANAGER
- Continue processing incoming ticket orders on weekly basis.
- Continue adding names to the master list of subscription sponsors.
- Total current ticket revenues; make that information available to the producer.

PARENT VOLUNTEER COORDINATOR
- Continue to contact all parents for volunteer positions.
- Contact parents of new student orchestra members.

PROPS CREW
- Continue attending scene rehearsals and using acquired props.
- Continually update the master props list for the production by act/scene.
- Continue to acquire additional props as needed.

COSTUME/MAKEUP CREW
- Crew provides cast with a comprehensive list of all personal items each cast member is expected to supply for himself. This list should have a firm completion deadline.
- Create checklist for collection of these items as they are brought in.
- Create an organized system of storage for all personal costume items.
- Attend cast rehearsals to collect and organize items as they are brought in.

STUDENT MUSICIANS
- Complete student bio form.
- Begin selling tickets and sponsor subscriptions.
- Place T-shirt orders.
- Become familiar with the music of the show through listening to the original cast recording or attending cast music rehearsals.

CAST
Principals
- Final week to learn new music with music director.
- Memorize all scenes that have been blocked.
- Memorize all major solos/duets.

Company
- Memorize all company musical numbers.
- Choreography of major production numbers begins.

Cast Costume Responsibilities
All cast members will be supplied with a list of required personal costume items.
- Acquire necessary items (shoes, tights or socks, undergarments, pants, shirt, hair accessories, makeup supplies) by deadline.
- Give items to costume crew as directed.

Week 6: Completing Act I

The focus of this week is to complete Act I. All Act I music should be learned and memorized, all major numbers choreographed, all principal scenes blocked and memorized, and all company scenes staged. Organize all Act I furniture, set dressings, and props; incorporate these items in the Act I run on Friday. Continue work on the set, publicity, and the playbill. Advertisement sales end this week.

GOALS

Incorporate as many elements as possible during the Act I run. Actors should wear their required shoes; any set, props, or costume pieces should be integrated into the run.

All members of the design team and all members of the student crews should attend the Act I run. During this rehearsal, any potential problems with design concepts will be apparent. But don't worry—there is plenty of time to negotiate compromises and reconsider specific elements of blocking, choreography, set, costume, or lighting concepts.

Reminder all cast and crew to complete paperwork in a timely manner and to continue selling tickets and sponsor subscriptions.

HIGHLIGHTS

- Final week of advertisement sales for the playbill.
- Producer conducts meeting of full design staff.
- Run Act I on Friday.
- All members of the design team and student crews attend the Act I run.
- Call-board photos for all students in the cast, crew, and orchestra.

PROFESSIONAL STAFF	STUDENT STAFF

PRODUCER
- Compare projected budget with updated total ticket revenue; make budget adjustments as needed.
- Conduct meeting of full creative/design staff.
- Place complete T-shirt order.
- Schedule call-board photos for all students in cast, crew, and orchestra.

DIRECTOR
- Attend meeting of full creative/design staff.
- Complete blocking for Act I scenes.
- Full run of Act I at end of week.

MUSIC DIRECTOR
- Attend meeting of full creative/design staff.
- Complete all Act I music.
- Full run of Act I at end of week.
- Distribute orchestra books to student musicians.
- Mail orchestra books to any professionally contracted musicians.

CHOREOGRAPHER
- Attend meeting of full creative/design staff.
- Complete choreography of production numbers in Act I.
- Full run of Act I at end of week.

SET DESIGNER
- Attend meeting of full creative/design staff.
- Continue construction.
- Attend full run of Act I at end of week using any part of the set that is available.

LIGHTING DESIGNER
- Attend meeting of full creative/design staff.
- Create lighting plot.
- Attend full run of Act I at end of week.

SOUND DESIGNER
- Attend meeting of full creative/design staff.
- Inventory available sound equipment.
- Determine budget for additional equipment.
- Begin to create sound design.

- All students continue selling tickets and sponsor subscriptions.
- Final week to sell advertisements for the playbill.
- All students take a call-board photo.

STAGE MANAGERS
- Create and post weekly rehearsal schedule that includes time and location of each rehearsal; agenda (music, blocking, choreography, etc.); and personnel needed for each day.
- Take attendance of cast at all rehearsals.
- Assist the producer in collecting student paperwork.
- Continue to attend all music, choreography, and blocking rehearsals; take notes of stage positions, entrances and exits, and all significant movement.
- Add all prop notes to working script.
- Add preliminary sound notes for Act I to working script, specifically solo (body) mikes and off-stage amplification needed.
- During full run of Act I at end of week, add set notes to working script.

CONSTRUCTION, PROPS, AND COSTUME/MAKEUP CREW CHIEFS
- Create and post weekly work schedule that includes time of each work session and personnel needed each day.
- Take attendance at all crew work sessions.
- Keep a record of any responsibilities assigned to a specific crew member.
- Continue to work closely with designers.
- Take notes in scripts at Act I run-through.

RUN CREW CHIEF
- Prepare script with notes for Act I run with available set.
- Use run crew during Act I run.
- Take production notes during Act I run.

CONSTRUCTION AND RUN CREWS
- Continue construction.
- Attend full run of Act I using any part of set that is ready at that time.
- Facilitate use of any completed set pieces.

PROFESSIONAL STAFF	STUDENT STAFF
PROPS COORDINATOR • Attend meeting of full creative/design staff. • Attend full run of Act I at end of week. **COSTUME DESIGNER** • Attend meeting of full creative/design staff. • Attend full run of Act I at end of week. **PUBLICITY COORDINATOR** • Incorporate all ads in final layout; finalize playbill design and layout. • Continue to create and proof playbill pages. • Complete design of playbill cover. • Coordinate call-board photo schedule with the producer. • Take the call-board head shots; get film developed. • Make follow-up calls to press to be certain the publicity packets were received. **TICKET MANAGER** • Continue processing incoming ticket orders on weekly basis. • Continue adding names to the master list of subscription sponsors. • Total the current ticket revenues; make that information available to producer. **PARENT VOLUNTEER COORDINATOR** • Finalize parent volunteers. • Create master list of volunteer responsibilities and assignments.	**PROPS CREW** • All Act I props should be completed; master props list should be organized. • Copy all Act I props notes from master list into the props script. • Attend all rehearsals; use props as needed. • Attend full run of Act I; take production notes throughout run. **COSTUME/MAKEUP CREW** • Assist costume designer as needed. • Collect and organize personal costume items of cast members. • Attend full run of Act I; take production notes throughout run. **LIGHTING CREW CHIEF** Take production notes in working script on stage placement of actors, possible use of spotlights, and scene changes during Act I run-through. **LIGHTING CREW** Attend full run of Act I; take production notes throughout run. **SOUND CREW CHIEF** Take production notes in working script on stage placement of actors, possible uses of solo (body) mikes, need for off-stage mikes, and uses of amplification for specific large areas during Act I run-through. **SOUND CREW** • Assist designer with equipment inventory. • Attend full run of Act I; take production notes throughout run. **STUDENT MUSICIANS** • Pick up orchestra book and begin individual practice. • Attend full run of Act; play music. **CAST** • Complete blocking Act I scenes. • Complete Act I music rehearsals. • Complete Act I choreography. • Integrate use of all rehearsal props. • By end of this week run Act I off-book with music, choreography, and props and with set as available. • All personal costume items are due.

Weeks 5 and 4: Completing the Playbill

Complete the playbill. If you've been creating pages for your playbill during the past four weeks, you've got a good start. Now it's time to include the advertisements and begin the process of proofreading the document.

The focus of the rehearsals during these two weeks is to build Act II. If you are producing a play, it is time to involve the sound crew in the rehearsal process. If you are producing a musical, you have a big job ahead of you. Since the cast already knows the Act II music, your focus should be on blocking scenes with principal characters, teaching new choreography, and staging scenes involving the company. Organize all Act II furniture, set dressings, and props; incorporate these items in the Act II run. Review Act I. Continue work on the set and publicity.

GOALS

Incorporate as many elements as possible during the rehearsal process for Act II. Actors should always wear their required shoes; any set, props, or costume pieces should be integrated into each rehearsal. The music director should begin including student musicians in daily rehearsals. Provide constant reminders to all cast and crew members to continue selling tickets and sponsor subscriptions.

HIGHLIGHTS

- Complete playbill.
- Costume fittings begin.
- Lighting and sound designers finalize their plots.

PROFESSIONAL STAFF	STUDENT STAFF

PRODUCER
- Compare projected budget with updated total ticket revenue; make budget adjustments as needed.
- Oversee and approve final playbill layout and design.

DIRECTOR
- Complete blocking for Act II scenes.
- Continue to review Act I.

MUSIC DIRECTOR
- Complete all Act II music.
- Rehearse with student orchestra members.

CHOREOGRAPHER
- Complete choreography of production numbers in Act II.
- Review all choreography from Act I.

SET DESIGNER
Continue construction.

LIGHTING DESIGNER
Complete lighting plot.

SOUND DESIGNER
Complete sound design.

PROPS COORDINATOR
- Oversee Act II props list.
- Coordinate and organize the use of Act II rehearsal props.

COSTUME DESIGNER
Begin costume fittings with available costumes.

All students continue selling tickets and sponsor subscriptions.

STAGE MANAGERS
- Create and post weekly rehearsal schedule that includes time and location of each rehearsal; agenda (music, blocking, choreography, etc.); and personnel needed for each day.
- Take attendance of cast at all rehearsals.
- Assist the producer in collecting student paperwork.
- Continue to attend all music, choreography, and blocking rehearsals, taking note of stage positions, entrances and exits, and all significant movement.
- Add all prop notes for Act II to rehearsal script.
- Add preliminary sound notes for Act II to rehearsal script, specifically solo (body) mikes and off-stage amplification needed.

CONSTRUCTION, PROPS, AND COSTUME/MAKEUP CREW CHIEFS
- Create and post weekly work schedule that includes time of each work session and personnel needed each day.
- Take attendance at all crew work sessions.
- Keep a record of any responsibilities assigned to a specific crew member.
- Continue to work closely with the designers.

CONSTRUCTION AND RUN CREWS
- Continue construction.
- Run crew members should facilitate the use of any completed set pieces.

PROPS CREW
- All Act II props should be completed; master props list should be organized.
- Copy all Act II props notes into the props script.
- Attend all rehearsals; use props as needed.

PROFESSIONAL STAFF	STUDENT STAFF

PUBLICITY COORDINATOR
- Continue to create and proof playbill pages.
- Create and insert all graphics for advertisements.
- Create a "thank you" column to recognize people, businesses, or organizations who have donated supplies or have shown support for your production.
- Finalize playbill design.
- Make an appointment at the printer for a meeting to discuss paper stock, ink color, due date for completed playbill pages, completion date for printed playbills.
- Work with the house staff to create attractive and complete call-boards.
- Take additional photos as needed.
- Store the completed call-boards in a safe place until opening night.

TICKET MANAGER
- Continue processing incoming ticket orders on weekly basis.
- Continue adding names to master list of subscription sponsors.
- At end of Week 5, give complete subscription sponsor list to playbill typist.
- Create addendum to playbill that includes a list of all additional sponsor subscriptions.
- Total current ticket revenues; make that information available to producer.

PARENT VOLUNTEER COORDINATOR
- Organize menus for tech rehearsal dinner and opening night dinner.
- Organize personnel and menu for refreshment sales.

COSTUME/MAKEUP CREW
- Assist costume designer as needed.
- Collect and organize personal costume items of cast members.

LIGHTING CREW
Attend all work sessions scheduled with the lighting designer during these weeks.

SOUND CREW
- Record all sound cues in script.
- Complete master sound cue list and identify all sound sources.
- Use all cues in daily rehearsals.

HOUSE STAFF
Work with the publicity staff to create attractive call-boards.

STUDENT MUSICIANS
Attend rehearsals with the music director as scheduled.

CAST
Rehearsals for Weeks 5 and 4 focus on building Act II. Some review of Act I should be included during these weeks.

Week 3: Completing Act II

The focus of this week is to complete Act II and to review Act I as many times as possible. This is a great week to concentrate on character development with all members of the cast. Since all actors can perform the entire play, they should have a more complete understanding of each character. The set should be nearly complete; all furniture should be present for daily rehearsals; all props should be available for daily use.

GOALS

Incorporate as many elements as possible during the rehearsal process for Act II. Actors should always wear their required shoes; any set, props, or costume pieces should be integrated into each rehearsal. The music director should continue to include student musicians in daily rehearsals. Remind all members of the cast and crew to continue selling tickets and sponsor subscriptions.

HIGHLIGHTS

- Run Act II.
- Review Act I.
- All members of the design team and student crews attend the Act II run.
- Lighting and sound designers place shop orders for rented materials.

PROFESSIONAL STAFF	STUDENT STAFF
PRODUCER • Compare projected budget with updated total ticket revenue. • Take completed playbill to printer. • Pick up T-shirts. **DIRECTOR** • Focus on completing Act II. • Review Act I. **MUSIC DIRECTOR** • Attend all rehearsals; continue to work on music as needed. • Continue to include student musicians in daily rehearsals. **CHOREOGRAPHER** • Attend all rehearsals. • Continue to rehearse choreography as needed. • Work with costume designer to be sure final costume design allows for necessary movement. **SET DESIGNER** • Continue work on set. • Coordinate final set concept with both lighting and sound designers. **LIGHTING DESIGNER** • Place shop order for rented lighting equipment. • Strike all lights currently hung on electrics. • Attend as many rehearsals as possible; begin making cue notes. • Final meeting to coordinate with set designer. **SOUND DESIGNER** • Place shop order for rented sound equipment. • Final meetings to coordinate sound expectations with set designer, costume designer, and music director.	All students continue selling tickets and sponsor subscriptions. **STAGE MANAGERS** • Create and post weekly rehearsal schedule that includes time and location of each rehearsal; agenda (music, blocking, choreography, etc.); and personnel needed for each day. • Take attendance of cast at all rehearsals. • Assist producer in collecting student paperwork. • Be sure rehearsal script is as complete as possible; include all blocking, choreography notes, musical cues, props and set notes, and preliminary sound cues. • Work with props crew chiefs to organize all props according to use: act/scene and stage right/stage left. **ALL CREW CHIEFS** • Coordinate individual notes and working scripts with those of stage managers. • Create and post weekly work schedule that includes time of each work session and personnel needed each day. • Take attendance at all crew work sessions. • Keep a record of any responsibilities assigned to a specific crew member. • Continue to work closely with the designers. **COSTUME CREW CHIEFS** • Use all available costumes in rehearsals this week. • Assign members of costume crew to specific cast members as dressers. • Purchase makeup supplies as directed by the costume designer.

PROFESSIONAL STAFF	STUDENT STAFF

PROPS COORDINATOR

Organize props according to their use in the show: act/scene and stage right/stage left.

COSTUME DESIGNER

- Use all available costume pieces in rehearsal.
- Final meetings to coordinate with sound designer, set designer, and choreographer.
- Continue building and fitting costumes as needed.
- Oversee dresser assignments.
- Oversee completion of actors' wardrobe worksheets.
- Oversee hair and makeup designs for each actor.
- Create a makeup supply list for the crew chiefs.

PUBLICITY COORDINATOR

- Take completed playbill to printer
- Work with ticket manager to create addendum for the playbill; addendum should be updated regularly and printed and photocopied as close to performance dates as possible.
- Advertise show within the school; promote production with signs and banners.
- Send an announcement of production to drama departments in other school districts.

TICKET MANAGER

- Continue processing incoming ticket orders on weekly basis.
- Continue adding names to addendum.
- Total current ticket revenues; make that information available to producer.

PARENT VOLUNTEER COORDINATOR

Confirm parent commitments for volunteer positions.

COSTUME/MAKEUP CREW

- Attend all rehearsals; use all available costume pieces and accessories.
- Each dresser works with assigned actors to complete wardrobe worksheets.
- Each dresser completes hair and makeup design for each actor.

CONSTRUCTION AND RUN CREWS

- Complete set.
- Split crew as necessary to assist director in rehearsals.

LIGHTING CREW

- Attend as many rehearsals as possible; take production notes throughout each run.
- Attend all prehang sessions scheduled with lighting designer during this week.

SOUND CREW

Attend as many rehearsals as possible; take production notes throughout each run.

PROPS CREW

- Attend all rehearsals; use all available props.
- Coordinate organization of props with stage managers.
- Compare notes in your rehearsal script with the stage managers' book.

HOUSE STAFF

Assist publicity staff as needed.

STUDENT MUSICIANS

Attend all rehearsals; play music.

CAST

- Work with assigned dresser to complete a wardrobe worksheet that details all parts of each separate costume and defines its use in production.
- Complete Act II.
- Review Act I.

Week 2: Teching the Show

Week 2 is a *big* week. During this week, all the separate elements of the production come together, and your artistic vision begins to come into view. Cast members have completed the task of learning the show. They now focus on finding a rhythm and tempo for their performance and creating the energy necessary for the production. This is a big week for the design team. The set should be nearly complete. The most critical jobs this week are loading in the lighting and sound and cueing the show. Final costume fittings and final hair and makeup styling will occupy the costume crew. The new elements this week are the addition of the lighting and sound equipment and the music rehearsal with the full orchestra. This is also the last full week for ticket presale. Remind all members of the cast and crew to continue selling tickets and sponsor subscriptions.

GOALS

If your rehearsals are well organized, you will have a much easier time adding all the technical elements to the production. The director, music director, and choreographer should give full attention to the cast during rehearsals on Monday, Tuesday, and Wednesday. All students should possess a clear understanding of the structure of the play and the purpose of their role within that structure. Props, set, and costume pieces should be a natural presence. The rehearsals should have a fluid feeling at this point. Later this week, the director and music director will devote more of their energy to the technical elements of the production. The sound, lights, complete sets and costumes, and musicians should add dimension and support to the work being done by the student actors.

COMMUNICATION MODEL

During this week, the director should begin communicating differently with the cast. All members of the cast and each crew should ask their questions of the student leaders: the stage managers and crew chiefs. The student leaders should be able to answer most of the questions posed to them. When the student leader cannot answer a question, he should direct the question to his designer; the designer should communicate with the director. This is the correct chain of communication for every production. It empowers the student leaders with the opportunity to lead and allows the director and designers to devote full attention to their jobs.

Members of the cast, crew, and orchestra	→	Stage Managers or Student Crew Chiefs	→	Design Staff: Set, Lights, Costumes, Props, Sound	→	Producer, Director, and Music Director

HIGHLIGHTS

- All rented lighting and sound equipment arrives.
- Orchestra rehearsal for full orchestra and all cast.
- Lighting cue sessions and cast light walking.
- Sunday tech rehearsal.
- Parent chaperones begin.
- Load-in for lighting and sound.
- Prepare dressing rooms.
- Costume parade.
- Sunday tech dinner.

PROFESSIONAL STAFF	STUDENT STAFF

PRODUCER
- Compare projected budget with updated total ticket revenue.
- Make arrangements for pickup of all rented lighting and sound equipment.
- Make arrangements for all necessary ladders, scaffolding, or hydraulic lifts to be present for the tech load-in.
- Pay all equipment rental bills promptly.
- Oversee needs of all staff.
- Confirm food responsibilities of parent volunteers.
- Oversee other parent volunteer responsibilities.

DIRECTOR
Look beyond the cast this week. Be sure the needs of each department are being addressed and that the production works as a whole; make adjustments as needed.

Monday: Run Act I.

Tuesday: Run Act II.

Wednesday: Run complete show.

Thursday:
- Attend orchestra rehearsal Thursday night; assist music director as needed.
- Work with lighting designer on focus and cue notes as needed.

Friday:
- Work with costume designer on costume parade and setting up dressing rooms.
- Work with sound designer on load-in as needed.
- Work with lighting designer on cueing Act I; oversee light walking by actors.

Saturday:
- Work with lighting designer during lighting cue sessions.
- Work with set designer on set placement during light cue session.
- Work with sound designer on sound concept, mike assignments, and sound balance in the performance space.
- Assist production stage manager with recording cues in script.

STAGE MANAGERS
Production Stage Manager
Monday: Run Act I.

Tuesday: Run Act II.

Wednesday:
- Run complete show.
- Work with student run crew chiefs to coordinate all possible set use during this week's rehearsals.

Thursday night: Attend orchestra rehearsal; assist music director as needed.

Friday: Attend costume parade and light cue session.

Saturday: Attend light cue for Act II.

Sunday: Attend tech rehearsal; call cues while sitting with director and lighting designer.

Assistant Stage Managers
- Create and post weekly rehearsal schedule.
- Take attendance of cast at all rehearsals.

Monday: Run Act I.

Tuesday: Run Act II.

Wednesday:
- Run complete show.
- Each assistant stage manager should specialize in one area, backstage right or backstage left, and mark their cue script accordingly with all cues: cast entrances, exits, props, set, costume changes, etc.

Thursday night: Attend orchestra rehearsal.

Friday: Attend costume parade and light cue session.

Saturday: Attend light cue session.

Sunday: Attend tech rehearsal and work from assigned backstage position.

PROFESSIONAL STAFF	STUDENT STAFF

Sunday:
- Run tech rehearsal.
- Focus all communication to members of staff, stage managers, and crew chiefs; transfer responsibilities to them.
- Assist production stage manager with calling cues.

CHOREOGRAPHER
- Attend rehearsals Monday–Wednesday.
- Attend Sunday tech rehearsal.
- Continue to rehearse choreography as needed.

MUSIC DIRECTOR
Confirm Thursday night orchestra rehearsal with any hired musicians.
Monday: Run Act I.
Tuesday: Run Act II.
Wednesday: Run complete show.
Thursday night: Attend and conduct orchestra rehearsal. Full orchestra (students and hired professional musicians) with full cast.
Saturday: Set up and organize orchestra pit for Sunday tech rehearsal.
Sunday: Attend and conduct tech rehearsal; student orchestra members only.

PROPS COORDINATOR
- Coordinate backstage props positions with set designer.
- Organize all prop preset positions and daily storage.
- Oversee purchase of perishable items.
- Oversee cleaning of food service items.
- Oversee use and storage of food items.
Monday: Run Act I.
Tuesday: Run Act II.
Wednesday: Run complete show.
Saturday: Supervise backstage preset of all props; oversee scene change strike/set job assignments.
Sunday: Attend tech rehearsal; supervise props crew.

ORCHESTRA MANAGER
- Assist music director with set-up and clean up for Thursday night's orchestra rehearsal.
- Assist music director with set up of orchestra pit.
- Coordinate with lighting crew chief to provide adequate lighting for all musicians in pit.

ORCHESTRA MEMBERS
Monday: Run Act I.
Tuesday: Run Act II.
Wednesday: Run complete show.
Thursday night: Attend orchestra rehearsal.
Saturday: Assist setting up orchestra pit.
Sunday: Attend tech rehearsal.

PROPS CREW CHIEFS
- Create and post weekly work schedule that includes time of each work session and personnel needed each day.
- Take attendance at all crew work sessions.
- Keep a record of any responsibilities assigned to a specific crew member.
- Split duties: One props chief assigned backstage right; one assigned backstage left. Scripts should be marked with notes accordingly.
Monday: Run Act I.
Tuesday: Run Act II.
Wednesday: Run complete show.
Thursday–Friday: Not in session.
Saturday: Attend lighting cue session; preset all props backstage for the Sunday rehearsal; make diagrams of each scene change; make large charts detailing each change and each crew member's strike or set responsibilities in that scene change; assign specific jobs to crew members.
Sunday: Attend tech rehearsal; use all props.

PROPS CREW
Monday: Run Act I
Tuesday: Run Act II.
Wednesday: Run complete show attend rehearsal; use all available props.
Thursday–Saturday: Not in session.
Sunday: Attend tech rehearsal; move all props as planned; each crew member will be assigned specific set or strike jobs for every scene change.

PROFESSIONAL STAFF	STUDENT STAFF
SET DESIGNER • Complete set. • Assist lighting designer with hang and focus (moving set pieces as needed). • Coordinate hanging of painted drops and scrims or rehanging soft goods with lighting designer. • Cleaning, spiking, and organizing as needed during lighting cue sessions Friday night and Saturday. • Oversee implementation of backstage rules of conduct. • Work with run crew chiefs to organize and assign scene change positions. • Work with lighting designer to install running lights backstage. • Work with costume designer to provide private backstage dressing space as needed. • Oversee and rehearse all set changes during the Sunday tech rehearsal.	**RUN CREW CHIEFS** • Create and post weekly work schedule that includes time of each work session and personnel needed each day. • Take attendance at all crew work sessions. • Keep a record of any responsibilities assigned to a specific crew member. **Monday:** Run Act I. **Tuesday:** Run Act II. **Wednesday:** Run complete show. Split duties: One crew chief remains with the set designer and half the crew to complete set; one attends rehearsals with director and uses half the crew to move available set pieces. **Thursday:** Assist lighting crew with hang and focus (moving set pieces as needed). **Friday:** Move and spike all set changes during lighting cue session; make diagrams of each scene change; assign specific jobs to crew members. **Saturday:** • Move and spike all set changes during lighting cue session. • Make large charts detailing each change and each crew members' strike or set responsibilities in that scene change. • Make signs as needed to post backstage rules of conduct. **Sunday:** Full tech rehearsal. Move all scene changes as planned; correct charts as needed. **RUN CREW** **Monday:** Run Act I. **Tuesday:** Run Act II. **Wednesday:** Run complete show. Split crew to complete set; assist director in rehearsals as necessary. **Thursday:** Assist lighting crew with hang and focus (moving set pieces as needed). **Friday:** Move and spike all set changes during lighting cue session. **Saturday:** Move and spike all set changes during lighting cue session. **Sunday:** Full tech rehearsal. Move all scene changes as planned; each crew member will be assigned specific set or strike jobs for every scene change.

PROFESSIONAL STAFF	STUDENT STAFF
LIGHTING DESIGNER • Hang and focus lighting. • Coordinate hanging of painted drops and scrims or rehanging soft goods with set designer. • Lighting cue sessions. • Work with director and production stage manager to finalize all lighting cues. • Work with set designer to install running lights backstage. • Work with music director to provide lighting in orchestra pit.	**LIGHTING CREW CHIEF** • Create and post weekly work schedule that includes time of each work session and personnel needed each day. • Take attendance at all crew work sessions. • Keep a record of any responsibilities assigned to a specific crew member. • Assist lighting designer in checking in rental equipment with shop order. • Attend all lighting crew sessions to hang and focus the plot. • Attend all lighting cue session to assist lighting designer as needed. • Create lighting cue sheet or spot cue sheets as needed. • Attend Sunday tech rehearsal and perform assigned job on the lighting crew. **LIGHTING CREW** • Attend all lighting crew sessions to hang and focus the plot. • Attend all lighting cue session to assist lighting designer as needed. • Attend Sunday tech rehearsal and perform assigned job on lighting crew.

PROFESSIONAL STAFF	STUDENT STAFF
SOUND DESIGNER **For a Musical** • Sound load-in. • Oversee final mike assignment chart. • Work with director, music director, and sound manager to achieve sound concept and balance for production. • Work with costume designer on body mike placement on actors. • Load in in-house communication system (headsets) as needed.	**SOUND CREW CHIEFS** • Create and post weekly work schedule that includes time of each work session and personnel needed each day. • Take attendance at all crew work sessions. • Keep a record of any responsibilities assigned to a specific crew member. **For a Play or Musical with Sound Effect Cues** • Make a master CD or cassette tape of all sound cues and music cues in the order they appear in production • Make back-up copy of each original master CD/tape **For a Musical** **Monday:** Run Act I. **Tuesday:** Run Act II. **Wednesday:** Run complete show: • Take production notes in working script on stage placement of actors, possible uses of solo (body) mikes, need for off-stage mikes, and uses of amplification for specific large areas • Assist sound designer in checking in the rental equipment with shop order. • Attend all sound crew sessions to load in and test equipment. • Create sound cue sheets or microphone charts as needed. • Take responsibility for daily battery changes and inventory of body mikes. • Attend Sunday tech rehearsal and perform assigned job on the sound crew. **SOUND CREW** • Attend all sound crew sessions to load in and test equipment. • Attend Sunday tech rehearsal and perform assigned job on the sound crew.

PROFESSIONAL STAFF	STUDENT STAFF

COSTUME DESIGNER
Monday: Run Act I.
Tuesday: Run Act II.
Wednesday: Run complete show.
Thursday: Final costume fittings.
Friday:
- Oversee costume parade.
- Oversee final organization and set-up of dressing rooms.

Sunday:
- Attend Sunday tech rehearsal—use full costume, hair, makeup.
- Oversee implementation of dressing room rules of conduct.
- Oversee final hair styling and makeup design.
- Additional costume work as needed during light cue sessions Friday and Saturday.
- Work with set designer for coordination of backstage costume changes.
- Work with sound designer for body mike placement on actors.

COSTUME/MAKEUP CREW CHIEFS
- Create and post weekly work schedule that includes time of each work session and personnel needed each day.
- Take attendance at all crew work sessions.
- Keep a record of any responsibilities assigned to a specific crew member.

Monday: Run Act I.
Tuesday: Run Act II.
Wednesday: Run complete show; use all available costume pieces; each dresser should update wardrobe worksheets for their assigned actors; assist all crew members as needed.
Thursday: Assist costume designer with costume fittings as needed.
Friday:
- Assist with costume parade.
- Assist in setting up and organizing dressing rooms.
- Make signs as needed to post dressing room rules of conduct.

Saturday: Assist designer as needed.
Sunday: Attend tech rehearsal; perform full duties as dresser.

COSTUME/MAKEUP CREW
Monday: Run Act I.
Tuesday: Run Act II.
Wednesday: Run complete show; use all available costume pieces; update wardrobe worksheets for assigned actors.
Friday:
- Assist with costume parade.
- Assist in setting up and organizing dressing rooms.
- Assist with implementing dressing room rules.

Sunday: attend tech rehearsal; perform full duties as dresser.

PROFESSIONAL STAFF	STUDENT STAFF

PUBLICITY COORDINATOR
- Continue to promote show within school and community.
- Continue to work with ticket manager to create addendum for playbill.

TICKET MANAGER
- Continue processing incoming tickets.
- Continue adding names to addendum.
- Total the current ticket revenues; make that information available to producer.

PARENT VOLUNTEER COORDINATOR
- Assign parent volunteer to assist costume designer during Friday's costume parade.
- Assign parent chaperones for lighting cue session on Friday night and Saturday.
- Assign parent chaperones for tech rehearsal on Sunday.
- Assign parent volunteers for tech rehearsal dinner on Sunday.

CAST
This week's rehearsals focus on putting the entire play together. It is important for each actor to experience the level of concentration, vocal stamina, and physical energy needed to perform the entire play.
Monday: Run Act I.
Tuesday: Run Act II.
Wednesday: Run complete show.
Thursday evening: Orchestra rehearsal for all cast and all musicians.
Friday:
- *Afternoon:* Complete costume parade.
- *Night:* Light walking for Act I during lighting cue sessions.

Saturday: Complete light walking for Act I; for all of Act II.
Sunday: Full tech rehearsal.

HOUSE STAFF
Assist publicity staff as needed.

Week 1: Curtain Up!

Performance week! This week includes two closed dress rehearsals, one invited dress rehearsal (parent photo night), and all performances. Your biggest challenge is to keep all members of the staff, cast, and crew focused on the same goal. During this week, people tend to feel tired and stressed. Your job is to be the cheerleader for your team. Keep everyone alert, aware of her responsibilities, and feeling confident. Team building is the priority for the director and producer throughout the week.

GOALS

Your primary rehearsal goal is to run the show in real time (no stopping unless for a true emergency) for all dress rehearsals. Take good notes during each dress rehearsal and share those notes with your staff, cast, and crew after the rehearsal is over. Make changes and adjustments as necessary from day to day to improve the production. After the final dress rehearsal on Wednesday night, *freeze the show*. That means *no more changes at all*.

Once you've completed the rehearsal process for your show, it is critical to establish clear goals for all members of the cast and crew for all performances. The performance goal most appropriate for students is the professional standard: to achieve as perfect a show as possible at each performance. This is the same goal held by every Broadway professional, both performers and technical personnel. It is a worthy goal to teach our students.

HIGHLIGHTS

- Parent chaperones continue.
- Dress rehearsals.
- Parent photo night.
- Opening night dinner.
- Cast party.
- Preparation for the strike.

WEEKLY SCHEDULE FOR PROFESSIONAL STAFF, CAST, AND CREWS

Monday–Tuesday:
- Dress rehearsals

Wednesday night:
- Final dress rehearsal
- Parent photo night

Thursday:
- Opening night performance
- Opening night dinner follows the show

Friday:
- Second performance

Saturday:
- Performance(s)
- If Saturday night is closing show, partial strike follows the performance
- Following the partial strike, cast party for all students in the cast, crew, orchestra, and their families

Sunday:
- Possible performance
- Complete strike

PROFESSIONAL STAFF	STUDENT STAFF

PRODUCER
- Compare projected budget with updated total ticket revenue.
- Oversee needs of all staff.
- Pick up completed playbills from printer.
- Approve and photocopy addendum for inclusion in the playbill.
- Confirm food and chaperoning responsibilities of parent volunteers.
- Confirm refreshment sale responsibilities of parent volunteers.
- Process checks to pay all hired staff immediately following strike at end of this week.
- Oversee and facilitate the strike.
- Make arrangements for all rented scripts, orchestra books, costumes, set pieces, props and lighting or sound equipment to be returned according to contract stipulations.
- Make arrangements for all borrowed costumes, props, set pieces or equipment to be returned in a timely manner.
- Oversee the Saturday night cast party for all student members of the cast, crew, orchestra and their families.

DIRECTOR, MUSIC DIRECTOR, CHOREOGRAPHER, PROPS COORDINATOR
Plan strike:
- Director oversees cast.
- Music director oversees orchestra members.
- Props coordinator oversees props crew.

SET, LIGHTING, SOUND, COSTUME DESIGNERS
- Monday–Tuesday dress rehearsals: Mask entrances and exits as appropriate for space requirements and production needs.

Plan strike:
- Set designer oversees run crew and construction crew; cast will assist as needed.
- Lighting designer oversees lighting crew; cast will assist as needed.
- Sound designer oversees sound crew.
- Costume designer oversees costume crew; cast will assist as needed.

PRODUCTION STAGE MANAGER
- Copy all final cues into a clean show cue script.
- Call all cues for dress rehearsals and performances.
- Assume leadership role during strike.

ASSISTANT STAGE MANAGERS
- Create and post a call schedule for the week.
- Take attendance of cast at all dress rehearsals and performances.
- Assume leadership role during strike.

ORCHESTRA MANAGER
- Assist music director with daily set up of orchestra pit.
- Assist music director with orchestra strike.

PROPS CREW CHIEFS
- Assist props coordinator with daily set up, clean up, and storage of props.
- Assist props coordinator with organizing properties strike.
- If Saturday night is closing show, complete props strike follows performance; assume leadership role during strike.

RUN CREW CHIEFS
- Assist set designer with daily set up, storage, and maintenance of set.
- Assist set designer with organizing set strike.
- If Saturday night is closing show, partial set strike follows performance; assume leadership role during strike.

LIGHTING CREW CHIEF
- Assist lighting designer with daily dimmer checks, focus notes, and maintenance of lighting design.
- Assist lighting designer with organizing lighting strike.
- If Saturday night is closing show, partial lighting strike follows performance; assume leadership role during strike.

PROFESSIONAL STAFF	STUDENT STAFF

PARENT VOLUNTEER COORDINATOR

- Assign parent chaperones for dress rehearsals Monday, Tuesday, and Wednesday.
- Assign parent chaperones for performances on Thursday, Friday, and Saturday.
- Assign parent volunteers to assist with box office help for each performance.
- Assign parent volunteers for organizing and running refreshment sales preshow, during intermission, and postshow.
- Assign parent volunteers to assist with Saturday night cast party for all student members of cast, crew, orchestra, and their families.
- Assign parent chaperones for Sunday strike.
- Assign parent volunteers to assist in returning borrowed or rented items.

TICKET MANAGER

- Continue processing advance-sale ticket orders through Tuesday. After Tuesday, suspend advance-sale orders; sell remaining tickets at the door.
- Wednesday: Do a final check of all reserved seating tickets. Be sure all presale tickets are in envelopes clearly marked with the patron's names. Sort all presale tickets alphabetically by performance night.
- Create standing-room-only tickets if needed.
- Prepare cash boxes for the box office.
- Confirm and assign positions to parent volunteers assisting with box office.
- Total current ticket revenues; make that information available to the producer.

PUBLICITY COORDINATOR

Complete addendum for playbill; get approval of producer, then photocopy as needed.

SOUND CREW CHIEFS

- Assist sound designer with daily microphone checks, battery replacement, and maintenance of sound equipment.
- Assist sound designer with organizing sound strike.
- If Saturday night is closing show, partial sound strike follows performance; assume leadership role during strike.

COSTUME/MAKEUP CREW CHIEFS

- Assist costume designer with daily cleaning, repairs and maintenance of costumes.
- Assist costume designer with organizing costume strike.
- If Saturday night is closing show, partial costume strike follows performance; assume leadership role during strike.

HOUSE MANAGERS

- Create and post call schedule for the week.
- Remind all house staff members of required attire.
- Take attendance of house staff at parent photo night and all performances.
- Work closely with ticket manager and production stage manager.

HOUSE STAFF

- Insert addendum into playbills each night.
- Set and strike call-boards each night.
- Seat audience.
- Assist with refreshment sales as needed.
- Pick up discarded playbills from the theater floor following each performance.

Postshow: The Strike

A production is never finished until the strike is over, everything is returned to its proper place, and order is restored. A good strike is well planned. It involves all members of the production team and is structured as an educational experience. Use this time to teach new vocabulary and appropriate safety etiquette for a strike. A strike can be dangerous. Be certain to have adequate adult supervision and use all trained staff in supervisory positions.

GOALS

Each crew should be assigned to strike all elements of its department. Since cast members will finish their strike first, they should assist other production departments. Cast members should be dispersed between the crews needing the most assistance: lighting, set, and costume/makeup.

Once the strike is complete, the director and producer should conclude the business paperwork in a timely manner: pay all staff, pay all bills, return rental equipment, and return all borrowed items. Most important, remember to send thank you notes to the people who were invaluable during the course of your production: your staff, generous donors, and parent volunteers. Once these obligations are fulfilled, it is time to start the next show!

HIGHLIGHTS

- Strike and restore in all departments.
- Return all rented and borrowed equipment and materials.
- Pay all hired staff.
- Pay all outstanding bills.
- Send thank you notes to all staff and parent volunteers.
- Balance budget.

STRIKE RESPONSIBILITIES BY DEPARTMENT

PRODUCER
- Oversee and facilitate the strike.
- Process checks to pay all hired staff immediately following strike at end of this week.
- Review final budget; balance the books.
- Make arrangements for all rented scripts, orchestra books, costumes, set pieces, props, and lighting or sound equipment to be returned according to contract stipulations.
- Make arrangements for all borrowed costumes, props, set pieces, or equipment to be returned in a timely manner.
- Send thank you notes to all staff and parent volunteers.

CAST STRIKE: Director oversees the stage managers and members of the cast during the strike.
Part 1
- Return all rented or borrowed costume pieces and accessories to dressers.
- Take all personal costume items and accessories home.
- Assist set/lighting crews with folding soft goods, painted drops, etc., as needed.
Part 2
- Assist lighting crew with coiling cable as needed.
- Assist any crew chief or staff member as requested.

ORCHESTRA STRIKE: Music director oversees orchestra members.
- Erase all pencil marks from each orchestra book.
- Strike and return all orchestra lights and electrical cords to lighting crew.
- Return all music stands, chairs, speakers, and other musical equipment to usual places.

PROPS STRIKE: Props coordinator oversees props crew.
- Discard all food props and wash food service plates, cups, and trays.
- Sort and package all borrowed or rented props.
- Return all personal props to company members.
- Return all repertoire props to usual storage places.
- Reorganize all props storage facilities and inventory supplies.

SET STRIKE: Set designer oversees run crew and construction crew; cast will assist as needed.
Part 1
- Remove and return any sound and lighting equipment incorporated in the set to those departments.
- Remove all furniture from stage area.
- Remove all fragile or breakable objects from stage area.
- Remove all set dressings (pictures on walls, curtains) from stage area.
- Strike, fold, and store all soft goods (painted drops, scrim, cyc, masking, etc.).
- Remove and disassemble any set pieces that interfere with lighting strike.
- Store and label for return all borrowed or rented set pieces.
Part 2
- Disassemble all set pieces and store good lumber, doors, and windows for future use.
- Remove all spike marks from the stage floor.
- Restore any soft goods removed or rehung for the production to usual places.
- Clean the stage; repaint black if possible.
- Reorganize all storage facilities and inventory supplies.

LIGHTING STRIKE: Lighting designer oversees lighting crew; cast will assist as needed.

Part 1
- Power off all lighting equipment from main power source.
- Disconnect and remove any lighting equipment incorporated in set.
- Strike, fold, and store all soft goods (painted drops, scrim, cyc, masking).
- Remove or disassemble any lighting equipment that interferes with set strike.

Part 2
- Strike all rented lighting instruments, cable, and other equipment; compare rental equipment with original shop order.
- Restore any soft goods removed or rehung for production to usual places.
- Rehang and focus all house units according to house repertoire design.
- Store all unused house units for future use.
- Reorganize all house lighting equipment and inventory cable, units, and supplies.

SOUND STRIKE: Sound designer oversees sound crew

Part 1
- Power off all sound equipment from main power source.
- Disconnect and remove any sound equipment incorporated in set.
- Remove any sound equipment that interferes with set or lighting strike.

Part 2
- Strike all rented sound equipment and cable (both amplification and house communication systems); compare rental equipment with original shop order.
- Restore all house equipment to usual places.
- Store all unused house equipment for future use.
- Reorganize all house sound equipment and inventory microphones, cable, and supplies.

COSTUME STRIKE: Costume designer oversees costume/makeup crew; cast will assist as needed.

Part 1
- Separate all rented, borrowed, and personal costume pieces and accessories.
- Return all personal costume pieces to company members.

Part 2
- Sort and package all borrowed or rented costumes and accessories for return; compare rental costumes to be returned with original rental agreement.
- Sort all repertoire costumes for cleaning.
- Clean all makeup supplies; discard depleted supplies as necessary.
- Clean dressing room areas; restore to normal use.
- Reorganize and inventory all costumes and makeup supplies.

HOUSE STRIKE: House staff reports to the producer
- Disassemble call-boards; return all photos and supplies to producer.
- Return all remaining playbills to producer.
- Assist set/lighting crews with folding soft goods, painted drops, etc., as needed.
- Assist lighting crew with coiling cable as needed.

GENERAL STRIKE ASSISTANCE

Parent volunteer coordinator
- Parent chaperones for Sunday strike.
- Parent volunteers to assist in returning borrowed or rented items.

ABOUT THE AUTHOR

Joy Varley has extensive experience as an educator, producer, director, composer, and perfomer.

Varley has been a public school educator for twenty-one years. She spent most of her career at the high school level, directing plays and musicals, teaching a variety of beginning- and advanced-level theater courses, and conducting choral performing ensembles.

Varley began her career as a teacher in Ohio, then moved to New York in 1982, where she served as the producer and director of The Theatre League of Westchester for five seasons and was co-creator of Sound Creations, a professional theater company, writing and producing nine original musicals for young audiences. She appeared as a leading performer in regional musical theater productions in the tri-state area and as a soloist at New York University, the Donnell Library, Northern Westchester Center for the Arts, Bronx Community College, and Lehman College. At Lehman College she premiered the songs of the late composer Ivan Wiener and conducted master classes in "The Care and Development of the Adolescent Voice." Varley has also performed with Robert Shaw at Carnegie Hall and at the Performing Arts Center in Akron, Ohio, and with Robert Page at Blossom Music Center in northeastern Ohio.

From 1996 to 1998, Varley worked at WPIX-WB11 Television in New York City where she served as creator and producer of "TEAM 11." She won an Emmy Award in 1997 for Outstanding Musical Composition.

Varley is currently the choir director of Byram Hills High School in Westchester County where she was named "Teacher of the Year" in 1993. She is recognized in *Who's Who in American Education*.